Amarantha

Chris Crockford

For Ginnie

And with Thanks to

Heather
Dave
Richard

Cover Design by Mike Smith

Find out more on Facebook.

Search for "Stones of Gunjai"

Also in the series

The Stones of Gunjai
The Crown of Gunjai
The Book of Carnothal

Prologue

Molly Kane was running for her life. She dived down a narrow alley that led away from the docks and she could hear it behind her. It's grotesque and keening howl cutting through the foggy London night like a knife.

Sensible people were indoors.

She was not being sensible.

Her husband Marcus was going to have a fit!

Well he would, if she lived long enough for him to find out what she was doing.

Ducking into a doorway, she tried to catch her breath, pushing her shoulder length, almost white blonde, hair out of her eyes. The eyes that had no pupils, just a dull whiteness.

She had been in India and lost her sight and when the powers of the Stones of Gunjai had fixed her, they had left them blank. Her sight was present, but her eyes were different. Not the sparkling blue they had been, just a blank white stare. One of the many reasons she didn't fit in.

She took a deep breath and tried to get herself together as from somewhere in the fog it howled again, this time accompanied by a horrible scream that cut off suddenly.

This was not good.

She reached over her right shoulder and drew the long, curved sword she had strapped to her back. The gems and finely worked silver in the hilt were worn smooth through use and the edge of the blade was lethally sharp.

She hadn't had the weapon for long. It had been a gift from her adopted sister and had originally belonged to a woman who knew how to use it. Molly wasn't too shabby with it but she lacked the finesse that years of hard training gave her and the blade still felt awkward in her hand, not the easy extension of her body that her sister made it look.

She stood in silence for a few minutes. The fog muffling any sounds and making it difficult to hear if the thing was still after her. She hoped not.

'How do I get myself into these things?' she asked herself.

Taking a deep breath, she stepped out into the fog once more. The doorway was quickly swallowed up by the thick mist and she headed back towards the river. She moved quietly, her booted feet making hardly any noise on the slick cobbles.

'Where are you?' she whispered.

As if to answer her question, the horrible howling sounded from somewhere nearby, but it was difficult to tell from what direction. The sound reverberated around the tightly packed buildings that made up this area of the docks.

She ran again, rounding a corner to come across the body of a young woman. This must have been who screamed. Molly slipped her sword back into its scabbard and knelt down.

One of her arms had been torn off and lay casually discarded on the road. What was more disturbing was that her heart, like all of the others, was missing. Just a huge hole in her chest where it had been torn out. Broken ribs jutted from the gaping cavity in her body and Molly felt her stomach flip.

She moved away from the body and into the mist once more.

It was close.

She knew it.

She could feel it.

From somewhere to her left it howled again. It was an unearthly noise filled with pain and anger.

'Where are you?' she said to herself again, slowly turning on the spot.

It erupted out of the fog from her left, catching her in the chest with its full weight and sending her tumbling backwards.

Molly hit the ground hard, cracking her head against the floor, but managed to roll to the right as a hand that ended in claws as big as her fingers raised sparks where they gouged the cobblestones.

Scrambling up, she ran again, trying to shake off the stars that were flashing in her vision.

This was definitely not good.

She pounded down the road, taking random lefts and rights in and out of the maze of alleyways that made up the dockyard, all the time acutely aware of the thing behind her. Its heavy footfalls loud as they stomped across the cobbled streets.

Molly vaulted a low wooden fence and found herself on a rotten, slippery, jetty. She turned to see if it was still following but the fog was thicker here on the river and she couldn't tell. It howled once more and she began to back away, breaking into a run as the fence exploded as the creature smashed through it.

Underneath her feet the old wood gave a warning creak, holding for a second before it gave way under the weight of the creature.

Molly looked down at the collapsing pier as the devastation caught up with her.

'Oh shi…' was all she managed before the planks under her feet disappeared and she pitched into the Thames, smashing into the edge of the pier on the way down.

Behind her, the thing went too as the old, rotten wood collapsed.

Molly hit the water hard. It was cold and dark and somewhere beneath her, she could feel the creature thrashing in the water.

She scrambled towards the surface, lungs bursting, eventually breaking through and splashing back towards the bank.

Gasping for breath, she hauled herself up and lay panting on the muddy bank for a moment.

Today had not been one of her best, that's for sure.

Hearing footsteps she looked up into the face of a man. His clothes were dirty and his face contorted into an ugly smile.

'Well if it isn't Molly Carter.' he said, 'I've been looking forward to seeing you again.'

She tried to sit up, but the man lashed out, punching her hard in the face, his dirty grin the last thing she saw before she blacked out.

Chapter One

Three Months Earlier
23rd of March 1819

Captain Phillip Lewis was sat in his cabin, a nearly empty brandy bottle on the table in front of him.

Blearily he tried to pour the rest of the amber liquid into his glass but only succeeded in emptying most of it over the stained and pitted wood. Cursing loudly, he dropped the bottle on the floor where it rolled with the storm driven pitch and yaw of the ship, clinking gently as it bumped against the legs of the desk.

He pushed his chair back and staggered across to the cupboard where he pulled out another bottle. There was a knock at the door.

'What?' he slurred, pulling the cork out of the bottle with his teeth.

The door opened to reveal his first mate, Collier, a gangly man with a dirty beard and lank hair.

Lewis spat the cork across the room and took a hefty pull from the bottle.

'What the hell do you want?'

The Captain sat down heavily, spilling more brandy on the table.

'Garring is dead.' said Collier flatly.

Through his alcoholic fug, he could see the blood splashed across Collier's face and clothes.

'What do you want me to do about it?' he muttered.

The first mate stormed in and snatched the bottle out of the Captains hands.

'You're supposed to be the bloody Captain! He's been aboard this ship for six years. Don't you care?'

Lewis stood up quickly, his face flushing with anger.

'How dare you talk to me like that.'

'You're bloody drunk!'

The Captain snatched the bottle back and sat back down, the fight having left him.

'Aye. I am.'

'We've got to kill it.

'Where is it?'

'Loose in the hold but we've shut and barred the hatches.'

'Then what's the problem? It's contained.' said Lewis, taking a swig.

'What do you mean "What's the problem"? It's killing the bloody crew while you sit up here and drink yourself stupid!'

From somewhere in the bowels of the ship came a chilling roar.

'It'll be alright, by this time tomorrow we'll have got rid of the bloody thing and we'll have been paid.'

'There won't be a ship by this time tomorrow. And even if there is there won't be anyone left to crew it!'

As if to emphasise the point, there was a scream from below decks and both men looked at each other.

'Alright.' said Lewis.

He staggered up and across to his bunk. Lifting the mattress, he took out a small chest, around two feet by one, which he unlocked using a key he had on a cord around his neck.

With exaggerated care, he placed a brace of pistols on the floor along with a powder horn and shot before he took out a small musical pipe that looked like it had been made of bone which he shoved into his pocket.

Picking up the pistols, the Captain unsteadily made his way back to his desk. Collier watched him for a moment as he tried to load the guns with shaking hands.

The first mate cursed and snatched the pistols from the Captain, loading them with a smooth efficiency that spoke of many years of practice. He threw one of them down on the table.

'Come on. If you can sober up long enough to shoot.'

Without waiting for a reply, Collier stormed out of the cabin. Lewis looked at the pistol for a second before taking a hefty swig from the brandy bottle.

He screwed his eyes shut and shook his head, trying to clear the haze from his mind and wishing, not for the first time in the last couple of months, that he'd never taken this job.

It had all started last year when he'd been asked to take his ship to the Far East, to Pannau, a small island off the coast of China and pick up a cargo. The request came via a lawyer, some stuck up bastard called Dickenson, who wouldn't say what the cargo was or who wanted it.

Initially he'd refused, but the amount of money on offer was substantial and with his debts, Lewis couldn't really say no.

The lawyer had given him specific instructions. Lewis was to sail to Pannau, meet a man called Cho, pick up the cargo and come back. If he made good time and the cargo was undamaged when they returned, then the fee would be doubled.

Lewis should have smelled a rat then. If it sounds too good to be true, then it is, and some bastard has it in for you.

They made respectable time and arrived just before December and as soon as they tied up, Lewis decided he didn't like the place.

It was, as Collier eloquently put it, a shit hole. It stank worse than the bilges and was full of thieves and cutthroats.

Not that the Captain was a prude or precious about such things, but he'd seen enough dives in his time to know that this was one of the worst.

The place thronged with people loudly selling their wares and seeing what they could steal.

Lewis and Collier had posted guards on the gangplank to try to deter any unwanted attentions and they had only taken half a dozen steps before they'd seen someone stabbed.

The pair had exchanged a glance that said, "Let's get out of here as soon as possible".

They were to meet the man Cho at a bar that edged the waterfront, if you could call a single room full of rats and murders a bar.

Sprawled on the pavement outside was a body, bleeding from a huge cut to his head. Collier had lent down to check if he was still alive, but Lewis had stopped him with a shake of his head.

'We don't get involved.'

They had walked in and the entire place went silent. All eyes were glaring at the westerners with a mixture of hatred and curiosity. Lewis walked to the bar.

'Cho. I'm looking for a man called Cho.'

The barman had grimaced and spat on the countertop in front of him before beginning to shout loudly.

'Captain.' Collier had muttered.

Lewis turned around to see the entire bar stand as one and a collection of blades drawn.

'Cho?'

The mob advanced and through a combination of shouting and pointedly waved knives, the pair were ejected from the bar and into the street.

'Well that went well.'

'Shut up Collier.'

'What now?'

The Captain had shrugged.

'No idea.'

'You don't think we've been sent on a wild goose-chase do you?'

'Shut up.'

They began to walk back to the ship. Around them the mood of the docks had changed and people were stopping what they were doing to spit on the floor in front of them.

'I get the feeling that this Cho feller isn't that popular.'

'Really?' Lewis had replied sarcastically.

They'd made their way back to the ship and waited.

Four days later, Lewis was sure they'd been set up. He'd had to ban shore leave for the crew as the first one to go to the docks had been stabbed to death. Lewis wasn't even sure if it was a robbery or something to do with this non-existent "Cho".'

The first mate had been stood looking out across the harbour when the Captain had gone up on deck. He went and stood next to him and took in the scenery for a while.

'He's not going to show is he?' Lewis had said.

Collier had shrugged.

'I know we'd better start getting some supplies on board, it's going to take us months to get back home.'

'We'll give him two more days, then we'll start sorting out and getting ready to head back.'

The first mate had left, leaving the Captain alone.

'When they got back to England,' he thought, 'he was going to find that bugger Dickenson and sort him out.'

The next day had dawned with the promise of heavy rain. Lewis hadn't even gotten out of bed when Collier had come barging into his cabin.

'He's here.'

'Who? And don't you ever bloody knock?'

'Cho. He's here and, well get your arse out of bed, you're going to need to see this.'

The Captain had jumped out of bed and headed out to see what was going on. And, as it turned out, it was almost a bloody riot.

The place was in uproar, it looked like the entire town was on the quay, shouting and waving blades and pitchforks. Stopped on the quayside were two carts. The first held one large crate while armed men were jumping down from the second.

The men rushed forwards, guns at the ready and began forcing the crowd back.

Stood in the centre of all this had been a smartly dressed Chinese man with an amused half smile on his lips.

He had greeted Lewis as he came down the gangplank, still tucking in his shirt.

'You must be Captain Lewis.' Cho had said, his English understandable but heavily accented. It was a damn sight better than Lewis' Chinese though.

The Captain offered his hand, but Cho just looked at it until Lewis felt uncomfortable and withdrew it. The Englishman got the feeling that he knew what a handshake was but just deigned not to reciprocate the gesture. Instead the man turned to the ship.

'This is a mighty vessel you have here. What is its name?'

'She's called The Amarantha.'

'I see. Is that good?'

'She's looked after us for a long time.'

'Very much good. As you see, I have been bringing the cargo. I would be liking your help in unloading.'

Lewis had glanced at Collier, who shrugged before going back aboard to rustle up some men. Cho continued to speak.

'This is for your care now. Being careful and do not opening the crate.'

Lewis had ignored him and gone to inspect the box as Collier re-joined them on the quay. The box was made of a sturdy hard wood and was taller than he was. He laid a hand on the box and it rattled under his touch.

'What the hell is in here?' he asked, placing an ear to the wood. Something inside snarled and the crate rocked dangerously. Lewis jumped back.

'Jesus.'

Collier had given him a dirty look. He didn't like blasphemy, and the Captain was sure he'd hear about how he was going to Hell later on.

Tell me something I don't know, he thought.

Shouting to his crew, they began to gather nervously around the crate. The first that went near it retreated quickly as the box rocked again. Lewis headed over to Cho.

'What's in there?' he demanded, pointing at the boxes.

The Chinese man smiled widely and took a small pipe from a pocket and put it to his lips. He blew hard, producing a shrill, piercing wail.

The contents of the box shrieked and thrashed wildly, so much so, Lewis thought the crate might topple over.

Cho blew again before shouting loudly at the box. It stopped rocking immediately. With another smile, the Chinese man gestured to the Captain and then pressed the pipe into his hands.

'What now?'

There was no answer, just another smile. Lewis turned to his crew.

'Get them loaded.'

With some trepidation, they began to get the box on board. It was safely stowed without further issue and leaving Collier to finish up, Lewis went to Cho.

'What's in there? Is it dangerous?'

'No. But I am suggesting that you may be good to go soon. Once I leave these people will not be nicely asking you to leave.'

'Why?'

'You're stealing their God.'

Lewis stared at him disbelievingly. The Chinese man smiled once more.

'The crate. Don't be opening it fully. The contents will be hungry but there is being a small door on the top. Feed it and it'll be being fine.'

He said, turning and walking away.

'What does it eat?' Lewis called after him.

The Chinese man turned back with a smile.

'Whatever it can get its hands on.'

Then, without a backward glance, he began to gather his men and they forced their way from the harbour through the crowd.

As Cho and his men left, the attention of the crowd turned to the westerners and their ship. Sensing the shift in hostility, Lewis hurried up the gangplank.

'Cut those lines, get us out of here.'

The crew did as ordered sawing through the mooring lines as bottles and rocks began to patter off the side of the ship.

Several men tried to jump aboard but they were swiftly overcome and thrown into the scummy water of the harbour.

Giving as much sail as he dared, Lewis guided the ship out of the harbour and into the stormy waters outside.

Their journey back home had been difficult. There had been the worst storms that the Captain and his crew had ever encountered, their ship tossed back and forth like a toy in bathtub, with several men being swept overboard.

At one point, one of the crew had tried to look in the crate. The thing inside had hissed and spat before blinding him with a lashing claw.

He'd fallen off the top of the box and broken his leg to boot. Lewis had been forced to put him ashore, leaving him in the care of a seaman's mission in Gibraltar.

After that, things had gone from bad to worse. The ship stank something terrible. Not just the normal stale smell of men and bilges but a foetid primal smell.

The food went off and the crew began to fall ill. Below the stinking decks there were mutterings of curses and bad omens, all blamed on the thing in the box.

It almost got to the point where Lewis had to put down a mutiny. Something he'd never have thought his crew were capable of. Five of the men had come to his cabin and demanded that he throw the thing overboard.

He met them and told them that if there was no cargo, then there was no money, but they'd persisted, getting violent and threatening. In the end, he'd had one of them flogged as an example to the rest. That man died within a day.

Then Lewis had hit the bottle. He drank heavily, his mood soured to the point where he locked himself in his cabin, letting Collier basically run the ship.

That had lasted until they were a day from England. A large storm had taken them and the crate had been smashed open and the thing escaped.

Collier and the Captain staggered across the deck as the ship rolled beneath them. Four men were lashing down the main hatch to the hold and as he watched, a clawed hand punched through the wood and grabbed one of the men by the ankle.

It dragged the screaming man down until his thigh jammed in the hole. Around him his shipmates panicked and tried to haul him out. There was a wet sucking noise and the man popped free, minus his leg.

He thrashed on the deck, blood pumping out to mix with the violent spray of the sea.

Lewis cursed and then shot the man dead. No-one deserved to die like that.

'Get the men up here. Grab boat hooks. Money be damned, it's going over the side.'

The men rushed to obey and formed a loose semi-circle around him. At his signal, the strappings were cut and the hatch flew open.

Before the thing had even got a claw out and onto the deck, Lewis put the pipe to his lips and blew as hard as he could.

With a pained roar, it flopped topside and the men charged it. Their boathooks and poles impaling the thrashing creature and with all their might, they heaved it over the side.

It disappeared in the stormy water with a splash and vanished from sight. Collier joined the Captain at the gunwales.

'What now?'

Lewis looked at his first mate.

'Follow me.'

Chapter Two

Brighton Bound
8th of June 1819

'I don't understand why he wants to meet me!' said Molly for the fiftieth time that day as the carriage carrying her and her husband Marcus rumbled through the London streets.

They'd been invited to dinner. Dinner with the Prince Regent no less.

Although, "invited" seemed too soft a word. Their presence had been requested in no uncertain terms and, as Marcus had said, "One does not turn down a dinner invitation from the future King."

They were headed to Brighton, apparently the Prince Regent had a house there and that's where he would be entertaining them.

The journey would take a while and Molly and Marcus' butler, Simcox, had arranged for an overnight stay at a coaching inn on the way. He, along with Molly's maid Gwen, had gone ahead earlier that day to make sure things were ready when they got there.

'I didn't need all this fuss.'

Marcus patted her on the knee.

'Why can't you just enjoy the ride? Don't worry about it.'

'That's easy for you to say, I've never met royalty before.'

'Neither have I.'

'You know what I mean.'

Her husband smiled.

'What about Nareema? She's a Princess. Daughter of a Maharajah.'

'She's different.' said Molly testily.

Marcus raised his eyebrows. Nareema was Mollys adopted sister.

The pair had been through a lot together in the search for the Stones of Gunjai and it was down to her that Molly had everything she did. Including her own title, Her Royal Highness, Princess Molly Kane of Sunjian.

A little over a year ago, Molly had been homeless and starving around the London dockyard. Nareema had rescued her and now she had everything she could ever want or need but, she was still having trouble adjusting to the life of a lady.

Marcus smiled to himself and Molly sighed, sitting back heavily.

'Look, I'm sorry. I'm absolutely terrified. What if I say something wrong? What if I upset him?'

'It's going to be fine.' he reassured her.

'But what if it isn't?'

Marcus moved and sat next to her, taking her hand in his.

'Trust me. It will be fine. I've heard that the Prince has fancies, he'll flit from one thing to another until he gets bored or distracted by something else.'

'So I'm just a fancy?'

'I'm afraid so.'

Molly made a face.

'Don't be like that. Just be yourself.'

'That's what I'm scared of being.'

Marcus squeezed her hand.

'It's going to be fine. We'll have a lovely dinner. I expect he'll want you to tell him your story, then we can go home.'

'Promise?'

'I promise.'

Molly nodded but she felt far from reassured.

They arrived at the coaching inn just before seven. Simcox and Gwen were waiting outside as the carriage stopped.

He was tall and imperious with receding hair and a hard face. He was dressed in an immaculate suit whilst Gwen was more homely with her long brown hair loose around her shoulders, while her deep green dress was well made and of high quality fabric. As befitted the maid of a Princess.

'Good evening Your Highness. Sir.' the butler said as he opened the door with a small bow.

Molly knew that this was all for show. When they were at home, he called her Molly. But appearances had to be kept up she supposed.

Technically she was a Princess with more money than she could hope to spend.

Technically.

Marcus got out and offered his hand. She took it and let him help her get out.

Molly looked around and then slipped on her glasses.

Thin silver frames held lenses of smoked glass. She didn't need them to see but they helped hide her white eyes. They were something that most people found disconcerting.

She looked at Gwen with a smile. The girl smiled nervously back.

'Your Ladyship.' she said with a curtsey.

'Hello Gwen. Trip down alright?'

'Yes Your Ladyship.'

The girl looked like she was going to say something else but Simcox interrupted her.

'I'm sorry Your Highness but the rooms that we have been able to obtain are far from suitable. It seems that a gentleman is travelling from London today with his daughter and has had his staff book most of the rooms. I did offer to pay for them but his head man was quite insistent that his master wouldn't like different accommodation.'

'I'm sure whatever we've got will be fine.' said Molly with a wink at Marcus.

'If you're sure…'

'I am. Come on.'

She strode off towards the inn with Simcox hurrying after her. It was quite a large two story building with a thatched roof. A stables and yard were around the back and a sign hung outside named it as "The Golden Lion".

Without waiting for a grand entrance, Molly pushed open the door.

The common room was plain but warm, a large fire burned in the hearth to the left while the rest of the space was taken up by tables and benches.

The place was busy but all conversation stopped as they walked in. Molly hesitated, suddenly not as confident as she had been and swallowed nervously before she took her glasses off. There were some hushed mutterings before from behind the bar, came the inn keepers' wife, almost dragging her husband and two young girls along in her anxiousness to meet a Princess.

The woman was plump with greying hair. She and the girls curtseyed and, after a surreptitious elbow to the ribs from his wife, the inn keeper gave a small bow too.

'We're so glad you chose our humble establishment for your stay.' said the woman, trying and failing, to sound more well-bred than she was. Molly smiled back.

'Thank you for making space for us.'

The woman flushed red with pride.

'I'm Fran Bloom and these are my daughters, Sarah and Jennifer.' The girls curtseyed once more. 'This is my husband, Harold.'

'It's pleasure to meet you all.' said Marcus.

'Thank you sir.'

There was an expectant silence before Mrs Bloom remembered what she was doing.

'Oh, my, what must you think of me. Your rooms are this way. If you'd like to follow me.'

She curtseyed again and led Molly across the room, leaving Marcus standing with Simcox and Gwen.

'Hadn't you better go with her Gwen?' asked Marcus pointedly.

She looked up at him, a flash of panicked embarrassment passing across her face.

'Of course sir. Sorry sir.'

The girl quickly followed, catching them up at the bottom of the stairs. Mr Bloom and his daughters smiled uncomfortably before they went about their business.

Marcus turned to Simcox.

'So how was your journey?'

'It was fine sir, although if I were you, I wouldn't eat the stew. I'm not sure whatever is in it should really be for human consumption.'

Marcus couldn't help but smile.

'Now If you will follow me please, I'll escort you to your room.'

'Aren't Molly and I sharing?'

'Ah, no sir. The inn only has one double room and as I said sir, someone else has already booked that. We've taken the liberty of preparing adjacent rooms for you and her Ladyship. I trust that is acceptable?'

'Of course.' replied Marcus, even though he was secretly disappointed.

'Very good sir.'

Mrs Bloom led Molly and Gwen upstairs. There was a wide balcony that overlooked the taproom below with doors leading off at various intervals. She stopped outside the door furthest from the stairs.

'Here you go Your Highness.'

She opened the door and Molly took in the room. It was quite small and only had a single bed. Her luggage was piled near the door and opposite was a window that overlooked the village green and pond outside. She looked questioningly at Gwen who shrugged slightly.

'Thank you.' she told Mrs Bloom as she entered.

'Can I get you anything else Your Highness? Drink? Food?'

Molly walked to the window.

'Yes. Please. I'll have some wine and whatever you happen to have cooked at the moment.'

The woman paled visibly.

'I'm not sure that would be suitable...'

Molly turned and flashed her a smile.

'What is it?'

'Stew, Your Highness. I could prepare you something else, the gentleman that booked the room along the corridor has sent instructions for...'

'No. Stew will be fine. And some bread to go with it please.' Molly turned to Gwen. 'Have you eaten?'

'Not yet Your Ladyship.'

'Please bring two plates of stew. I'm sure it will be more than sufficient.'

'Are you sure?'

'Yes. Please.'

The woman curtseyed once more and left, looking visibly shaken and muttering to herself.

'Shall we have a wager on what's in the stew?' Molly asked with a mischievous grin.

'I'd rather not if it's all the same. Do you think it'll be alright to eat?'

'It'll be fine.'

Molly sat on the bed. It sagged alarmingly and Gwen grimaced.

'I'm sorry about the room your Ladyship, this was the best they had. The others are already taken by some posh nob and his staff. They wouldn't give up the double room, even when Mr Simcox offered to pay their bill. To be honest, his staff were quite rude about you.'

'Really? What did they say?'

Gwen blushed.

'I couldn't possibly repeat it.' she said miserably.

'I bet I've been called worse.' laughed Molly.

She stood again and went back to the window, looking out across the green.

'So are you going to tell me what's up?'

'Nothing Your Ladyship.' Gwen replied quickly.

Molly turned and fixed her with a penetrating stare.

'Don't give me that. Something is wrong and I want to know what. Also, my name is Molly.'

Gwen looked down, wringing her hands together uncomfortably. She still wasn't use to calling her Molly. It didn't sit right. She was her maid and it didn't feel right to be so informal.

'I'm waiting.'

'You know my sister is getting married.' the girl said, without looking up.

'Yes.'

'Can I, um, is it still alright for me to go?'

Molly almost laughed.

'Is that it?'

Gwen nodded, still staring at the floor.

'Of course you can go. I said you could, didn't I?'

'Yes, but then all of that stuff at the abbey happened and I thought…'

'You thought what?'

The girl shrugged miserably and Molly sighed.

'Gwen, look at me.'

Molly waited until she had her full attention.

'Look. You should know me by now. I said you can go. What happened at the abbey wasn't nice but I don't need looking after all the time. I'm a big girl and I can take care of myself.'

'But the master said…'

'He said what?' Molly asked pointedly.

Gwen looked down again.

'Nothing.' she muttered.

'No, come on. He said what?'

There was a tense silence before Gwen spoke.

'He told me that I'm your maid and I need to start acting like it. I should look after you and not let you go off getting into trouble.'

Molly could tell the girl was on the verge of tears.

'Did he.'

Gwen nodded.

'What else did he say?'

'Nothing.'

Molly didn't believe her but said nothing else.

'I don't want to be fired.' said the girl eventually, 'I like this job. I…'

'Gwen.' snapped Molly sharply. 'Stop it. Leave Marcus to me. For now, you're going to do as I say, and what I say is that you're going to your sister's wedding, you're going to have a wonderful time and not worry about a thing. Is that clear?'

Gwen nodded once more.

'I said, is that clear?'

'Yes, Your Ladyship.'

'Good. Now stop moping. Why don't you go downstairs and see how the stew is coming along.'

The girl left, seemingly anxious to be away. Molly waited until the door was closed before looking out of the window again.

She was furious. How dare he go behind her back like that. And threaten Gwen with being put out on the street! He had no right.

Molly was gripping the window frame hard enough to turn her knuckles white. Around her the temperature in the room was beginning to fall and pattern of frost began to form on the glass.

How dare he!

There was a knock at the door.

'What?' she snapped angrily.

It opened and in came Gwen, closely followed by Mrs Bloom.

'Oh, it's cold in here.' said the innkeepers wife with a shiver, 'I'll get you some more blankets.'

Mollys foul mood began to lift slightly, and as it did so, the temperature began to rise.

Mrs Bloom had her husband drag a small table upstairs along with two of the stools from the bar so that Molly and Gwen could eat in her room.

They were tucking into their stew, which consisted mostly of potato as far as Molly could tell, when Marcus knocked on the door.

'May I come in?'

'Of course.' Molly said icily.

Gwen jumped up.

'I'll go and see if Mr Simcox needs any help.'

'Nonsense.' said Molly. 'Sit down and finish your stew.'

As if to emphasise the point, she poured the girl a cup of wine from a stoneware pitcher.

'Drink?'

Marcus shook his head.

'No. Thank you.'

Molly finished her cup of wine, stood and took Marcus' arm, swiftly guiding him towards the door.

'We're going for a walk, and no, I don't need you to come with me. Finish your stew, finish the wine too if you want. I'll see you later.'

'Very good your Ladyship.'

She sat back down as Molly and Marcus left.

'She seems awfully nervous today.' commented Marcus as they strolled out of the inn.

'Wouldn't you if you'd been threatened with being thrown out onto the street?'

'What?'

'She told me Marcus. What do you think you were doing? She's my maid…'

'Yes.' he said, cutting her off, 'Your maid. She's paid to look after you. And, in my opinion, she's not doing a very good job of that.'

'I don't need looking after.'

'Ladies of your standing…'

Now it was Molly's turn to interrupt.

'I don't have a standing. And besides, it should be my choice who I employ.'

'No. As the…'

Molly turned to him angrily.

'If you say, "Master of the house" then I'll knock you in that pond.'

'Molly. Don't be like that.'

'Like what?'

He sighed.

'Like this. Angry.'

'Angry? How else do you expect me to feel? You're trying to fire my maid.'

'I'm not trying to fire her. I just suggested that she take a little more care in her duties. That's all.'

'That's not what she thinks. She was kidnapped and almost murdered! That wouldn't have happened if she hadn't been working for me.'

'Now you're being silly.'

'Silly?'

Molly bit back her next words and stalked away before she said something that she'd regret later.

Marcus sighed once more and went after her.

'Molly, wait.'

He caught her up by the pond.

'Look. I'm sorry. Gwen is paid to look after you and she's not doing that.'

'I don't need looking after.'

'I know.'

'Then why should I have a maid at all?'

Molly picked up a stone from the ground and hurled it into the water.

'Well?' she demanded when no answer was immediately forthcoming.

Marcus shook his head.

'You're a Princess. A lady. You need to have staff to do things for you. I don't know a single other lady that doesn't have at least one maid.'

'I am not a lady.'

She threw another stone, this one was propelled by a ferocious gust of wind and hit the water with the force of a cannon ball, sending a huge waterspout into the air.

'Molly. Calm down. Look at me.'

Gently Marcus reached up and turned her round so she was facing him.

'I'm sorry.'

Molly sighed and pinched the bridge of her nose.

'No. I'm sorry. Look, Gwen is a good girl. She does help me and do things for me. I'll not see her thrown out because I can't let her help more. I owe her that much. *We* owe her that much.'

'Very well. Just let her do her job.'

'I'll try. But I'm making no promises. I'm so use to doing things for myself that letting someone choose my clothes seems unnatural.'

'Alright. But…'

'But nothing.'

Marcus nodded then offered her his arm. She took it with a small hesitation and they began to walk around the village.

'Gwen is going to her sister's wedding next month. I've already promised that she could go.'

'Alright.'

'She's going to be away for a few days. Maybe a week.'

'We can hire in someone else temporarily.'

'No. I'll manage.'

Marcus didn't say anything else. He didn't want to get into another argument.

He could see Molly's point of view. She'd had next to nothing for nearly all of her life and was fiercely independent, but that had changed now.

She was a lady with a house, money and titles. She didn't aught to be cooking or cleaning or the other hundred and one things that she did that Gwen should be doing. That's why he'd spoken to the girl. But Molly didn't see it like that. She never would.

Together they wandered around the village, their moods lightening as they took in the evening air. The village wasn't very big and seemed to have sprung up around the coaching inn. There was a blacksmith and a few houses dotted around the village green and pond but nothing bigger than the inn itself.

The evening was quite pleasant, but the wind was picking up a little as they came back. Outside the inn was large coach and horses. Four, put upon looking men were unloading case after case and box after box.

'Who needs that much luggage?' asked Molly as they neared the carriage.

'I couldn't possibly say dear…' said Marcus with a smile and feigned air of ignorance.

Molly grinned and playfully punched him in the arm.

'Stop that. You keep telling me I'm a Princess. So I'm allowed to bring luggage.'

'I never said a thing…'

Both smiling they headed into the common room to find a well-dressed gentleman shouting at the innkeeper and his wife.

Two other men, servants by the look of their clothes were stood nearby. From the look of their faces, they'd been the target of the shouting moments before.

'And another thing,' he yelled. 'I don't believe that my room has been cleaned for at least a month.'

'But sir,' replied Mrs Bloom. 'That room was cleaned this morning, especially…'

'I seriously doubt that, woman.' putting a distasteful spin on the word "woman". 'The dust on the floor is quite upsetting my, um, daughter.'

As if on cue, a young woman, at least half the shouting man's age came in, pushing her way past Molly and Marcus to hook an arm in his. She whispered in his ear.

'Very good my dear.' he replied before rounding on the poor innkeepers again.

'I demand another room.'

'There isn't another one sir. That's the best we have.'
He blustered with rage for a moment

'Well damn it, get it cleaned.' he yelled.

'Is there a problem here?'

Both the man and the young woman turned to look at Molly. She was smiling sweetly.

'Who are you?' he demanded.

Marcus stepped forward as he felt Molly tense.

'I say sir, please show some manners. You are addressing my wife. Her Royal Highness, Molly Kane of Sunjian.'

A grin of realisation passed across the man's face.

'Ah, so you're the pretend Princess then are you?'

He whispered to the young woman who giggled.

'How dare you sir!'

Molly put a hand on her husband's arm and stepped forward.

'Don't Marcus. I don't think that this gentleman needs any help to look silly in front of all of these people. He's doing quite a good job of it himself.'

The man was outraged. He stepped up close and pointed a finger at Molly.

'Now listen here, you little...'

He never finished his rant as Molly grabbed the outstretched finger and bent it back, twisting the man until his arm was behind him.

'I would greatly appreciate it if you didn't point at me again.' With a shove, she turned him around to face the innkeeper and his wife.

'I think you owe these hardworking people an apology, don't you?'

'I don't think...'

She shoved his arm further up his back and he cried out in pain.

'What was that?' she asked.

'I'm... I'm sorry.' he blurted out.'

'For what?'

'Shouting. Being rude. I'm sorry.'

'See, that wasn't so hard now was it?'

She let go and shoved him forward.

'Mrs Bloom. I believe that that the good gentleman here is very pleased to have a room, especially the best one in the establishment. Furthermore, he and his...' Molly eyed the young woman, '...his daughter would be very grateful to you for some of your fine stew for their dinner this evening. Isn't that right?'

The man was massaging his shoulder and looked fit to explode with anger, but the young woman put a restraining hand on his arm. He glared at her for a second before spitting out the words.

'Of course.'

He turned and stormed up the stairs with the young girl and staff following on closely behind. As soon as they heard the door slam, Molly let out a sigh.

'If she's his daughter, then I'm a Frenchman.'

She looked round. The entire common room was staring at her in disbelief. Marcus on the other hand had a sly smile on his face.

'What?' she asked innocently. 'Manners don't cost anything.'

Marcus shook his head as Mrs Bloom came up to her.

'Thank you, Your Highness. He's stayed here before and he's always a right pain in the arse.'

The woman realised what she'd just said, covered her mouth and blushed furiously.

'Don't worry about it.'

She looked around the room before shouting.

'While I'm here, who'd like a drink?'

A cheer of appreciation went up from the people in the room and Molly grinned.

It was fully dark. The moon was high but that didn't worry him, the shadows on the stairs were enough.

The blonde princess with the funny eyes had bought drinks and then gone up to bed. That was hours ago and now the place was empty.

Cautiously he crept along the landing and stopped outside her room. Pressing his ear to the wood, he couldn't hear a thing.

Hopefully she was sleeping and he'd be able to see what he could get his hands on before she woke up. He smiled to himself, but a rumbling stomach put paid to that.

As soon as he'd seen her come to the inn he knew that he'd have a chance to steal something. She didn't look to be the careful type and besides, he was almost past the point where he cared if he got caught or not. He'd not eaten for three days and whatever he could find would go some way to fixing that.

Taking a deep breath, he opened the door a fraction. She hadn't even locked it! She was just inviting him in. Begging to be robbed.

Peering in, he could see that the window was open, and she was fast asleep with her luggage open near the door.

If he was quick, he could get in and out in under a minute. Pushing the door wide, he crept in and began to look through the cases.

'Are you looking for anything in particular?'

He almost cried out and span around quickly. She was standing right behind him! He backed away, fumbling for a knife at his belt but she had a long curved sword in her right hand which she brought up quickly.

He bumped into the wall and the point stopped less than an inch from his throat. He hadn't even heard her move. There was no way she could have gotten across the room without him hearing.

'Drop your knife on the floor. Slowly.'

Moving with exaggerated care, he pulled the dull and rusty blade from his belt and dropped it on the floor.

'Good. Now, tell me what you were doing going through my things?'

He began to form some story in his mind, but she just looked at him. The blade didn't waver, and she stared with blank white eyes. He almost felt as if she were reading his soul.

Behind her, a gust of wind blew in, and the clouds slipped from the moon, casting its rays across the room. The sudden change in light gave her a ghostly appearance, nightdress and hair blowing in the breeze. All the time, the point of the blade didn't move.

'I'm waiting.' she said, taking a small step and resting the point of the sword against his adams apple. It was incredibly sharp.

He decided that honesty was probably the best policy.

'I... I was going to rob you.'

'Really.'

He went to nod then realised that he'd more than likely impale himself on the blade.

'Yes.' he stammered.

'Why?'

As if in answer to the question, his stomach rumbled loudly. She laughed softly to herself.

'Wait there.'

She lowered the blade and turned around. Seeing his chance, the thief took a step towards the door but a sudden wind, stronger than he'd ever experienced, sprang out of nowhere and slammed him back against the wall, pinning him in place.

The Princess looked over her shoulder.

'I said, wait there.'

He wasn't sure, but he could have sworn that her eyes were glowing blue. Maybe it was a trick of the light. Maybe he was just hungrier than he thought and it was playing with his mind. A moment later she came back and the wind vanished.

'Here.' she said, handing him a small leather pouch.

Gingerly, he reached out and took it. It was heavy and full of coins.

'What's your name?'

In a state of shock, he just looked at her. She narrowed her eyes and brought the sword up once more.

'No. Please. My name is John. John Warner.'

'Well John Warner. My name is Molly Kane. Do you know how guilty I'd feel if I killed you now?'

John shook his head.

'Not very, but it would make a mess.' she said, before she lowered the blade once more.

'I'm going to check up on you John Warner and if I find you stealing again, then you'll regret it. Is that clear?'

He nodded.

'Good. Now get out of here before I change my mind.'

John went to move but she raised the sword again.

'Actually, I've got a little job for you. Do you know that big carriage that lord what's his face came in?'

'Yes.' he stammered.

She smiled widely.

Molly watched the man almost fall over himself to get out of the room. Honestly. If he'd have just asked, she'd have given him some money. Maybe she'd have a word with Mrs Bloom in the morning. There might be a job he could do.

She slipped her sword into its sheath and sat down on the bed. It creaked alarmingly and she sighed. There probably wasn't much more sleep she was going to get.

Standing up, sword in hand, she went out of the room and down to the taproom. The place was empty, so she threw a little wood on the embers of the fire, helped herself to a mug of ale and sat down.

Mrs Bloom came out early, rousing her daughters along the way.

'Come on. Get up. We've got to clean down the common room before breakfast.'

Blearily the girls rose and dressed while their mother went into the bar. Sat on the floor near the fireplace was the Princess and alongside her was a long sword.

'Your Highness?'

The girl looked around at her.

'Morning Mrs Bloom.'

'What are you doing down here?'

The Princess shrugged.

'Couldn't sleep. I hope you don't mind but I helped myself to a drink.'

She waved an empty tankard in the air.

'No. No. Not at all.' replied Mrs Bloom vacantly.
'Thank you.'
The Princess turned back to stare into the fire again.
'If you don't mind me asking, are you alright?'
'Yes.'
She sighed and stood up, brushing herself off but only managing to smear a large sooty mark across her nightdress.
'Bugger.' she said exasperatedly.
Mrs Bloom put her hand across her mouth, shocked. The Princess picked up the sword with a grin.
'Don't look like that. I bet you've heard worse.'
The innkeeper's wife didn't know what to say.
'Do you need an odd job man around?' she asked the stunned woman. 'Someone to help with the fixing bits and pieces?'
'We could do with some help with the roof I suppose. Harold isn't as young as he use to be...'
'Good. I've got the perfect man for the job. He's called John Warner. He needs some work and some food. Can you do that for me?'
Mrs Bloom nodded.
The Princess had grinned widely, patted her on the arm in a friendly manner and then went back upstairs.
Mrs Bloom watched her go.
'Well I never!'

Marcus and Molly were ready to leave when the posh man and his "daughter" came down. He looked at Molly with disdain.
'Leaving already?'
'Yes. Not all of us can sit in bed until midday.' she called back with a grin.
He scoffed and turned away but the young girl kept Mollys eye for a moment. Something unsaid passed between them and she looked down.

'Come on.'

Marcus took her arm and guided her out of the door.

'Did you see her?' ask Molly as they walked towards their waiting carriage.

'Who?'

Molly poked him in the ribs.

'The daughter.'

'Yes? So?'

'Did you see a bruise on her face?'

Marcus frowned and opened the door for her.

'No.'

Molly climbed in.

'I'm sure there was a bruise. I'm going to have a look.'

'Don't.'

He put a hand on her arm and stopped her.

'No. Don't. Leave it.'

'But...'

'No Molly.'

Now it was her turn to frown. She sat down heavily.

'Well, he'll have a nice ride to where-ever he is going.' she said.

'What?'

Molly grinned.

'What have you done?'

'I've not done anything.'

He looked at her.

'Molly...'

'Alright. I might have paid someone to fill the space under his seat with manure.'

'You did what?'

'I only said I might have.'

He shook his head in disbelief but couldn't help but smile.

'Honestly.'

'Well the man is an arse. He deserves it.'

Marcus shook his head again and banged on the side of the carriage to signal the driver they were ready to leave.

They arrived in Brighton a little after four in the afternoon. Molly almost gasped as they approached.

'I thought you said it was a house.'

'Well, its close.'

'No it bloody isn't!'

The structure in front of them was one of the most impressive that Molly had ever seen. A huge building made of grey stone, with thin towers at the corners and a massive central section that had a roof shaped like a giant onion.

Smaller areas also had the same style rooves and it reminded Molly of the buildings she had seen in India, but even Nareema's palace paled in comparison to this.

The carriage rumbled through the gates and into the immaculately tended gardens, guards snapping to attention as they passed. Molly swallowed dryly and took a deep breath. Was she ready for this?

Marcus smiled at her.

'Calm down. You'll be fine.'

The carriage stopped outside and a finely dressed servant opened the door. He bowed low as they got out.

'Your Highness. His Royal Highness, Prince George, the Prince Regent, welcomes you to the Pavilion. If you will please follow me.'

He led them in, through an expansive hall, up an enormous staircase, to a suit of rooms.

'Your luggage has already been brought up and your staff are lodged downstairs. If you require anything then please ask.'

'Thank you.' said Marcus.

The man bowed once more and then left, closing the door behind him.

Molly wandered around in a slight daze. There were four rooms. A big bedroom with a sizeable fourposter bed, a dressing room, bathroom and a parlour for entertaining.

'Well this is something.' said Marcus, admiring the very ostentatious, Indian inspired décor.

'I think I'm going to be sick.'

'Why? It's not that bad.'

Molly sat down in a large leather armchair in the parlour.

'No. It's all this.' she said, gesturing around. 'My stomach is doing flips! I wasn't expecting anything so, so grand.'

'Well he is going to be the next King of England.'

'Oh dear.'

Molly slumped forward and rested her head in her hands.

'I'll get you a drink of water.'

'I could do with something stronger than that.'

Marcus pulled a blue silk rope and somewhere down below a bell rang to summon a servant. While they waited, he rubbed a hand across her back.

'Just breathe. I don't think there's anything to get worked up about.'

Molly didn't argue but was far from reassured.

Chapter Three

Royalty

Molly and Marcus were dressed in their finest. Marcus in the uniform of a General of the Royal Guard of Sunjian, given to him by Nareema, Mollys adopted sister.

Brilliant white jacket and trousers with gold piping and a wide royal blue sash running from his right shoulder to left hip. The sash was edged in silver and had a large, star shaped, silver brooch pinned at the top.

At his side hung a heavy curved sword, its highly polished scabbard covered in deeply engraved whorls and lines.

He looked stunning although the right sleeve was pinned up, hiding the fact he had lost his right hand to the evil Tong Li during their quest for the Stones of Gunjai.

Molly wore a silver off the shoulder gown with wide skirts. It was trimmed with fine lace and teardrop shaped pearls. Mollys dressmaker, Mrs Hopkins, had outdone herself.

Gwen, had done her hair, pinning it up and topping it off with a silver and diamond tiara. Around her neck she wore a heavy silver and diamond necklace with matching earrings.

Long silver silk gloves and a matching wrap was draped across her shoulders, almost, but not quite, hiding her tattoo.

The deep and intricate tattoo that covered her entire back was of a huge eagle with its wings curving up across her shoulders and upper arms.

It was her mark.

Her link to the Darkness.

It was given to her by the Daughters of Kali when she was in India and had hurt beyond belief when she got it.

Pinned to her left breast was a small silver brooch shaped like a bird in flight and on her left wrist was an exquisite silver bracelet with a perfectly cut sapphire set into it.

'Do you think this is too much?' she asked Marcus.

He shook his head, beaming with pride.

'You look lovely.'

She'd blushed.

'Although, I hope you'll try not to ruin this one?'

She stuck her tongue out at him. He was right, she didn't have a good track record when it came to fine dresses. They always seemed to end up torn or covered in dirt and blood.

'That's not very ladylike.' he told her as he gave her a kiss.

'I'm not a lady.'

'No.' he said, 'You're a Princess.'

'I'm not sure I'm one of those either.'

'Nonsense.'

She smiled tightly.

'Are you ready?' he asked, offering her his arm.

'I'm never going to be ready.'

'You'll be fine.'

He led her out of the room and down the stairs. At the bottom, they were met by a liveried servant.

'Please follow me.'

The man led them into an enormous room with an amazing painted fresco on the ceiling featuring jungles and elephants. The jungle looked light and airy, obviously the painter had never seen a real jungle, thought Molly. It certainly hadn't looked like that when she'd been there.

There were fifty or so other people in the room, chatting in small groups. All were dressed in their finest. There were military men, resplendent in their uniforms and medals and others in finely cut suits.

Molly absently wondered how many of the women there were actually married to the men they were with. She'd heard stories about the posh men and their mistresses.

She mentally shrugged the thought away and took in the women more closely. Jewellery and fine silks seemed to be the order of the day, along with flamboyant feathers from exotic birds.

Not one of them would have seen a hard days' work or hunger in their lives and Molly instantly began to hate them all.

Their escorting servant stopped in the doorway and whispered in the ear of another man. This one, while still obviously a servant, was dressed in a gold tunic with braiding. He nodded to the first man and then glanced at Molly and Marcus.

'Ready?' asked Marcus, squeezing her hand.

'For what?'

The golden liveried servant stepped forward, cleared his throat and announced them to the room.

'Her Royal Highness, Lady Molly Kane of Sunjian and her husband, Sir General Marcus Kane.'

All conversation stopped and everyone turned to look. Molly blushed furiously at the attention.

'This is just like my first ball. I didn't like it then either.' she whispered.

Marcus smiled at her and escorted her in.

'Let them stare.'

'But that's exactly what they're doing!' she hissed back, unconsciously clinging onto his arm like a drowning woman.

'Calm down.'

He let go of her hand and took two glasses of champagne from a servant bearing a tray as around them the conversation began again. Molly blushed further as she knew that they were all talking about her.

'I don't know if I can do this.'

'Of course you can.' said Marcus with a smile as he handed her a drink.

'Then why do I want the ground to swallow me up?'

'Take a deep breath and forget them. You're a Princess. You outrank them and they'll be falling over themselves in a moment just to speak to you.'

As if to confirm Marcus' words, a handsome man in an army uniform stepped up. He was in his early forties with greying hair and a wide moustache. Bright blue eyes held a mischievous sparkle and he smiled widely.

'Your Highness.' he said, bowing low and, as he straightened, he gently took her hand and kissed it.

'Sir.' said Molly, taken aback.

The man turned to Marcus and saluted crisply.

'Major Harry Gould at your service sir.'

'Major Gould.'

He offered Marcus his left hand to shake, obviously having taken in Marcus' missing right.

'I thought I'd get my introduction in early.' he said, before leaning in conspiratorially, 'Before the rest of the fops and dandies with their painted mistresses get to you.'

Molly looked down but couldn't help but smile.

'Ah. Told you.' he whispered as a small group of women bustled forward.

They all curtseyed deeply before the oldest of the group, somewhere in her fifties Molly judged, spoke.

'Your Highness. It is a great pleasure to meet you. We've heard so many stories.'

Molly smiled tightly. What sort of stories, she wondered.

'Hello.' she muttered unenthusiastically.

The woman opened her mouth to say something else, but a blazing fanfare erupted from the doorway, cutting her off.

Molly turned to see two more golden dressed servants holding long trumpets. The announcing man moved to the centre of the doorway.

'His Royal Highness, Prince George, the Prince Regent.'

The servant stepped aside and in he came. Nearly everyone in the room bowed or curtseyed, staying down until the Prince was ready. Nearly everyone.

Molly stood open mouthed.

The Prince was a large man. Not muscular but he had a certain, weight, about him. His face was dominated by a large nose, under which the podgy flesh of his chins wobbled. A mass of dark brown hair covered his head, but his bright blue eyes were focused and sharp.

He was dressed in a black jacket and trousers with a silver brooch on his lapel. While around his neck hung a pendant on a red silk ribbon.

He took a sip from a golden goblet he had clutched in his right hand before taking in the room.

Molly felt a gentle tug on her dress and she glanced down to see Marcus bowing low.

'Molly…' he hissed.

She looked at him and then up again at the Prince Regent. He had noticed that she was the only one in the room not bowing to him and a wry smile passed across his lips before he came over to her.

'Molly!' hissed Marcus again but it was too late, the Prince Regent was stood in front of them.

He smiled at Molly before dipping his head in a very slight bow.

'You must be Lady Kane.'

Molly looked at him, mouth still open. There was another, not so gentle, tug on her dress and she remembered where she was. Dropping into a small and ungainly curtsey she stammered.

'Yes Your Highness.'

The Prince Regent smiled again, as if enjoying some personal joke before he turned to the still bowed assembly.

'Rise my friends.'

There was a stilted pause as the rest of the people in the room straightened. The Prince Regent turned once more to Molly.

'I'm sorry Your Highness, I….'

He smiled once more and offered her his hand. Molly didn't know whether to take it or kiss it. In the end she did the former.

He nodded and led her out of the room and into another across the hall. This was just as large and as fabulously decorated as the last but had a small stage at the far end with lots of chairs set looking towards it, a bit like a theatre.

Behind them, the other guests followed. The Prince Regent led her up to the stage and helped her step up.

'I gather you have quite a tale to tell.' he said, 'My guests and I would like to hear it.'

He went and sat in the large chair in the middle of the room while the rest of the guests sat around him, leaving Molly stood on the small stage.

There were many hushed conversations until the Prince Regent raised a hand and an expectant silence fell. Molly could feel the hundred pairs of eyes on her as they waited. She licked her lips nervously, mouth suddenly dry.

'May I, um, may I have a drink please?'

'Of course.' said the Prince Regent and with a wave, ushered a servant forward. The man handed Molly a silver goblet containing a deep red wine.

She took it with shaking hands and a small terrified smile before taking a sip. Glancing to the side, she saw Marcus stood near the edge of the stage. He smiled encouragingly.

She could do this.

Snatches of impatient conversation were building from the back of the room.

She could do this.

Lifting the cup of wine to her lips she drained it in one and handed it back the servant before letting out a long breath.

'My name…' she faltered and looked at Marcus.

He smiled once more and nodded, willing her on.

Taking another deep breath, Molly started again, gaining courage with every word.

'My name is Molly Kane. I am the adopted sister of Her Royal Highness Princess Nareema Kareen Vashti, first daughter of the Maharajah of Sunjian. I am a Daughter of Kali and I was the Keeper of the Stones of Gunjai.'

She let that sink in for a second, the quiet conversations ending until the room was entirely silent.

'A year ago, I had nothing. This is my story…'

Chapter Four

Dinner Conversation

Molly finished speaking and stared out at the crowd.

They were silent now, the gasps of astonishment and snatches of conversation that had accompanied the story were gone.

She could feel them waiting for something.

Waiting for the Prince Regent.

Slowly, he handed a nearby servant his wine cup before standing up. He glanced around the room once, then smiled and began to applaud. This was the signal and soon, the entire room was on its feet and clapping.

Molly felt herself blush.

'Bravo, what a story. What a story.' intoned the Prince Regent.

Gradually the applause died down and the Prince Regent turned to his guests.

'We have been heartily entertained, now let us be heartily fed!'

He walked up to the stage and offered Molly his hand. She took it and he helped her down.

'Come my dear.'

The Prince Regent led Molly once more.

They headed out of the room and down the corridor to an enormous dining room. The table was laid with all manner of fruits and exotic looking foods.

Prince George led her along the table, gently depositing her six seats from the end before he took up his place in a large chair at the head of the table as the assembly began to file in.

Marcus was seated opposite her but the table was so wide and full of glasses and cutlery that speaking to him was almost impossible.

To her left sat a stiff woman in a blue dress with matching feathers in her hair. She looked at Molly and smiled but it didn't reach her eyes.

She didn't like Molly and her manner said everything that she needed to know.

'Very nice story.'

Molly looked up at the man sitting down on her right. It was Major Gould.

Despite herself, she could feel her cheeks redden.

'Thank you, sir.'

'Call me Harry.'

She blushed further. There was something disarmingly handsome about him and she could feel herself getting flustered.

'You told it very well.'

'It's as much as I remember.'

A servant poured them both a large glass of red wine. Molly picked hers up and drained it in one. Major Gould smiled.

'I've not seen a lady drink like that before.'

'Then you don't know the right sort of lady.'

He looked at her for a second before he burst out laughing.

'I probably don't.'

The woman on the other side sniffed and tutted loudly. Molly gave her a glance and a frown. At the head of the table, the Prince Regent was tucking into a large pie.

Servants began to circulate, depositing more food and drink in front of the guests. A thick soup was handed to Molly. She eyed it suspiciously.

'What's this?'

The Major looked up from his own bowl.

'Soup a la Flamond.'

She looked at him blankly.

'It's a creamy vegetable soup. It's got onions, carrots, lettuce and a few other things in it. Then the finish it off with egg yolks and cream.'

Molly tried it. It wasn't that bad.

'You seem to know a lot about it.' she said between spoonful's.

The Major shrugged.

'I pick the odd thing or two up. Besides, it's one of my favourites.'

Across the table, Marcus was in an animated conversation with a man to his right.

'Your husband seems to be enjoying himself.' commented the Major.

Molly smiled as she watched her husband.

'Yes. We don't go out much.'

Harry looked at her quizzically.

'A Princess and a General? I'm surprised you don't have dinner invitations coming out of your ears. Especially with the stories you tell.'

She shrugged sadly.

'We get a lot of invitations.'

'Then why not take them up?'

Molly put her spoon down, suddenly she didn't feel that hungry.

'Honestly? I'm scared.'

'Scared? I…'

'Major.' interrupted Molly, 'I'm not used to this. A year ago I truly had nothing more than the tattered dress on my back. I don't know how to behave, I don't have the manners, the..' she struggled for the word '… the etti… um…'

'Etiquette.'

'That's it. Etiquette. I'm not educated. I don't fit in.'

She looked down at her hands. Across the table, Marcus caught her eye.

'Is everything alright?' he mouthed.

Molly nodded and smiled sadly. Next to her, the Major topped up his wine from a decanter then refilled Molly's.

'I wouldn't worry about it.' he said kindly. 'Have a drink, enjoy the food and be grateful you don't have to pay the bill.'

Molly laughed, her mood rising.

'I'm sorry. I've been so nervous about today, I'm all over the place. It's a bit like when I met Marcus' parents for the first time.'

'Really?'

'No.' she said with a shake of her head. 'There's no thirty-foot tall monster trying to kill me.'

Major Gould looked at her as if he couldn't decide if she were joking or not. Eventually he shrugged.

'Well, the night is young.'

More food was delivered. There were plates of duck, saddles of lamb, pies, vegetables and more wine than could be good for anyone.

'Have you seen any fighting Major?' asked Molly, placing her knife and fork on the gilt-edged plate.

'Some.'

'Marcus was a Waterloo. He hasn't said much about it.'

'It wasn't a very nice place. Battles always sound more exciting than they are. The reality is far from pretty.'

Molly picked up her glass and had a sip.

'Most things are. What part of the army are you in Major?'

'Logistics.'

'I'm sorry, I don't know what that means.'

He laughed.

'I move things about. Make sure people are where they should be and they've got what they need.'

'A stores-man?'

'Something like that.'

'Oh.' replied Molly.

They lapsed into an uncomfortable silence, broken after a second by a huge guffaw of laughter from the Prince Regent. Molly looked at the Major.

'I'm sorry.' she said.

'What for?' he enquired, puzzled.

'I'm sure there's lots more to you than that. I'm not very good at this whole thing.'

He patted her on the hand and she blushed.

'You're doing marvellously.'

There was another silence.

'If you don't mind me asking, why is a stores-man at a dinner with the Prince Regent?'

'That's a very observant question.'

Molly shrugged.

'I like to know what's going on.'

'You're a very clever woman.' replied the Major.

'Thank you. But you still haven't answered my question.'

He smiled his charming smile.

'Ah, dessert.' he said, changing the subject.

A servant cleared their plates while another deposited a glass dish in front of them containing some small white balls.

'What's this?' asked Molly, distracted slightly by the contents of the dish.

The Major smiled at her.

'Ice cream.'

He picked up a spoon and had a small taste.

'Rose flavoured if I'm not mistaken. Try it. I'm sure you'll like it.'

Very tentatively Molly picked up her spoon and tried a tiny bit. It was the most extraordinary thing she'd ever had. It was cold and creamy with a gentle flowery hint.

Across the table from her, Marcus was watching and smiling widely, his own spoon in his hand. Molly took another, larger, spoonful.

'Slow down,' said the Major, 'You'll get a headache.'

Molly grinned like a child, spoon in her mouth.

Next to her the woman tutted again and spoke in a hushed tone to the person next to her. Molly didn't catch all of the conversation but the words "Pretend Princess" were obvious.

She tried to ignore the rising anger she was feeling and concentrate on the food.

'That was amazing.' she said, as she cleared her dish and, much to the visible horror of the woman on her left, she pulled off one of her gloves, licked her finger and ran it around the bowl until nothing was left.

The Major watched her with amusement.

'Good isn't it. Not sure how they make it but I do find it most palatable.'

She glanced at the Majors dish, it was still mostly full.

'Are you going to eat that?'

He laughed and pushed it towards her.

'Be my guest.'

She took it with a smile, which fell quickly at another loud tut from the woman on the other side of her. Molly carefully put the spoon down and turned to face her.

'Yes?' she asked. 'Do you have anything to say?'

'No Your Highness.' she replied, although her tone suggested otherwise.

'If you have a problem with me, then say it.' snapped Molly, 'Otherwise will you kindly shut the hell up.'

The woman blanched as around them the temperature fell dramatically. A strange knot of discomfort, almost like fear, began to form in those guests that were sat nearby.

'I'm waiting.'

The woman swallowed dryly, unable to find any words to placate the hard look on Mollys face.

'Molly.' said Marcus loudly and sternly.

Those guests that weren't close looked around and a silence descended on the whole room.

She held the woman's gaze for a moment before looking away. The silence and sense of fear began to slowly lift. Molly pinched the bridge of her nose.

'Are you alright?' asked the Major.

She smiled tightly.

'I have a bit of a headache. I think I may go and lie down.'

'Here, have a drink.'

He picked up her glass and was surprised to find that the wine inside was frozen. He opened and closed his mouth a few times.

'Good night Major.'

She stood and went to the Prince Regent, curtsying awkwardly.

'Your Highness. Please excuse me. I'm not feeling that well and am going to retire for the evening. It has been a pleasure to meet you.'

'Nonsense.' he exclaimed. 'We're going to have dancing and music!'

'Thank you but no. I can't.'

He opened his mouth to reply but she had already turned and was walking away.

Around the table, everyone watched her go. Marcus made his excuses and followed, catching up with her in the hallway.

'Molly. Are you alright?'

'Just a bit tired Marcus.'

He didn't look convinced.

'It's something else too. Did you feel it?'

'Feel what?'

He lent in and whispered, as if saying it would transport them to that foul realm between life and death where the souls of the dead walked.

'The Darkness.'

She looked at him as if he were mad.

'Don't be silly. I can only go there if I summon my eagle and I've only done that a couple of times since we got back from India. I don't like it. It scares me and…' she tailed off, the harrowing thoughts that ran through her head more than visible on her face.

'Come on let's go.' he said, trying not to let his own troubled thoughts show. He offered his arm and she took it with a sad smile.

As they began to walk back to their rooms, there was a polite cough and call from behind them.

'Your Highness?'

Molly turned around. She really wanted to go to sleep. The meal had been extravagant, she had eaten far too much and she had a furious headache.

Behind them was the servant who had initially carried the dinner invitation from the Prince Regent. He short and round with a badly fitted wig perched on his head that looked like a mushroom. The man sauntered over and bowed low.

'My name is Harrington and I was wondering if I, ah, may trouble you for a moment or two of, ah, your time.'

'Can it wait until tomorrow?' she asked.

He smiled, the corners of his mouth turning up and out and giving Molly the impression of a toad. A toad under a mushroom.

'It, ah, won't take a moment, I assure you.'

She looked at her husband, who shrugged. In the end, she sighed.

'What do you want?'

He smiled again.

'Please follow me.'

The man led them down a few corridors to a more spartan area of the building. These corridors were draughty and were made of stone devoid of the decoration and decadence of the rest of the place. He showed them into a small, windowless room with a desk and three chairs.

'Please sit.'

Marcus pulled the chair out for his wife and then sat himself. Across the desk, the slimy man sat on his own chair.

'I'm sorry to interrupt your, ah, evening Your Highness but I was wondering if, ah, you could help me with a little issue.'

Marcus frowned at him

'What sort of issue?' inquired Molly.

'Ah, well, it's quite delicate but I'm sure a woman of your, ah, talents, will be able to resolve it with the minimum of fuss.'

Molly looked at her husband.

'Just tell me what you want please.'

The man smiled his toady smile.

'Sir Wilfred Hancock owns quite a large area of the dockyards and, ah, is responsible for a lot of money coming into this country. He, ah, has been having a little trouble lately and I was wondering if you would, ah, take a look into it for me.'

'What sort of trouble?' asked Marcus suspiciously.

Molly sat forward on her chair.

'The sort of trouble that causes his workers to have their hearts ripped out.'

'What!'

'Absolutely not!' said Marcus.

The man smiled once more.

'With the greatest respect sir, I, ah, that is, the Prince Regent and the Crown, was asking your wife. Not you.'

Marcus bristled with anger.

'How dare you sir…'

Molly laid a hand on his arm.

'I can't.' she said.

'There would be a suitable, ah, recompense. A large estate and castle in Scotland along with its associated titles of course. That and, ah, the thanks of the Crown...'

Molly shook her head and stood.

'No.'

The man smiled tightly.

'Of course. Thank you for your, ah, time. If you will please follow me, I will, ah, show you to your rooms.'

He stood and without another word led them upstairs to their suite. He bowed low before leaving. As soon as the door closed behind him, Marcus erupted.

'The cheek of the man...'

Molly smiled.

'Let it go. It seems your aunt Sarah was right. Maybe I have got a reputation.'

'He wanted you to go after something that's killing people.' raged Marcus, ignoring her completely. 'Tearing their hearts out! Who does he think he is? Who does he think you are?'

'What sort of question is that?'

'What?' asked Marcus, blindsided by her response.

'Who does he think I am? Who do *you* think I am?'

'I...' he began to reply, flustered by the change of direction in the conversation.

Molly shook her head.

'It doesn't matter.'

Later that night, Molly lay awake. The moon was high and bright, casting its rays into the room and making it almost like day. Next to her, Marcus was snoring lightly. Carefully, she slipped out of bed and padded to the window.

Below her the extensive gardens were immaculate in the moonlight. She rested her head on the window. Who was she? *What* was she? She didn't know any more. Was she a Princess or just playing at it? The pretend Princess?

She sighed and turned away from the window. She needed to think. Hardly making a sound, she left the room and headed to the gardens.

The grass was damp and cool beneath her bare feet as she walked in the moonlight. Behind her, the Pavilion was large and imposing, its southern face deeply in shadow. Idly, Molly picked her way through the garden, not really paying attention to where she was going.

She was brought up short when a voice shouted from the shadowy depths of a stone building near a wide lake.

'Halt.'

Two soldiers emerged into the moonlight. Both carried guns and one was quickly stubbing out the remains of a cigarette. They moved cautiously towards her and she caught a whiff of alcohol on them.

'What're you doing?' demanded the first one.

'Just out for a walk. I should be getting back.'

The men looked at her, taking in her thin nightdress before they glanced at each other and the first one grabbed her arm.

'I don't think so. You're coming with us.'

Molly shouted and reacted instantly, driving her fist into the side of his head. He cursed and let her go. She pivoted and kicked the musket from the hands of the other before punching him hard.

He staggered back and Molly moved away from them, ready for more trouble.

The soldier who grabbed her cursed again and raised his musket.

'You're going to regret that.' he snarled.

'Really?' she said.

Molly span around as from behind her came a loud crack of a gun. Standing there was Major Gould. He had a smoking pistol in his hand, pointing towards the sky.

'Is there a problem here?'

Immediately the soldiers snapped to attention.

'We've found an intruder sir. She was resisting…'

'I hardly think that Her Royal Highness is an intruder.'

'Sir.'

The Major winked at Molly as from near the building, another group of soldiers came running. They skidded to a halt.

'Is there a problem sir?'

'Yes. These two men. They're on a charge. Dereliction of duty, being drunk and assaulting a member of the Royal family of Sunjian.'

'What?' cried the soldier who had grabbed Molly.

'Get them out of here.'

'Yes sir.'

The men were dragged away, protesting their innocence as they went.

Molly looked at the Major.

'Thank you.'

He slid his pistol into his belt.

'No harm done. But I wouldn't advise that you go wandering around in the dark in your nightgown in future. Some of the men might get the wrong idea.'

She looked down and flushed with embarrassment which was made worse by his disarming smile. Casually he slipped off his jacket.

'May I?'

She didn't know what he meant until he draped it over her shoulders.

'You don't want to be catching a chill now, do you?'

She shook her head.

'Come on, let's get you back.'

He offered her his arm and after a moments' hesitation, she took it and allowed herself to be led back towards the building.

'So what are you doing out in the dark?'

Molly shrugged.

'I couldn't sleep.'

'Ah. Probably too much ice cream.'

There was an embarrassed silence.

'What about you?' she asked, trying to fill the void.

'Me? I was just taking some air.'

'Oh.'

He looked at her and she blushed again.

'I may need to get the Captain of the guard to review the men in the morning.'

'Why?'

'Well two of them just got beaten up by a girl.'

She looked at him sharply with a flash of anger.

'I mean no offence Your Highness but to look at you, you wouldn't seem the type to be able to take on two soldiers.'

She looked back down at the floor.

'Well...' she muttered. 'They shouldn't have grabbed me...'

'And I expect they're regretting it now. More so in the morning.'

'What're you going to do to them?'

'They'd been drinking. I could smell it a mile off. Drinking whilst on duty is forbidden and they know it. I will see that they're suitably punished.'

'Oh. I didn't mean to get...'

'No. Don't fret Your Highness. You are not responsible for them. They're grown men and will have to face the consequences of their actions.'

They walked the rest of the way to the Pavilion in silence. He patted her arm in a friendly manner as they reached the stairs.

'There we are, all safe and sound. Is there anything I can get for you?'

'No. Thank you.'

She slipped his jacket off and handed it back.

'I will see you in the morning. Maybe I could persuade you to give me a demonstration of your fighting skills before you head back to London?'

Molly blushed again and looked at the floor.

'I don't know about that.' she replied sheepishly.

The Major smiled and saluted crisply and clicked his heels together.

'Good night Your Highness.'

'Good night Major.'

'Please. Call me Harry.'

He smiled once more before tuning on his heel and heading away. Molly watched him go before letting out a breath she didn't know she had been holding. Her heart was pounding in her chest. Taking a long breath, she headed back to bed.

Chapter Five

Taking the Job

After she had returned to bed, Molly had slept badly, her dreams troubled to the point that Marcus had woken her up before her tormented thrashing and painful sobs woke the whole pavilion.

So, it was with an aching tiredness and blinding headache that she met Gwen the next morning. Molly was sat in one of the leather armchairs massaging her temples when the girl came in.

'Good morning Your Ladyship.'

'Stop with the Ladyship stuff Gwen. I'm not feeling that well.'

The girl wrung her hands.

'The Prince Regent is taking breakfast on the terrace this morning and he has requested that you and the master join him.'

Molly sighed heavily.

'I've taken the liberty of picking you something to wear.'

'Thank you.'

'Would you like me to help you dress?'

Molly shook her head and stood up.

'No. I'll manage.'

'Very good Your Ladyship.'

'Actually, there is something you can do for me. I want you to go and find Simcox. We're going home this morning and I don't want to stop on the way. We're just going straight back to London. Can you sort that out?'

'Of course.'

The girl curtseyed and left. Idly Molly wondered how she managed to do it without looking like a fish flopping on a quayside, something that she herself always felt she looked like.

Marcus was already dressed when she went back into the bedroom.

'How are you feeling this morning?'

'Tired.'

He smiled tightly, her nightmares had been better recently but last night, well he was worried.

'We're to have breakfast with the Prince Regent apparently.' Molly told him.

'Then you'd better get dressed. Gwen has already chosen something for you.'

'I know. She told me.'

Trying to summon some enthusiasm Molly went into the dressing room.

Hanging by the wardrobe was a pale blue dress edged in fine lace. It was beautiful but probably not what Molly would have picked.

She would have gone for something simple but then again, she was having breakfast with the future King. Shaking her head and trying to clear the settling fog in her mind, she began to dress.

Breakfast had been pleasant, the morning sunshine doing wonders to lift Molly's spirits. They had given their thanks to the Prince Regent and had left as quickly as they dared, Molly keen to be home.

The Prince Regent had invited them back as he had wanted to hear more about Molly and her stories and they'd had to agree just to get away.

As she and Marcus walked through the hall they met Major Gould coming the other way.

'Leaving so soon?'

'Yes. I'm not feeling that well today.'

'I'm sorry to hear that. I hope your adventures last night had nothing to do with it.'

Molly shook her head and Marcus frowned but said nothing. The Major smiled and bent to kiss her hand.

'It has been a pleasure and an education to meet you Your Highness.'

Despite herself, Molly couldn't hide her blushes. The Major straightened and offered his hand to Marcus.

'General. I do hope to meet you and your charming wife again.'

'Thank you Major.' said Marcus, shaking the proffered hand.

They both watched him leave before heading out to the carriage.

The trip home was long and uncomfortable. Marcus was silent for quite a lot of the journey, at least until they were a few streets from their house.

'So are you going to tell me what "adventures" you were having with Major Gould last night? Are they the reason you've started having bad dreams again?' asked Marcus pointedly.

'You know why I have bad dreams.'

He didn't say anything.

'Don't be like that Marcus.'

'Like what?'

'Jealous.'

He made a harrumph noise and folded his arms before turning to stare resolutely out of the window.

Molly sighed.

'I couldn't sleep so I went for a walk in the gardens. I bumped into some of the soldiers that guard the Pavilion. They thought I was an intruder. One grabbed me and…'

'He did what?'

'He grabbed my arm so I punched him. The Major stepped in and stopped things getting out of hand. Then he escorted me back. That's it.'

Marcus looked at her but said nothing.

'Oh, stop it. I can take care of myself you know.'

'By attacking soldiers.'

'He grabbed me! What did you expect me to do?' she snapped.

'Sometimes I think you go looking for trouble.'

'I do not!'

'What about that business in the village? You certainly…'

'That was not my fault.'

'I never said it was. What about India?'

Now it was Mollys turn to remain silent.

'I could have saved you from the pain and nightmares. But no. You had to go after the Crown on your own.'

'I wasn't on my own and no, you couldn't have saved me. He'd have killed you.'

'But I could have tried…'

'No Marcus.' she told him with an iron certainty.

He sighed. He *would* have been killed. Malor had only kept Molly alive so she could be a sacrifice to his dark Gods and cement his power over the Stones of Gunjai. He looked out of the window.

'Sometimes I think that you seem to have a casual disregard for your own safety.'

'And what is that supposed to mean?' she demanded.

'You go heading off into the dark without a thought to what's out there or who's going to get hurt.'

Molly opened her mouth to snap a reply, but in the end, she just huffed, folded her arms and glared out of the window. As much as she wanted to deny it, he was right, but it hurt to be told that.

They travelled the rest of the way in silence, staring out of opposite windows, both too stubborn to admit they were wrong. As soon as the coach had stopped outside their home, Molly was out and through the door.

Gwen and Simcox had arrived not too much before them and the girl tried to talk to her but, Molly just swept past and through into the garden to the summer house.

It was called a summer house, but the interior was far from standard. It was large and open plan with a woven reed mat on the floor. The far wall held a large array of weapons, most of which Molly was scared to touch.

A large padded sack hung from the ceiling and in the far corner sat a stout pole with other smaller poles jutting out of it at odd angles. It was to this that she headed.

Taking a deep breath, she began striking the smaller poles using her hands and forearms. The wood rattled from the force of the blows for a few seconds before she shouted out in anger and punched the main pole as hard as she could.

Pain flashed along her arm as the wood resisted her blow and she cursed loudly.

Turning away from the poles she cradled her right hand with her left as Gwen tentatively knocked before coming in.

'Are you alright?' the girl asked.

Molly bit back a sharp retort. It wasn't her fault.

She nodded as the girl came over.

'Yes. I'm fine. Marcus and I have had a little disagreement. That's all.'

'Let me have a look.' said Gwen, reaching up to take Mollys hand.

'I said it's fine.' snapped Molly.

Gwen took a surprised step back. There had been a flash of something in Molly's eyes. Something dark against the usual dull white. She swallowed nervously and bobbed a curtsey.

'Very good Your Ladyship.'

The girl turned to go and Molly sighed.

'Gwen. I'm sorry. Please.'

She sat down heavily on the floor as Gwen came back over.

'Do you want to talk about it?' she asked, sitting down opposite her.

Molly shook her head.

'No.' she replied softly.

They were silent for a moment.

'I'm sorry. I'm quite tired.' said Molly eventually.

'Are you having the, um, nightmares again?' Gwen asked tentatively.

Once more, Molly shook her head.

'No.' she lied, not wanting any further fussing. 'Not for a little while.'

'That's good.'

The nightmares were terrifying and last night had been the worst for a while. She and Marcus had travelled to India in search of the Crown of Gunjai and during their search, Molly had been taken captive by a man possessed by an ancient spirit.

He'd hurt her for the fun of it and she would often wake up with his laughter in her ears and the pain wracking her body.

'Am I normal?' she asked.

Gwen looked at her.

'What do you mean?'

'I mean. Do you think I go looking for trouble? Should I stop all this?'

She gestured to the racks of weapons on the wall.

'Do you want to?'

'I don't know.'

Gwen looked at her hands for a moment.

'If you didn't do it, what would you do?'

Molly shrugged.

'Learn to be a lady I suppose. Fit into my station in life.'

'Be seen and not heard?'

She shrugged again and idly picked at the mat on the floor.

'If you weren't you, then I'd be dead.' said Gwen matter-of-factly.

Molly looked up.

'That's a bit of an exaggeration.'

'It isn't. The Grand Master would have killed me and that thing would be loose.'

Molly shook her head but Gwen was right. If she hadn't been there, the scarred man would have murdered Gwen and released the demon Carnothal into the world. Then who knows what would have happened?

'I mean, you use what you can do for good. Right?' asked Gwen.

'I don't know. I just do what's necessary.'

The girl stood up.

'I'm not an expert on these things. Maybe you should talk to the master... I mean your husband about it.' said Gwen, hurriedly changing her description of Marcus as she caught Molly's look.

Molly didn't like to think of herself as Gwen's mistress or Marcus as her master even though the girl was in their employ and that was how things were done. Gwen got up.

'I'll go and see if dinner is ready.'

'Thank you.'

Molly watched her go before she stood up. Not for the first time since she got back from India, she wished her Nareema was here. She could talk to her about this stuff.

She sighed sadly. What was she going to do?

The next day and after another sleepless night troubled by black nightmares, Molly and Marcus went for a walk. The park was always nice at this time of the year and the summer sun was high and warm.

'I'm going to go and see Uncle Tobias.' said Molly.

Marcus looked at her.

'I promised to tell him what happened with the search for the Crown. And well, to be honest, it's a story he's going to love.'

Tobias Callahan was not in any way related to Molly. She'd met him through Nareema as they searched for the Stones of Gunjai. He was an academic and scholar and he knew more about the Stones than anyone. His scatty and eccentric nature was truly endearing and Molly had promised to visit to tell him of their adventures.

'Very well. We'll go...'

'I'm going on my own Marcus.' she said, interrupting him.

'What?' he asked in disbelief. 'I couldn't possibly...'

She stopped and turned to him.

'I need to think, Marcus. I need some time to work out who I am.' She looked down. 'To work out *what* I am.'

'You're you and I love you for that. I'm sorry about yesterday. I just get so worried about you.'

She smiled sadly.

'I'm sorry too. Honestly, nothing happened the other night that I couldn't handle. I can take care of myself.'

'I know. It's just, the nightmares...'

Molly looked down again.

'They're getting better.' she lied.

'Really?'

'I think so.'

They began to walk along again.

'You should talk to me about them. About India.'

'I will. When the time is right.'

'You can't keep it bottled up...'

'I know. I need to be clear in my head first. Then I'll talk to you about it. I promise.'

Marcus frowned.

'I promise.' she repeated, placing a hand on his arm.

'Very well.'

They ambled along in a companionable silence.

'I'm still going to see Uncle Tobias.'

Marcus nodded.

'Are you sure you don't want me to come with you?'

Molly shook her head.

'No. Thank you. I need to do this on my own.'

'I assume Gwen is going?'

'I wasn't going to…'

Marcus turned to his wife.

'I insist. If you must go halfway across the country, then at least take your maid with you. It is unseemly for a lady of your standing to travel without a servant.'

She laughed.

'You sound so pompous. I don't have a standing.'

'Pompous! I am not!' he protested.

She elbowed him in the ribs.

'Yes you are, Sir General Marcus Kane.'

'Well I have every right to be pompous. I'm married to you. Your Royal Highness, Lady Molly Kane of Sunjian, Daughter of Kali and Keeper of the Stones of Gunjai. If that doesn't give me the right, then I don't know what does!'

She laughed.

'What time is it?'

Marcus took out his pocket watch.

'It's… Hey!'

Molly snatched it out of his hand.

'You forgot to add "one-time thief" to the list.' she said with a smile before running off a few paces.

'Give that back.' he said, his own grin nearly as wide as hers.

'Come and get it.' she replied, before turning and running off through the park.

Marcus counted to five and then gave chase.

'Now are you sure you've got everything?'

'Yes. Don't fuss.'

Molly lent out of the carriage window and gave her husband a kiss.

'Gwen and I will be fine.'

'I still think I should be coming with you.'

'No Marcus. Honestly.'

He sighed theatrically.

'We'll be back in a few weeks. I promise we'll be on our best behaviour.'

Before he could say anything else, she banged on the side of the carriage and it began to pull away.

'Miss you already!' she shouted as it left him standing in front of their house.

As soon as he was out of sight, she pulled her head back inside and sat down. Gwen was sat on the seat opposite and looking nervous.

'Are you sure this is a good idea?' the girl asked.

'Nope.' said Molly. 'It's a bad idea but it's the right thing to do.'

Gwen frowned.

Two days before, Molly had got her to take a letter to Harrington. She had handed it to an aide and waited for a reply. After three hours of standing around a draughty corridor, she had been summoned to see a short man in bad wig.

He'd sat across a large desk and regarded her critically. Gwen looked at the floor, feeling like she was being judged. Eventually he'd spoken.

'Tell your mistress that I'm, ah, grateful for her involvement in this matter. Please ask her to meet me here at, ah, ten o'clock on Wednesday. Do you understand the message?'

'Yes sir.'

'Repeat it.'

Gwen had swallowed nervously and repeated the message.

'Good.'

He'd looked down at his desk and began to make some notes on a piece of paper. A few seconds later, he'd looked back up again.

'Are you still here? Get away with you girl!'

'Yes sir.' Gwen had replied hurriedly before leaving.

She'd almost run from the building, there had been something in his tone that she didn't like. Something that gave her the impression he would have her killed her as soon as look at her.

Caught up in the fear, Gwen didn't notice the two men who followed her. They're clothes were well made but just rough enough to blend in. They kept a respectful distance but tracked her all the way home.

Chapter Six

Regrettable Actions

'So here you bloody well are.'

Captain Lewis lifted his weary and drink fuddled head from the table to stare at his first mate.

'Sod off.' he said before slumping back down.

The older man smiled and sat down.

'You ain't my Captain any more. You can't give me orders.'

'Just leave me alone.'

'What, so you can wallow in self pity for a bit longer?' he asked, picking up a half empty bottle and taking a swig.

Lewis didn't answer.

'You think you've got the monopoly of feeling sorry for yourself? I've lost my livelihood.'

The Captain sat up.

'And I've lost my bloody ship! It stinks worse than a shit heap and even if I had the bloody thing, I can't get a crew. No-one will go near it. They think it's cursed.'

Collier shrugged.

'Maybe it is.'

'Just piss off will you.'

The first mate took another swig.

'I heard that they took the Amarantha. It's a shame. She was a good ship.'

Lewis snatched the bottle back.

'She was. Contaminated, they say. A danger to health. What would they bloody know?'

'What're they going to do with her?'

'Don't know. Don't bloody care.'

'That's a lie.'

'Is it? They've got her tied up down at the wharf near the Osser warehouses.'

'I know the place. That's where they go before they're sent to the breakers.'

'Like me. That's where I should be going.'

'I'm fifty three! How'd you think I'm going to find another ship?'

'Why should I care?'

'I thought we were friends.'

Lewis took a long swig.

'What do you want me to say?'

They lapsed into a tense silence.

'Was it worth it?' asked Collier eventually.

'No. Money's gone. Paid off that fat bastard Porkonicov.'

'Now you're drinking yourself to death.'

'Yeah, and I want to do it in peace. So for the final time, sod off and leave me alone.'

'You need to sort it out. You're a good sailor. You can get another ship.'

'I can't.' said Lewis bitterly. 'That lawyer, Dickenson, he's seen to that. No-one will touch me with a pole. Can't even get a punt on the river. I'm cursed. Just like my ship. Just like you.'

'But we delivered...'

'We didn't. Not the full cargo. Not nothin'. Now if you've finally finished, I want to be left alone.'

Lewis took another drink before resting his head back on the table. Collier watched him for a minute before he shook his head and walked away.

The carriage rumbled along for a few miles until Molly banged on the side. The driver immediately stopped and she got out.

'Pass me my things please.'

Gwen lifted the seat of the carriage and took out a black leather backpack along with a long wooden box which she passed to Molly.

73

'I still don't think this is a good idea.'

'No. Well, I'm doing it.'

'But…'

Molly shut the carriage door but Gwen opened the window immediately and lent out.

'Enough. I'm going to do this. You just take the carriage and have a nice time seeing your family. There's enough money in the luggage to keep you entertained and not want for anything. Spoil them. I don't expect to get any of it back. The carriage will come and pick you up in a couple of weeks.'

'But…' Gwen said again.

'Trust me. Driver, please go.'

Before the girl could say anything else, the carriage began rolling off and Molly had turned and walked away towards the river. Gwen watched until she couldn't see Molly any more before sitting down heavily. She had a feeling that this wasn't going to end well.

Wednesday came and Molly attended her appointment with Harrington. She was met at the gate and escorted through a bewildering number of corridors before being shown into a large room.

Four expansive windows filled the south side while the rest of the room was covered in heavy dark panelling. It had expensive carpeting and a large fireplace took up most of the east wall.

'Mr Harrington will be with you shortly.'

The servant left, closing the door behind him. Left alone, Molly wandered around. Three large armchairs sat near the west wall and a big desk with a couple of uncomfortable looking seats were in front of the fireplace. To her left was a wide sideboard with a selection of expensive looking decanters and glasses carefully arranged on it. Not knowing what to do, she sat down.

A few minutes later, the door opened once more and she stood up as a man was shown in. Much to her surprise, it was Major Gould.

He seems as shocked to see her as she was to see him.

'Your Highness?'

'Major Gould. What are you doing here?'

'I was about to ask you the same thing.'

'Mr Harrington asked me to come.' she said.

The Major's brow furrowed in confusion.

'Your Highness, I don't...'

'It's just Molly.' she said, interrupting him, 'I don't like titles.'

The Major laughed.

'Molly it is then, and I insist you call me Harry. Did Harrington tell you what this was about?'

'He mentioned some deaths...' she replied vaguely.

Harry frowned.

'I'm not sure that you're the right person to be looking into this.'

'Well neither are you. What's a stores-man got to do with this?'

The Major grinned.

Drink?'

'No. Thank you.'

He nodded.

'Do you mind if I have one?'

'Why would I mind?'

He grinned again and she couldn't stop herself blushing.

Going over to the sideboard, he helped himself to a large whisky from a decanter.

'Are you sure I can't tempt you?' he asked as he poured.

She shook her head. Nerves had kicked in and she thought that if she were to have anything, she may not be able to keep it down. Her stomach was doing flips.

'Probably wise.'

He took a sip and sighed appreciatively.

'Harrington is many things, but he does keep a good drop of scotch.' The Major took another sip and smiled at Molly.

'Don't look so nervous.'

She looked at her hands in her lap.

'I'm not sure what I'm doing here. It all seemed so clear cut the other day but now? I don't know…' she looked up, '…and you didn't answer my question. I've got form for this sort of thing but what are you doing here?'

The Major looked puzzled once more and opened his mouth to reply but he was interrupted as the door opened and in bustled Harrington.

Once again, Molly was reminded of a toad in a wig as he smiled humourlessly.

'Your, ah, Highness. Major Gould. Thank you so much, ah, for coming.'

He sat down behind the large desk and looked between the two. Molly felt way out of her depth but the Major just sipped his drink as this was the most natural thing in the world.

Harrington cleared his throat.

'I'd offer you a, ah, drink but you seem to have, ah, helped yourselves.'

Major Gould raised his glass in a mock toast.

'As of this morning, I have had some more disturbing news. It's not just the holdings of Sir Wilfred Hancock that have been, ah, under…'

The Major put his glass down and interrupted him.

'Come on Harrington. Get down to it. Her Highness and I don't have all day.'

He caught Mollys eye and gave her a knowing wink and she couldn't help but smile a little. Harrington bristled.

'Major Gould. I am trying to explain what, ah, is going on!'

'Well make it quick, there's a good chap. Her Highness and I have a lunch to attend.'

Molly looked at him in surprise and he winked again.
The man behind the desk frowned.

'If you would let me finish, the attacks, ah, that I have alluded to, now seem to no longer be isolated to just the holdings of Sir Wilfred. They are, ah, spreading all along the dockside and I have received petitions from many of the, ah, owners…'

'What about the people who live there and don't own warehouses or ships?' asked Molly.

Harrington looked at her as if she were mad.

'I'm sorry?'

'There are lots of people who live around the docks. What about them?'

'Well naturally…'

'You don't care, do you?'

'Your Highness…'

Molly stood up, nerves replaced by an unexpected anger.

'You don't care because they don't make you any money.'

'I assure you, ah, that is not the case. Sir Wilfred…'

'Where is he?' she demanded.

'He is, ah, waiting for you at his, ah, properties by the waterfront. I have a, ah, carriage outside waiting to take you, ah, there.' Harrington said, surprised by her forthright attitude and anger.

Without another word, Molly stormed from the room, slamming the door behind her. Major Gould finished his drink and stood.

'Nice scotch. Better get on with it then.'

'Major Gould.'

The soldier turned back.

'I haven't given Sir Wilfred any, ah, specifics as to who will be attending him this afternoon. Neither have I mentioned this to the other half dozen gentlemen you will be seeing. It may be beneficial, for the time being at least, to try, ah, not to advertise the exact nature of who the Princess is.'

The man looked at him in silence for several seconds before he nodded once and then left without another word.

Harrington watched him leave. Reaching across his desk, he rang a small bell and a second later another man came in through a hidden door in the wood panelling.

He was dressed in scruffy, but not dirty, clothes and of average height, but there was a steeliness about him in the way he walked. A diagonal scar ran across his face from just above his left eye and down across the bridge of his nose while his dark hair was ruffled and stuck out at awkward angles from underneath his hat.

Harrington waited until he had sauntered across the room and was stood in front of his desk.

'Mr Potts. Follow them and if she looks like, ah, being a problem, kill her.'

The man nodded.

'What about her maid?' he asked, his voice like gravel.

'I've got a lad following her. She's left London and is heading north.'

Harrington considered this for a moment.

'No. Leave her be for now. Concentrate on the Princess.'

Mr Potts nodded again.

'And the Major?'

'I know your history with, ah, Major Gould and I trust you to use your discretion and act as you see fit. If he were, ah, to say, have an accident, then I'm sure he wouldn't be mourned for too long.'

A sly smile graced the lips of Mr Potts.

'As you wish.'

He left and after the door had closed, Harrington shook his head. This had seemed like a good idea. Send a monster to catch one.

Chapter Seven

Sir Wilfred Hancock

Molly was stood in the hallway when the Major came out. She was angry. She'd lost her temper. Again. He smiled at her.

'I thought you'd be on your way to see Sir Wilfred by now.'

Molly blushed embarrassedly which made her feel like a child who has had a tantrum for no reason.

'I would have.' she said, looking down before muttering, 'If I knew how to get out of here or where the carriage was.'

The Major grinned and offered her his arm.

'If you will allow me.'

She hesitated before sighing and slipping her arm through his.

'Don't let Harrington get to you.' he said, as they walked out of the building. 'The man is a complete arse who couldn't find his breeches without a map.'

They stopped outside, a thin drizzle had begun to fall so they dashed across to the waiting carriage, the Major opening the door before helping Molly in.

'It's probably nothing. Just some rival or another trying to strongarm his way in.'

'But he said that people had had their hearts torn out.' she replied as he climbed in and sat opposite her.'

He shook his head.

'I wouldn't expect so. It would take considerable force to actually tear someone's heart out. It'll have been some fighting and a little spilled blood. You mark my words.' Harry raised his eyebrows. 'I take it you're not adverse or scared of a little spilt blood?'

Molly looked him in the eye.

'No.'

'Somehow, I didn't think so.'

They rode along in silence for a few minutes.

'So, who is this William Handcork then?' asked Molly.

'Sir Wilfred Hancock.' corrected the Major. 'I don't know really. He made a lot of money importing goods from India and the Far East. I do know that we probably should have let Harrington finish though.'

'Sorry.' said Molly. 'I just couldn't stand him any longer. He makes my skin crawl. There's something about him that I just don't like. He hadn't even considered that there might be other people around the docks that might be scared, hurt or even worse. There are other people in the world you know.'

'There are.' agreed Harry. 'but sadly, none of them give him money. That's what it's all about I'm afraid. Harrington has the ear of the Prince and that gives him influence. He's probably on the payroll of Sir Wilfred and he's being pushed to do something about it.'

Molly frowned.

'That doesn't mean I have to like it.'

'No. I don't either.' said Major Gould, sitting forward. 'When we get there, let me do the talking. I do know that Sir Wilfred is an old man. He won't take kindly to being talked at by a woman.'

'I won't...' began Molly angrily.

The Major held his hand up and she stopped talking.

'I mean that as no slight, Your Highness. Things will be easier. That is all. I would also suggest you keep your temper in check, regardless of what he says.'

She looked at him in surprise.

'Don't look like that. I've only known you for a few days and in that time, you've got into a fight, stormed out of a meeting and now you're angry with me for telling you what to do. You may not agree with it but that's the way it's going to be.'

She folded her arms and glared at him.

'Do I take your sullen silence to be an agreement?'

'I don't know.' she muttered, 'What does "sullen" mean?'

He looked at her for a second as if trying to work out if she were being serious before laughing and shaking his head.

'Don't laugh at me.' she said angrily.

'I'm not. On my honour, I'm not. I fear that Harrington may have thrown you to the sharks.'

'What's that supposed to mean?'

'It means that beating the hell out of it won't make it go away. Sir Wilfred, Harrington and people like them swim in different circles to you. You're a small fish in a very big and dangerous pond.'

'What about you? How much knowledge of this does a stores-man have?'

Harry sighed.

'I didn't think I'd be telling you this so soon.'

'Telling me what? For God's sake, just tell me!'

'I work in military intelligence.'

'Is there such a thing?' she asked with a raised eyebrow

'Yes,' replied Harry with a laugh. 'It's my job to find things out. Things that can affect the security and sovereignty of the Crown.'

'So you're a spy?'

He shrugged.

'So who are you spying on? Sir Wilfred?' he didn't answer, so she narrowed her eyes at him as an uncomfortable thought crossed her mind. 'It's me isn't it? You're here to watch me?'

'Your Highness…'

'Don't give me that. Just tell me.'

'These are political games my dear. Games I don't think you're equipped to deal with. I've been politicking for most of my life in one way or another. You on the other hand…'

'So I'm just here to be spied on and get eaten by the political sharks?'

'No. I don't think so, but Harrington wanted you involved for a reason. I have suspicion that I know what that reason is, but I want to be sure.'

'You're going to spy on me.'

'No. If I was, I wouldn't have told you, but I can't deny that you have come to my attention.'

'Is that why you were in Brighton?'

'Partially. But I couldn't turn down the chance to get a seat at one of the Prince Regent's banquets. It was quite a spread.'

'But why spy on me? I'm no one in particular.' she said exasperatedly.

'Really? A homeless girl who suddenly becomes a Princess with more money that she can spend. A Princess with a growing reputation for fighting monsters? Your work at Brillington Abbey sounded very fanciful but that many eye witnesses and the evidence we found in the catacombs was quite solid. That I expect is why Harrington wants you here. You're the only one that will have seen anything like this before.'

'So I'm going to be your monster hunter?'

'No. As I said, there isn't a monster. It's just some unruly land grab attempts. You're going to be there to…'

'To what? Be pretty on your arm?'

Harry smiled.

'A job for which you are more than qualified, I assure you.'

Molly sighed and slumped back against the seat.

'Now don't be like that. When we get there, I'll talk to Sir Wilfred. You just have a look around.'

'What if someone notices?'

'Then you're just a silly girl who doesn't know any better.'

She made a dissatisfied noise.

'Just play your part. Let me handle the rest.'

He glanced at her hands.

'Ring.'

'What?'

'Wedding ring. Take it off.'

She looked at him in shocked surprise, covering the ring protectively with her other hand.

'What?'

'You're a pretty young girl, and if you can use that to your advantage then do. The wedding ring is a giveaway that you may not be who you seem to be.'

'I didn't think we'd be…'

'For now I think it would be prudent for you to remain as anonymous as possible. So take the ring off.'

She did as she was told. Not liking it one bit but seeing the wisdom in the plan.

'Can you do anything about your eyes?'

Molly huffed.

'Why don't you just drop me here and you can do it by yourself.'

'Don't be like that. You're going to be able to get into places that I can't. I need you with me.'

She sighed and took her glasses out of her pocket. They were silver framed with lenses of smoked glass.

'Better?' she asked angrily as she slipped them on.

The rest of the journey was in stony silence. The carriage stopped outside a pair of large gates in the centre of a high wall with a smaller, man sized door in the left hand side gate.

After a few seconds, the big gates opened and they rumbled into a large courtyard. A huge L shaped warehouse sat in front and to the left of them while the river was to the right.

'I'd wait there if I were you.' Harry told her as he got out, 'It's raining.'

'What? And miss all the fun?' she replied sarcastically.

He shook his head before he offered his hand to help her out.

As she stepped from the carriage, an old man came out of the building to the left. He was wearing a very expensive but severe suit and used a silver topped cane to walk. A hooked nose sat in the middle of his stern face, and although his body was bent and showing the signs of age, his eyes were distrusting and serious.

A respectful step behind him was a young man. He was well dressed, with his dark hair slicked back and the same nose and eyes as the older man. His hands were clasped behind his back and he looked nervous. The old man took them both in at a glance before pointing at the Major with his walking cane.

'You took your time.' he snapped.

His voice matched his body, old but with a sneery, snide tone.

'My apologies Sir Wilfred…'

'Who's this?' the old man demanded, cutting him off and pointing at Molly with his stick.

She bobbed a small curtsey.

'Hannah, sir.' she answered quickly, before the Major could say anything. 'I'm Major Gould's daughter.'

Sir Wilfred looked between them both for a second.

'What's she damn well doing here? This isn't a family outing.'

'I don't like being on my own sir, I…'

'I wasn't talking to you, you insolent child,' said Sir Wilfred, talking over her and pointing at her with his stick, 'I'm not in the slightest bit interested in anything you've got to say. Women and children should be seen and not heard. Better still if they're seen as little as possible.'

With that, he dismissed Molly as irrelevant and turned to the Major.

'Well come on then. I haven't got all day.'

'I'll wait in the carriage, father.' Molly said with a forced sweetness as she tried to hide her anger at the old man.

The Major gave her a sideways glance.

'Very good dear.'

'Oh no she won't' snapped Sir Wilfred. 'I'm not getting my damn carriage out for this. You can take me to the wharf and I'll show you what happened last night. She'll only get in the way. She can wait here in the yard.'

The old man then promptly pushed past her and heaved himself into the carriage. Molly and the Major exchanged a glance before he nodded once to her.

'Behave yourself.'

'I will father.' she said, giving him a quick peck on the cheek.

He frowned and then climbed in the carriage.

'We won't be too long.'

'Have fun.'

The carriage began to circle the yard as it turned around and she couldn't help hearing Sir Wilfred begin to harangue the Major.

'Fun? What does she think this is? It's a place of business sir, and it is no place for women. You should teach that child some manners…'

Molly was glad when the coach rumbled out of the yard. She really didn't like that man.

Shaking her head, she looked around, almost jumping with fright when she saw the young man still standing behind her.

'I'm sorry. I didn't mean to startle you.'

'That's alright. You were so quiet, I didn't know you were there.'

The man smiled tightly.

'We haven't been formally introduced.'

He held his hand out.

'My name is Geoffrey Hancock.'

Molly looked at his hand for a second before she shook it.

'I'm Hannah. Hannah Gould.'

'Delighted to meet you. Your father has gone to… well, he's gone to see what happened last night. It's just down the wharf. May I suggest that you be careful here. This is a working warehouse and there are all sorts of dangers around and about. We don't want you to hurt yourself or have any accidents, do we?'

'Of course. I'm sorry.'

'No need to apologise.'

There was an uncomfortable silence and Geoffrey looked at his feet as if trying to source some inner courage before he finally asked,

'Would you like a cup of tea?'

'Thank you. That would be nice.'

'Very good. I'd invite you in but father says that women shouldn't be in the workplace. It distracts the men and they aren't productive.'

Molly couldn't help but raise her eyebrows in surprise.

'And do you think that?' she asked.

Geoffrey looked at his feet again for a moment, as if trying to work out what to say.

'Well, if you don't mind me saying so, you are very pretty and, if I'm not being to forward, that I haven't been able to take my eyes off you since you arrived. So, in that respect, yes, he is right.'

He smiled warmly.

'I'll have some tea brought out directly.'

'But it's raining. You wouldn't want me to catch a cold, would you?'

She could see the inner turmoil in his face.

'Father said…'

'Do you always do what your father tells you?'

Geoffrey looked towards the gate and then at his feet again.

'I suppose it is raining and it would be impolite for me to leave you standing in the cold. But you must do as I ask and be careful. Father will be most displeased if he were to find you in the building.'

'Of course Mr Hancock.' she replied as sweetly as she could manage.

'I'll be a moment. I just need to make sure things are proper and ship shape.' he said, before nodding and striding quickly towards the building.

Molly waited until he went in and the door closed before she began to look around. The yard was huge, at least two hundred feet to a side, with a cobbled floor. Crates and bales were piled up near the wall while a long pontoon stuck out into the water.

Surprisingly, there didn't seem to be anyone else around. Cautiously, she moved across to the crates and, finding nothing interesting, she headed into the building in front of her. Something didn't feel right.

There were a pair of large doors with a smaller door to the side. Both were locked tight. She moved towards the river, climbing on a pile of crates to peer through a high window.

The glass was dirty and she couldn't see anything more than some more boxes just inside. Frowning, she climbed back down again, heading back towards the doors when from the river came a loud splash that caused her to spin around.

The yard was silent and even the ever-present sounds of London seemed to shrink into the background. Cautiously she walked to the pontoon. The river water was dark and lapped against the bank like treacle, oozing with an oily sheen covering the surface.

The splash sounded again, from somewhere under the pontoon and she move along to try and see underneath. Seeing nothing, she moved further down and climbed up on a pile of crates, leaning right out over the river.

'What are you looking for?'

Molly cried out in surprise and pitched forward but was grabbed around the waist and hauled back before she fell in.

She turned quickly to see Geoffrey. He smiled nervously.

'Are you alright?'

Molly took a breath and composed herself.

'Yes. Yes, I'm fine. Thank you.'

'What were you looking for?'

'I heard a noise…'

'Ah. Probably rats.'

'Rats?' she said, faking fear.

Rats didn't bother her. She didn't like them, but being homeless around the docks for years had desensitised her to their presence. They were just another thing that went along with the streets.

'Yes. They come from the river.'

He looked at her.

'Miss Gould, tea will be ready shortly.'

Geoffrey hesitated before speaking again, his voice quavering with nerves.

'Would it be improper for me to join you for tea?'

Molly almost laughed at the ridiculousness of the question but caught herself just in time, instead replying with a girlish giggle, 'That's *very* forward of you Mr Hancock.'

'I'm sorry.' he said quickly, 'I mean no offence. Please…'

She giggled again and laid a hand on his arm and he visibly tensed.

'I'm sure my father would be please to know that someone is with me. I don't like being on my own. Although I do hope your intentions are honourable.'

'What? Of course. I wouldn't dream…'

'Well then that's alright then.'

Geoffrey smiled widely.

'You do me a great honour miss Gould. If you will please follow me.'

He turned away and Molly shook her head. This wasn't as easy as she'd first thought. Maybe she could get him to tell her something. He seemed nice enough. A bit desperate for company but she suspected so would she if she had Sir Wilfred for a father. He didn't look like he got out much.

'Miss Gould?'

She snapped out of her reverie and hurried across the yard to where Geoffrey was holding a narrow door open for her.

'Thank you.'

The door opened into a well-furnished office with a large heavy desk and chair. To the left were a couple of wide leather armchairs.

'Please take a seat.'

Molly smiled at him and did as he asked, absentmindedly taking her glasses off. She instantly regretted it as she heard Geoffrey gasp in shock.

'Good God! What happened to your eyes.'

She cursed under her breath.

'I hurt them.' she said. 'While I was in India.'

That much at least was true.

In a second, Geoffrey had knelt by her side and taken one of her hands in his with a look of honest concern on his face.

'You poor thing. What happened?'

Molly sighed inwardly

'I don't really like to talk about it. I was just... Ill.'

Geoffrey hesitated before speaking.

'Was that, um, when you lost your mother?'

'What?' she replied, surprised by the question.

'I'm sorry. I don't mean to pry but you said you don't like to be left on your own, which is why you came today with your father. That would suggest that your mother is no longer around or you could have stayed with her.'

'He's smarter than he looks.' thought Molly.

She looked down while she decided what to say. Geoffrey took her silence as having dredged up some old, painful memories and squeezed her hand while giving her an "I understand" smile.

'My mother died years ago.' he said. 'Father and I have been alone since. But we have work to take our minds off it. How must you cope with such a loss?'

'Mr Hancock. I miss her but she wouldn't want me to brood endlessly about it.'

'Will you tell me what happened?'

Geoffrey moved to the other armchair, never letting go of Molly's hand and forcing her to turn to face him. He sat in patient silence while Molly tried to work out what on earth to tell him.

'Mother and I were in India with father while he was in the army.' she said eventually. 'We both caught a rare fever and neither of us was expected to live. I got better. Mostly. It hurt my eyes and I couldn't see for weeks. Mother didn't get better.'

There was a long, uncomfortable silence, broken only by the ticking of the mantle clock. Eventually Geoffrey smiled.

'You are a remarkable woman Miss Gould, dealing with your loss like that. It is very brave of you. I can't say I know any girls that would be so forthright. You are a very brave girl Miss Gould.' he hesitated as he plucked up the courage. 'May I call you Hannah?'

'Now you're being very forward Mr Hancock.' replied Molly with a coquettish smile, trying to ignore his condescending nature.

He apologised hurriedly.

'I'm terribly sorry. Please forgive my… I didn't mean to…'

'It's alright Mr Hancock.'

Geoffrey licked his lips and glanced at the clock.

'May I show you something?'

The carriage rumbled along towards the wharf. Harry was sat opposite Sir Wilfred and vainly trying to ignore the man. It wasn't easy.

'Well, we can't do much about the poor excuses we have for children can we. Other than to show them a firm hand, which is what I suggest you do with your daughter sir. You'll regret it when she becomes wilful and disobedient, you mark my words.'

The old man punctuated the last phrase with a sharp tap on the carriage floor with his walking cane. Harry smiled tightly.

'Very good Sir Wilfred. I will talk seriously with her later.'

The old man made a dismissive harrumph noise.

'Sir Wilfred,' ventured the Major, 'Could you tell me what has happened?'

'What's happened! It's that bastard Marshall. He's still sour about that business with the Frenchie buggers. He's behind this. Sending out people to kill my workers! Half of the layabouts haven't bothered to turn up. Well when they do, they're going to get their marching orders and that's a fact. If I had my way, I'd give them a damn good thrashing to boot.'

'I understand Sir Wilfred but…'

'You don't understand anything. Your type never do. Don't understand business. So busy running around in your uniforms and kowtowing to the likes of Harrington that you don't know what it's like to do a day's hard graft.'

Once more, Harry smiled tightly. Frederick Marshall was on his list to see this afternoon. He'd been suffering the same attacks as Sir Wilfred but the old man wouldn't have it. Also, the Major suspected that Sir Wilfred would soil himself when faced with enemy cannon and cavalry charge. No, there was something else at work here.

He rubbed his chin thoughtfully.

'When did this all start, Sir Wilfred?'

'Couple of months ago. My foreman didn't turn up for his shift. A couple of lads found what was left of him a street away from the yard. His widow came to see me, expected me to pay for the work he'd done. The cheek of the woman. It's not my fault that she has so many bloody children and I damn well told her so!' he rapped his cane on the floor once more.

The carriage stopped, sparing Harry from having to ask any further questions. Sir Wilfred leant out of the window and shouted at the driver.

'Well don't just sit there man, open the damn door!'

Hurriedly, the driver dismounted and did as he was told, Harry unable to miss the dirty look he gave Sir Wilfred as the old man exited.

'I hope you've a strong stomach.' he told Harry before walking briskly away.

The Major looked around. They were at a small wharf. Nearby were a selection of dirty, red brick warehouses and tied up at an old pontoon were a couple of ships. The closest, "The Amarantha" looked like she'd seen better days.

'Come on then, I haven't got all day.' shouted Sir Wilfred from the doorway of the nearest warehouse.

Harry hurried over to an angry look from Sir Wilfred.

'Well, here we are. Get looking.'

With a frown of his own, the Major entered.

Geoffrey had stood and, still holding Molly's hand, led her into the warehouse. The lower floor was packed tightly with containers and all sorts of boxes. He'd grinned nervously before leading her up to the second floor.

'Where are we going?'

'I want to show you something. Father will be very cross if he finds out, but I think we've got time.'

Almost dragging Molly along, he unlocked a small, but heavily re-enforced door on the landing, pushing it wide so Molly could enter.

'What… Oh my….'

The room was vast. Taking up the entire floor of the warehouse and an ornate ironwork ceiling that stretched into the story above, it was carefully set out. Highly polished wood covered the floor and every ten feet or so, there was a cabinet or glass encased pedestal.

'This is fathers collection.'

There were suits of armour, weapons of all sorts, stuffed animals in human like poses and a myriad of other things.

Molly pulled away from Geoffrey and walked up to a waist high case containing three swords. She reached out to touch the glass but recoiled in shock as Geoffrey smartly rapped her on the back of her hand.

'Don't touch.' he admonished sternly.

Molly glared at him but he didn't seem to notice.

'What is this place?' she asked, still smarting from the smack.

'Father collects things from around the world. He likes to look at them. I'm not allowed in here normally but I do come and look when father is out. Come and look at this…'

Geoffrey took her hand once more and led her along to a stone pedestal. Sat upon a bed of red velvet was a golden necklace with a small jewel hanging from a pendant.

'This is from India. I thought you might like to see it.'

'It's very pretty.' ventured Molly.

'Pretty?' laughed Geoffrey, 'This is one of the Stones of Gunjai. They're magical gems that can control the very elements themselves! Father paid a handsome sum for this.'

Molly looked at him and had to restrain herself from laughing in his face. She'd been the keeper of the real

Stones and this one wasn't even a good copy. Whoever had sold this to Sir Wilfred had seen him coming.

'Does it work?' she asked innocently.

'Work?'

'Yes. Can it control the, um,' she remembered she was supposed to be playing the role of a silly girl and had to change tack. 'Can it control the elephants?'

Geoffrey looked at her and then burst out laughing.

'Elephants? Oh Miss Gould, you are a one. I can see that I'm going to have to teach you a lot of things.'

'Excuse me?' she asked. What did he mean "teach her"?

'Come, we better be getting back before father returns.'

He grabbed her hand again and led her out of the room, carefully locking it behind him.

Molly was once more stood outside when the carriage rumbled back into the yard. Geoffrey had given her some tea and then ushered her back out. He was stood nearby with a knowing smile on his face.

The carriage stopped and the driver jumped down to open the door for Sir Wilfred. The old man looked at Molly and then at his son.

'What're you smiling at?' he snapped.

Geoffrey's face dropped quickly.

'Nothing father.'

'Good. Keep it that way.' he turned to Molly and pointed at her with his walking cane.

'You girl. I hope you've not been leading my son astray.'

'No sir.' she replied as meekly as she could manage.

'I think you should be leaving. Your father is waiting for you.'

Molly hurried over to the carriage and glanced in. Major Gould was sat, ashen faced and staring at her.

'Get in please.'

She turned to Geoffrey.

'It was a pleasure to meet you Mr Hancock.'

'The pleasure was all mine Miss Gould.'

He offered his hand to help her into the carriage.

'Perhaps I could see you again. With the permission of your father, of course.' he said quickly with a glance at the Major.

Molly gave him a shrug and a smile before she sat opposite the Major. Geoffrey shut the door behind her.

Almost immediately, the driver cracked the whip and the coach turned and headed out of the yard, leaving Geoffrey looking disappointed.

Neither said anything until the carriage was well clear of the docks.

'So?' asked Molly.

Major Gould took a deep breath and rubbed his eyes.

'Harrington was right. Something has been…'

'Been what?'

'It's not pleasant. I'd rather spare you the details.'

She looked at him with an amused smile.

'Major. I'm sure I can handle the details. Do you know what I did on my wedding day? I said, "I Do", to my husband and then killed a thirty-foot tall, skinless demon with claws as big as my arm.'

He looked at her as if she were mad.

'Really?'

'Yes. Really.'

She folded her arms across her chest and waited expectantly for the Major to speak.

'Well… Don't say I didn't warn you.' he said eventually. 'Harrington's information was correct. Whatever has been doing this has been tearing the hearts out of the poor, unfortunate, victims.'

Molly sat, stony faced, and listened as he told her what he had seen. Sir Wilfred had instructed one of his men to take the Major to a small storehouse just down the wharf that had been the scene of the latest attack.

There he found a body. It had been covered by a sheet but the force of the trauma caused was evident. Something had smashed his ribcage open and pulled out his heart.

'Could he have been shot?'

Major Gould shook his head.

'No. Something that would do that much damage to his chest would have blown a hole in his back bigger than my fist. There was nothing there.' he shook his head and sighed.

'I think that this may be too much for you my dear. I don't know why Harrington got you involved. A lady such as yourself…'

'And that is precisely why I think he did. I'm not like any lady you know Major.'

He shook his head.

'Still, I think it best…'

She smiled at him.

'No father. *I* think it best if we do this together.'

The Major had to smile.

'I've never been a father in my life! Well, not that I know of anyway.'

Molly raised her eyebrows at him and he grinned.

'So, daughter of mine, what did you find out in the yard?'

'Nothing. Everything was locked up tight. There was no-one around. The place felt deserted. Something wasn't right.'

'What about the son?'

'Geoffrey? He seemed a bit strange but I don't think he gets out much.'

The Major made a thoughtful noise.

'Anything else?'

'Sir Wilfred has got a collection.'

'Collection? What of?'

Molly shrugged.

'I don't know. Things!'

'Like?'

'Stuffed animals, swords, jewels, old pots. Things! Geoffrey was very secretive about it all. I don't think he was supposed to be in there, let alone showing me. Then there was the splashing in the river.'

Puzzled, Harry lent forward as Molly continued.

'There was a splashing noise, under the pontoon. Geoffrey said it was rats.'

'It probably was. They're all over the place.'

Molly shook her head.

'It'd have to be a bloody big one. I've never seen a rat splash that much.'

He shrugged.

'Maybe.'

'What are we going to do now?'

'Well I've got to go and see the next five men on Harrington's list this afternoon.'

'What about me?' asked Molly.

'Well, fun though it has been to have a daughter for a while, I think you should be getting home.'

'No.' she replied hurriedly.

'Why ever not?'

'Harrington wanted me to help so you're not going to get rid of me that easily, besides, I want to go back to Sir Wilfred's yard and have a look around. Later. When it's dark. Something didn't feel right and I want to know what it is.'

'That's not...'

'I know it's not a good idea. But I'm still doing it.'

He made a face.

'If you *were* my daughter, I'd have a few things to say about that.'

'But I'm not. At least, not as far as you know.'

He laughed.

'Touché. So if you don't want me to take you home, where do you want to go?'

'I thought you told Harrington we were going to eat?'

'Then eat we shall.'

'And while we're at it, you can tell me what "tooshay" means...'

Chapter Eight

Investigations

Major Gould pressed himself against the brickwork. Night had drawn in and a heavy fog had settled, blanketing the river and surroundings like snow. Why he'd agreed to this he didn't know.

That damn girl had him wrapped around her little finger and he wasn't even sure how it had happened. He wasn't even sure that she knew that she was doing it.

They'd had a nice lunch and then they'd gone to see the other on men Harrington's list. They'd all told more or less the same story as Sir Wilfred, there had been violent deaths and they were all blaming one another.

Again, he'd left Molly alone to have a snoop around but she'd found out nothing more than they already knew. Only Sir Wilfred seemed to have something unusual going on.

After that, he'd once more offered to drop her home. She refused and got him to drop her near a run-down dress-makers shop close to the river. The paint on the woodwork was peeling and the whole area seemed rough. Far too dangerous for a lady.

'Meet me by the warehouses at about eleven tonight.' she'd said before disappearing inside the shop.

Now he was here. Waiting. From somewhere above, there came the dreadful shriek of a bird, but it wasn't anything he'd heard before and, he hated to admit it, it put the fear of God into him.

Moving as cautiously as he could with his back pressed to the wall, he edged along until he could see the warehouses across the road with their high wall and gates. They loomed out of the fog but he couldn't hear any noises from the other side.

The screech sounded again and he fancied he saw a dark shadow pass overhead but that thought was lost as the edges of fear crept up on him. He could feel them gnawing at him, filling him with the desire to run.

Pushing those thoughts down, he pulled back into the shadows as the small gate across the road opened a crack.

'Major?' came a hushed call.

He moved forward, surprised to see Molly in the doorway. Hurrying over, he joined her in the yard, pushing the gate closed as he came in.

'How'd you get in here?' he asked before he took in her attire. 'And what are you wearing?'

She smiled and gave him a little twirl.

'You don't want to know how I got in, trust me. And as for this? It's practical and comfortable.'

'But it's...'

'Don't be a prude.'

He shook his head. She was dressed in a black leather jumpsuit with sturdy boots. A long knife was strapped to her thigh and the hilt of a long sword protruded over her right shoulder. The Major looked at her for a second but her face was unreadable.

'You've done this before, haven't you?'

'Not really. But I bet you have. You're supposed to be the spy.'

'I am not a spy.' he protested but she just smiled at him. 'Do you know how to use that?' changing the subject and pointing at the sword at her back.

Molly grinned and drew it with a flourish before offering it to him hilt first.

'A bit. It was a gift.'

He took it and swished it through the air. The blade was well balanced and grip set with silver and precious gems.

'Who the hell gives a girl a sword as a present.'

'My sister.' she replied smugly as she took the sword back and slipped it back into the scabbard.

They moved across to the farthest warehouse.

'Does this place seem empty to you?' Molly whispered as they neared the building.

'I was thinking something similar. For someone with Sir Wilfred's' money and empire, this place should be heaving.'

Molly moved ahead, climbing on a pile of crates to look through the windows.

'It looks clear.'

Below, the Major moved across to the door.

'Locked.'

Molly bit her lip and looked around before drawing the knife from her thigh.

'What're you doing?'

She reversed the blade and drove the hilt into one of the panes of glass. It shattered and she reached in to undo the window catch.

'You can't do that!'

Molly looked at him as she slipped the knife back into its sheath.

'I've already broken in once and besides, it was like that when I got here.' she smiled. 'So, are you coming or what?'

Without waiting for an answer, she heaved the window open and disappeared inside. Major Gould shook his head before following.

He dropped the few feet onto the floor and looked around. The warehouse was dark and he couldn't see the girl anywhere.

'Your Highness?' he hissed, almost jumping out of his skin when she replied, her voice right next to his ear.

'My name is Molly.'

He span to see her standing beside him.

'Good God! You nearly gave me a heart attack! You're going to be the death of me.'

'I hope not. Come on.'

Together they moved through the warehouse.

'This way.'

Molly led the Major through the tightly packed crates in the warehouse and up to the second floor, stopping outside the small re-enforced door.

The Major looked at Molly for a second before reaching into his jacket pocket and pulling out a small cloth roll. Carefully unwrapping it, he took out a couple of long, bent pieces of thin metal.

'Keep watch.' he told her as he turned and began to pick the lock.

'That's an interesting skill for a Major.' Molly noted.

From where he was crouched in front of the door, Harry smiled.

'I'm full of interesting little skills.'

'I wouldn't mind learning that when you've got a few minutes.'

He stood as the lock clicked open.

'I don't think a respectable lady such as yourself needs to learn how to pick a lock.'

Molly smiled at him.

'Who said I was respectable? Or a lady?'

She moved past him to open the door.

'We'll that's something.' said Harry as he entered, closing the door behind him.

'It's something that looks like a load of old tat to me Major.'

'My name is Harry.' he said, mimicking her tone from earlier, 'Let's have a look around.'

Cautiously they moved further into the room, the fog outside the windows making the place feel dank and dirty.

Molly picked up a small clay cup from a wooden pedestal. It was old and hand made.

'What's this?'

'Put that down.' hissed Harry.

She shrugged and went to put it back on the plinth but a noise from far across the room made her jump. It was just on the edge of hearing but sawed at her mind like a razor.

Harry didn't seem to hear it. It sounded once more and bit deeply in her head she couldn't stop herself from flinching.

The crash that the cup made as it hit the floor and shattered echoed around the room. Molly cringed and closed her eyes.

'Oops.'

Harry came over.

'What are you doing?'

She shrugged again.

'Sorry.'

The Major lent over the pedestal, there was a small card stuck on the side.

'The Cup of Christ.' he read.

'What's that?'

'Well, if the card is right, then you've just broken the cup that our Lord and Saviour drank from at the last supper. The Holy Grail.'

'Is that bad?'

'Don't touch anything else.' he said as he walked away.

Molly hurried to catch him up.

'Was it important?'

'Probably not, but you might have just smashed one of the most important religious relics in history.'

'Oh.' she said. 'I did say I was sorry.'

'Be more careful. Come on.'

'What are we going to do?'

'Have a look around and then get out of here.'

'But what about…'

'Forget it.'

'Major, did you hear a noise. Just before I, uh, I had the accident?'

Harry shook his head.

'What noise?'

'I don't know. It was like…' she tapered off before shaking her head. 'It doesn't matter.'

'Just be more careful. Please. We don't want any more priceless antiquities damaged, do we?'

He moved away again. Molly bit her lip thoughtfully before she turned towards where she thought the noise had come from.

In the far corner there was a plinth, empty apart from a red velvet cushion. There was no card on the side. Cautiously, Molly picked up the cushion and looked underneath.

Nothing.

She put it back down again and glanced around before leaning back on the pillar. It dropped two feet into the floor with a click before there was a soft grinding noise and part of the floor dropped away to reveal a set of stone steps spiralling down.

'Major.' she called quietly. 'Come have a look at this.'

He hurried over.

'What have you done now.'

She frowned and folded her arms defensively.

'I haven't done anything.'

'Don't look like that.' he said.

'Like what? You just assumed that I've broken something else.'

'I never said that.'

She frowned again and put a foot on the top step but the Major put a restraining hand on her arm.

'I think it best if I go first.'

'Why?'

'We don't know what's down there.'

She smiled.

'No. We don't do we.'

Without another word, she pulled away and went down. Harry rolled his eyes and muttered under his breath.

'Damn girl.'

'Hey, there's a lantern here.' she called up.

He followed and caught her up ten steps down. She'd taken a battered looking lantern from a niche in the wall and was lighting it.

'I still think I should be going first.'

'That's nice.' she told him with a grin, although the lamplight made it look menacing and he felt his heart beat hard.

The narrow stairs wound down, and by the time they reached the bottom Molly guessed they were well below ground level.

At the bottom was a short, damp corridor with a low ceiling that was barely wide enough for Harry to walk down. At the far end, just visible in the dull yellow light from the lamp was a heavy iron door. The mouldering brickwork was slimy to the touch, with an unhealthy green moss growing from the cracked blocks.

With a look at each other, they started forward, trying to ignore the heavy smell of mould in the air.

'I'm not sure I like this place.' said Molly quietly.

'Neither do I.' replied the Major.

The door was rusty but had been re-enforced with fresh iron bands across it. A new, sturdy looking, lock had also been recently added by the look of it.

'What now?'

The Major squeezed past her, uncomfortably aware of her pressing against him as they moved.

'Don't worry about it father.' she whispered in his ear, as if she had been reading his mind and, despite himself, he blushed furiously.

Trying not to pay attention to the huge grin he knew she had on her face, he knelt and began to pick the lock.

Molly watched him work, holding the lantern low so he could see what he was doing. Idly, she wondered what her own father had been like. She'd never known him but if he was anything like the Major, then she wouldn't have been disappointed. However, she suspected he wasn't. Probably some poor drunk or criminal.

She shook her head to brush away the suddenly sad thoughts that had ambushed her as with a definite "click", the lock opened. Harry put away the lockpicks and put his shoulder to the door.

It was heavy and creaked on rusty hinges. As soon as it was open they were both assailed with a heavy stench of mould and decay. Molly covered her nose.

'Maybe you don't want to go in there.' suggested Harry.

She shook her head and went through the door.

'What? And let you have all of the stinky fun?'

The room beyond was quite large, around forty feet to a side, with a ten foot square area in the far corner enclosed in heavy iron bars and another solid looking door in the right hand wall.

Past the bars, more than half of the floor was taken up by a stagnant and smelly pond with a gate at the far end that looked like it dropped down into the water. To the left, on their side of the bars, was a cog and wheel that seemed to operate the wall mounted gate on the other side.

Cautiously, they moved to the bars. There was a low gate set near the wall with a huge padlock on it. Whatever was in the cage, wasn't supposed to get out. The rest was more slimy brick with a pile of dirty rags and blankets gathered in the corner near the gate, like a nest.

Various bones were scattered all around the nest, some still having the vestiges of flesh still clinging to them. They both looked at each other and Molly shrugged.

'What do you...' began Harry but Molly shushed him into silence.

'Can you hear that?'

Harry frowned at her.

'I can't hear a thing.'

'Sshhh.'

Handing him the lantern, she drew her sword and crept over to the other door. Pressing her ear to it, she was sure she could hear crying coming from the other side.

She reached towards the door handle when it began to turn on its own.

'Oh shit.' she muttered.

Harry looked at her in disbelief as she dashed across to him, unceremoniously grabbing him by the jacket and hauling him back through the door to the low tunnel. Molly heaved it shut.

'Quick. Lock it.'

Harry was there in a moment and began to lock the door.

'I think we may have outstayed our welcome.' he said as the lock clicked back.

'Right,' said Molly. 'I say we run like hell. How does that grab you?'

'As plans go, that's not very original but...'

He didn't have time to finish his sentence before Molly grabbed his jacket once more and dragged him down the corridor and back up the stairs.

Emerging back into the collection room, Molly turned to the stairwell. Just visible was the top of the plinth that had covered the entrance.

Not knowing what do to or how to close it, she stamped on it as hard as she could and much to her relief, was rewarded with a click and grinding noise as it rose back out of the floor.

'Time to go.' she said, slipping her sword back into its scabbard.

They pounded their way back through the warehouse and through the still open window. Neither stopping until they were out of the yard and heading down the foggy road.

Eventually, the Major ducked into a doorway to catch his breath. Molly fell in beside him.

'Well we know there's something going on alright.' she said.

Harry nodded, trying to still his pounding heart. He wasn't as young as he use to be. Taking a deep breath, he got himself under control.

'Where did a lady like you learn language like that!'

'Don't be a prude.' she replied with a grin, 'and besides, it fitted the situation.'

'It did, but I don't like to think a lady should say anything like that. I should wash your mouth out.'

Molly laughed.

'Sorry father.'

Harry smiled too, the adrenaline wearing off slightly.

'I think maybe I should come back tomorrow with a few soldiers and see what we can see.' he said after a moment.

'What about me?'

'You my dear girl, are going to stay out of this.'

He saw the look that crossed her face.

'Don't argue with me. Just do as you're told. Sir Wilfred is up to something and the proper authorities will investigate this further.'

'But I can help.' she protested.

'I know you can, but you're not going to. Do you understand?'

She frowned at him.

'Come on. Let's get you home.'

'I can find my way from here.' she said snootily before stalking off into the fog. The Major called after her.

'Molly!'

There was no answer.

'Damn girl.'

Chapter Nine

Old Friends

Molly walked through the fog, keeping to the darker areas of the streets as she threaded her way back to Mrs Hopkins shop. The old woman was letting her stay there while she dealt with this Sir Wilfred business.

It was away from Marcus, who definitely wouldn't approve, and close enough to the docks so she could do some good.

But she wasn't doing any good, was she?

Major Gould had practically written her off and told her not to get involved, even after what they'd found. She didn't like it.

Passing the mouth of an alley, she heard crying.

'It's none of my business.' she told herself.

She closed her eyes. It wasn't anything to do with her. She shouldn't get involved.

'Damn it.' she whispered before drawing her sword and moving quietly into the alley.

It was narrow, muddy and littered with the detritus of the dock. Cautiously she walked along, sword held ready in her hands. About half way down was a girl, sat in the mud and crying.

She was about Molly's age with dark hair and dark eyes. A burgeoning black eye covered the left side of her filthy face while her once green dress was worn and tatty. Molly recognised her instantly.

'Ruth?'

The girl looked up in surprise and shock at the voice.

'Don't hurt me.' she pleaded, shuffling away, seeing only a woman in black with a sword held next to her. Molly put the sword away and crouched down beside her.

'Ruth, it's me. Molly. Molly Carter.'

'Moll?'

Ruth flung herself at Molly, almost knocking her over into the mud. In response, Molly put her arms around the girl and held her while she cried.

The tears didn't last long and Ruth pushed herself away and wiped her face with the back of her hand.

'What's going on?' asked Molly.

'Just being silly really' she replied with a sniff. 'Old Porky said I owed him money. Sent his boys over and they took all I had. It was only a few pennies but still... They gave me a black eye as a reminder and I did a runner before they could take anything else.' she sniffed again before adding, 'I hope the beast gets the old bastard.'

'Beast?'

'You know? The beast. The thing that's been stalking the docks. It's killed half a dozen people. Tore their hearts out, so they say.' she looked at Molly. 'Where've you been? What're you wearing and why have you got a sword? I thought that Gatling brothers had got you.'

Molly smiled.

'They almost did. Two of them are dead now.'

'I heard that too. Someone said a for'n woman killed them. Cut their heads off before drinking their blood.'

'Not quite.'

Molly couldn't hide a grin as she helped her friend up.

'Where are you staying?'

Ruth shrugged.

'No place in particular. They've started checking the hay lofts now and chucking anyone they find out, unless they can pay for the privilege that is, or are offering other services.'

Molly frowned. She knew exactly what "other services" she meant.

'And you haven't got any money.'

Once more, Ruth shrugged.

'No.'

'Come on.'

'Where?'

'Somewhere safe.'

They walked through the fog in silence. Molly could tell there were hundreds of questions that Ruth wanted to ask but wouldn't. Not yet. Eventually they came upon their destination and Ruth pulled up short.

'Mad ol' Hopkins' place? Are you crazy? She'll go spare if we break in there.'

'We're not breaking in. I've got a key.'

'What?'

'Come on.'

Molly led her friend around the back and into the small yard behind the dress-makers shop before letting them into the kitchen.

'Shhh.'

As quietly as they could, they found and lit candles which dispelled the night, but tiny wisps of fog crept in through the poorly fitting windows.

'Sit down.'

Molly pointed to the kitchen table and Ruth did as she was told.

'How'd you get a key to Hopkins' place?'

'She gave it to me. I'm staying here for a few days. I've got some stuff to sort out.'

'Like what?'

'Hungry?' asked Molly, changing the subject quickly.

'Starving.'

'When did you last eat?'

'Dunno,' said Ruth. 'Day before yesterday I think.'

Rooting around in the pantry, Molly returned with a loaf of bread, some cheese and a couple of bottles of ale. She passed the food and one of the bottles to Ruth who looked at her as if she were mad.

'We can't. She'll be furious. Remember when you stole that pie…'

'Yes, and she and I have had words about that.'

They both turned at the new voice to see a small thin woman with grey hair and knowing eyes standing in the doorway.

'Now I know I said *you* could stay here but I don't remember saying you could turn my kitchen into a doss house while you were at it.'

Molly stood up.

'I'm sorry. She needed help and…'

Mrs Hopkins sighed.

'Don't make too much noise and I want the place spotless when I come down in the morning.' she looked Ruth over. 'If you're still here, I expect I can find you something cleaner than that sorry excuse for a dress you're wearing.'

'But I can't pay. I've got…'

'Who said anything about paying?' she said with a gap-toothed smile before pointing at Molly. 'Besides, I expect her Highness here will be able to cover the cost of a thousand dresses. Now I'm going to bed. I don't want to be woken up again. Understand?'

'Yes Mrs Hopkins.' said Molly with a smile.

As soon as the old woman was out of the room, Ruth turned to her friend.

'What's going on? Why did she call you that? Where *have* you been for the last year?'

Molly pulled the stopper out of the bottle and took a hearty swig.

'It's a long story. Eat up and I'll tell you all about it.'

'So you're a Princess?' asked Ruth.

They'd finished the bread and cheese and were on their third bottles of ale. Molly had stoked the fire and both were sat on the floor nearby, enjoying the warmth while Molly was absentmindedly cleaning her sword.

112

'Apparently so. It was a gift. Alongside a title and a house and a few other things.'

'Well I'll be.'

Molly shrugged.

'It's not all it's cracked up to be.'

'What? I'd give my right arm to have even half of what you've got. You've fallen on your feet there and that's a fact.'

'I suppose.' replied Molly, staring into the fire.

'Then why aren't you happy?'

'Who said I wasn't happy?'

'It's written all over your face.'

'I am. I am happy. It's just that…'

'What?'

'I don't know.' admitted Molly. 'I don't fit anywhere anymore.'

Ruth finished her bottle.

'You never did!'

'Hey! Less of that.' replied Molly with a smile.

'Sorry your Highnessness.' replied her friend with a mock bow.

They went silent for a few moments, staring into the fire.

'So what are you doing here and not lording it about in your house and sat in your parlour counting your money?'

'I don't sit and count my money.'

'I would.'

'You can't count.'

Ruth nodded and looked down, idly fiddling with the empty bottle in her hands.

'No. I can't. But I'd like to learn. And to read and write.'

'Maybe I'll teach you.'

'Really?'

'Why not?'

Ruth took Molly's bottle off her and took a swig.

'Don't know. It doesn't seem to be important.'

'It is.' replied Molly. 'Tell me about this "beast".'

Ruth shrugged.

'It started a couple of months ago. Something is around the docks. People are scared to go out at night. There's some hushed-up talk about it coming from one the big warehouses. You know the ones, with the big gates and high walls.'

'I know them.'

'They say it came from forn' parts on a ship. It eat all the crew and then drifted for years before it was picked up. Now it lives in the warehouses, killin' anyone it wants. I heard that it rips people's hearts out.'

'It's probably nothing like that.' lied Molly, a horrible feeling forming in the pit of her stomach.

Ruth took a pull from the bottle and handed it back to Molly.

'Don't know, I've not seen them afterwards. I've heard it though.'

'Heard it?'

'Yeah. It's horrible. Like a scream. Set my teeth on edge.'

The girl shuddered involuntarily.

'So what *are* you doing back here?'

'Nothing much,' said Molly with a smile. 'Help me get this tidied away and then I think we should get some sleep.'

Ruth gave her a sideways, "I don't believe you", look before helping Molly with the bottles and dishes.

It was late the next morning when Molly and Ruth surfaced, having shared Molly's bed in the spare room. Mrs Hopkins gave them a critical stare before ushering Ruth off into the shop with instructions for Molly to make some tea.

Twenty minutes later, the girl returned, beaming with pride at the new dress she had. It was a lovely pale blue and cut from expensive cloth.

'That should do you for a while.' Mrs Hopkins said as she followed her into the kitchen. 'I'll send you the bill shall I?'

'Of course. Thank you Mrs Hopkins.' Molly replied.

'Oh, some posh bugger left this for you.'

The old woman passed Molly a thin envelope with a heavy wax seal.

'What is it?'

'How should I know? He was tall man with a droopy moustache. Said you should meet him later.'

Molly frowned as read the letter and slipped it into her pocket.

'What is it?' asked Ruth.

'Nothing. I'll pour shall I?' she said dismissively, pouring tea for all of them

No sooner had they sat down, when the shop bell rang. Mrs Hopkins sighed and stood up.

'Never a bloody quiet moment.' she muttered, heading through the curtain that separated the shop from the kitchen.

There was a moments silence before the old woman spoke. Her voice was unnecessarily loud.

'Ah. Hello Mr Simcox, what can I do for you today?'

Molly almost dropped her cup.

'What's the matter?' Ruth asked her as Molly darted up and peeked through the curtain.

'Shhh.'

Joining her friend and the curtain, Ruth looked through.

'Who's he? A bit well dressed for this place.'

Molly moved away from the curtain.

'It's my butler.' she whispered.

Ruth broke into a grin.

'What? Really?'

'Yes. Really. Now be quiet.'

'What's the problem?'

'He doesn't know I'm here. If he finds out, he'll tell Marcus.'

'Your husband?' asked Ruth.

'Shut up!'

Back in the shop, Mrs Hopkins spoke,

'I'm sure I can manage a cup of tea Mr Simcox. Let me go and make sure everything is tidy…'

Molly cursed and grabbed Ruth's hand, almost dragging the poor girl out of the back door and into the yard, stopping only to grab the two teacups that were on the table. She shut the kitchen door, set the cups on the floor and then headed out of the gate.

'I don't see what the problem is,' said Ruth as Molly hauled her down the road, 'If he's your butler, then just order him not to say anything.'

Molly headed into an alleyway and pressed herself against the wall.

'It's not that simple. I'm supposed to be in Somerset. Not in London. He'd feel it his duty to tell Marcus. He's that sort of man. A kind and gentle man but very…'

'Nosey?'

'No. Honourable.'

Molly cursed again and began to head down the alley and away from the shop. Ruth hurried to keep up.

'So what're you doing here then? If your husband and servants think you're across the country…'

'Not all of them. Gwen knows what I'm doing.'

'Who's Gwen?'

'My maid.' said Molly, lifting her skirts to cross a particularly muddy patch.

'You've got a maid?'

Behind her, Ruth grinned and followed.

'Come on. Tell me. We've known each other for years…'

Molly stopped and let out an exasperated sigh.

'Alright, but not here. Let's find somewhere to go and I'll tell you. You've got to keep it a secret though.'

'I will.'

'I mean it Ruth. It's important.'

There was something in Mollys voice that made Ruth hesitate, her smile dropping slightly. This *was* important.

'I swear on my life.'

Molly sighed again before heading off with Ruth trailing behind.

Chapter Ten

Meetings

The pair went to a tavern near the river. The expensive cut of their clothes got a few odd looks and the barkeep had initially refused to serve them until Molly pushed a few coins across the bar. After that, they took a couple of ales and steaming plates of stew and sat at a table in the corner.

Molly watched Ruth finish her meal before ordering her another. She remembered what it had been like to be hungry all the time.

'So, what on earth is going on?' asked Ruth between mouthfuls.

'The beast. I'm supposed to find it and stop it.'

Ruth nearly spat out her stew.

'What? It's supposed to be killing people.'

'I know. What I'm about to tell you is a secret. It can't go any further.'

'I swear. On my grave, I promise.'

Molly looked around before leaning in and telling her all that had happened since she met with Harrington a few days previously. Ruth sat in engrossed silence until Molly sat back.

'That's quite a story.' she said eventually. 'Did you really meet the Prince Regent?'

Molly nodded.

'Wow.'

A shadow fell across their table and they both looked up into the faces of two heavy set men. Both were scruffy and had the look of people who were used to having their own way.

'What's this?' said the closest, a waft of stale breath washing over the women. 'New dress. Ale? Food? Were you holding out on us yesterday? Mr Porkonicov isn't going to like that.'

He grabbed Ruth by the arm and hauled her out of her seat.

'Get off me! I don't owe him anything.'

'Well he begs to differ and was disappointed by the poor offering that you handed out yesterday. Said we were to give you a more permanent reminder of what happens to little sluts who take what they shouldn't.'

'I haven't got any money!'

'Let her go.'

Molly slowly stood, the men watching her in amusement.

'Well if it isn't Molly Carter. I think you have a debt to pay to Mr Porkonicov too. He'll be so happy we found you.'

'I said, let her go.' there was a real menace to her words but the men just grinned.

'And why would we want to do that? Grab her, Bill.'

The second man went to grab Molly but she snatched up the metal tankard she had and smashed him in the side of the head with it. He fell backwards with a curse.

'Let her go. This is your last chance.'

'You're going to pay for that. Maybe Mr Porkonicov will be nice enough to let us have you when he's finished.'

Molly slipped the glasses from her face and the nasty grin on their faces slipped a fraction.

'Ruth. When I say, run.'

Around them, the bar was silent. Money changed hands on the outcome as the crowded pub watched intently.

Moving slowly, Molly slid out from the other side of the table into a clear space. Bill smiled to reveal brown and rotting teeth.

'Come here.'

He darted forward, only to find Mollys tankard coming the other way. It contacted sharply with his nose, breaking it for the umpteenth time. He stepped backwards as blood covered his face.

'Little bitch!' he roared and swung a fist at Molly which would have taken her head off if it had connected. The punch hit nothing but air as at the last second, Molly dropped to a knee and punched him as hard as she could in the groin.

He doubled up, eyes uncrossing only long enough to see a Molly grasp the tankard with both hands and swing it upwards. It caught him under the chin and snapped his head backwards. He let out a little moan and then tipped sideways into another table, smashing it in half.

The man holding Ruth looked on in disbelief for a second before Molly lashed out, stamping hard on the side of his knee. There was a horrible snapping sound and he went down with a howl of agony.

'Ruth. Run.'

The other girl twisted out of the mans' grasp as Molly grabbed a small wooden stool and smashed him in the face with it. He span on the spot and before he'd stopped moving, Molly had grabbed Ruth's hand and was dragging her through the crowd and out into the road.

At the back of the inn, Mr Potts watched them go. Well, that had been interesting. She handled herself pretty well for a girl. Mr Porkonicov's men should learn to be more careful.

Picking up his hat, he collected his winnings from the still stunned patrons of the bar and left with a smile on his face. Maybe he'd have to have some fun with those two after all.

They'd run maybe three streets before Ruth pulled Molly into an alley near the docks.

'How the hell did you do that?' she gasped.

'Practice.'

Her friend looked at her with a mixture of fear and awe.

'I've never seen anyone stand up to Porkies men like that.'

'They should've done as I asked.'

Ruth was sure she saw a flash of black pass across her friend's eyes. It was there and gone in a moment but she was sure it was there. Molly screwed her eyes shut and pinched the bridge of her nose.

'Are you alright?'

'I've got a bit of a headache and I could do with a lie down.'

She took a deep breath.

'Come on.'

Molly headed away, one hand on the wall to steady herself. Ruth followed.

'Are you sure you're alright?'

'Yes.' she snapped.

'Well it don't look like it to me.'

Ruth grabbed her arm and dragged her over to a pile of wooden boxes where she sat her down.

'I'm sorry. I sometimes have trouble with my temper.'

Ruth looked at her quizzically for a moment.

'Well you sure showed those bastards.'

Molly smiled tightly then closed her eyes.

'Maybe you should go back to Mrs Hopkins…'

'No.'

'Moll…'

'No. I can't. I have things to do.'

'You always were stubborn. Well I can't let you go off on your own in this state. I'm coming too.'

'No…'

Ruth stood straight and folded her arms with a determined look on her face.

'Go back to Mrs Hopkins. You'll be safe there. I'll be back later.' Molly told her.

'No.'

'Please?'

Molly held her friends gaze for a moment before she sighed.

'Fine. Come on then.'

'Where are we going?'

'Well I want to find out some more about this beast. I'm going down to the docks. Maybe people around there can help.'

'They might.' replied Ruth, reservedly.

'You don't sound sure.'

'You've not been here for a year. What with the beast and Porkie, this place has changed. People aren't so talkative. 'specially not to strangers.'

'I'm not a stranger!'

'The Molly I knew wouldn't have just beat up two men.'

Seeing the look on her friend's face, Ruth crouched down and took Molly's hands.

'Look. Moll, you've been away. You've changed. You may not see it, but I can. There's a confidence you've got that you didn't have before. Things round here have changed too. Porky runs this area now. He's got people scared. The beast has got people scared too.'

'How'd Porky do that. Last I heard he was going up against the Millers. They were set to destroy him.'

'Well they would have done, if some of Porkies men hadn't set fire to their building with them inside. Not a one made it out alive. He took over all of their businesses and that was that. He's the fat king of the docks now. Even Jack Gatling has thrown his lot in with him.'

'Why doesn't anyone do anything about it?'

'Moll, that's the most straight laced thing you've ever said! replied Ruth with a grin. 'Like who? The posh folks don't give a damn and Porkie is wise enough to leave the big warehouses alone. He don't want the kind of trouble they can dish out. Since he don't bother them, they leave him alone, which pretty much gives him the right to do what he wants.'

Molly frowned.

'Alright. So I probably didn't do a good thing when I…'

Ruth shook her head but couldn't hide the smile.

'Probably not, but they had it coming.'

She straightened.

'Well, things round here haven't been the same since you left, Moll. Quieter for one. But it's good to have you back.'

She offered Molly her arm and with a shake of her head and grin of her own, Molly stood and together they walked off towards the dockyards.

John Warner licked his lips nervously. The dockside market was busy, bustling with people and the air was loud with the calls of the market sellers and hawkers. He'd already managed to lift a couple of coin purses and was now eyeing up another likely target.

The man was stood outside a small shop and looking at a pile of books with his back to him. Should be easy.

Moving out into the crowd John moved across to the man, he glanced around once more before gently lifting the tails of the mans coat and going for his wallet.

'What did I tell you about stealing John Warner?'

The voice was loud and he snatched his hand back as the man turned around to see what the shout was.

Panicking slightly, John looked around.

It was her! The blonde Princess. He'd recognise her anywhere. She was halfway across the market.

How the hell had she seen him?

The man he had tried to rob was glaring at him but couldn't prove a thing.

'Oi, wait there.' she yelled.

She began to move through the throng towards him, but instinct took hold and he turned and ran.

Molly and Ruth were stood near a fruit and vegetable stall when Molly had seen the thief. She was sure it was the man from the inn and a shout across the market had proved it.

He'd turned around, seen her and then in a blind panic, began to run.

Grabbing a swede from the stall she hefted it and with a deft overhand throw, lobbed it towards the retreating man.

Behind her glasses, her eyes flashed blue, as did the sapphire on her bracelet and the thrown vegetable suddenly picked up speed as if it was caught in a ferocious wind. It hurtled down and with unerring accuracy, smacked the man in the back of the head.

He staggered two steps and then went down in the road. She paid the man for the swede and turned to Ruth.

'Come on.'

Her friend looked at her in awe.

'How the hell did you do that?'

Molly didn't answer, she was already pushing her way through the crowds to the downed man.

He had groggily managed to pull himself up to his knees when she reached him. Hauling him up by his jacket, she dragged him into the mouth of a nearby alley.

'Ruth, keep watch will you.'

'Why? What are you going to do?'

'Just do it please.'

Her friend frowned but did as she asked while Molly moved further down the alley with the thief.

His senses began to return but she twisted him and slammed him face first into the wall.

Slipping her hand into a pocket of her dress, she drew a short knife and pressed it against his back.

'I told you I didn't want to find you thieving again, didn't I John?'

'I din't have any choice.' he protested.

Molly span him around to face her and pushed him back against the wall before taking her glasses off.

'Why didn't you take the job at the inn?'

'It weren't for me.'

'So thieving is? What happened to the money I gave you?'

'I was robbed. I…'

Molly pressed her knife against his throat.

'I don't take kindly to be lied to John.'

'I lost it.'

'Lost it?'

'I like a game of dice…'

'You bet it away?'

He looked at her pleadingly.

'Please don't kill me.'

Molly sighed angrily and stepped back.

'I'm not going to kill you. But you are going to do some work for me. My friend Ruth will take you somewhere and find you something to eat. Then you're both going to go and find out what you can about the beast that's been around the docks.' she raised the knife. 'Don't even consider running on me John. If you do, I'll find you and then you will regret it. Is that clear?'

He nodded frantically. She may only be a slip of a girl and he should have been able to take her with one hand behind his back but there was something about her that scared the living daylights out of him.

'Yes miss.'

'I mean it John.'

'Yes miss. I promise miss.'

Molly slowly lowered the blade, never taking her eyes from the man. She sighed and pinched the bridge of her nose before calling Ruth over.

'Ruth, this is John. I want you to go and find him something to eat. Then the two of you, go and find out

what you can about the beast. Meet me at the Lion on
Cripple Street this evening.'

'Moll…'

'Please Ruth. I need to go and speak to someone.
Here…' she handed Ruth some coins.   'That should see
you alright.'

Ruth looked at the money in her hand. It was more than
she'd ever held. Molly turned back to John.

'Remember what I've said John.'

He nodded vigorously.

'Yes miss.'

'Now go on. Get out of here.'

Molly waited until Ruth and John were out of the alley
before she screwed her eyes shut and massaged her
temples. She really did have a bad headache.

'You're late.'

Major Gould snapped his watch shut and stood as Molly
came walking across the park.

'I don't have a watch.'

He shook his head with a dismissive sigh before offering
her his arm. She slipped her arm through his and they
began to walk. The day had clouded over and there was a
deep chill in the air.

'There'll be more fog later I expect.' said the Major.

Molly didn't reply.

'Your Highness, please…'

'Yesterday you didn't want me anywhere near this.
What's changed?'

Harry looked down.

'Harrington has said that you're to be involved. I've told
him that I think it's a bad idea but he is most insistent.
Still, that doesn't explain what you're doing at a tatty
dressmakers.'

'I don't want Marcus to know.' she said offhandedly.
'Now what have you found?'

The Major made a face.

'I still think this is no business for a lady…'

'Oh father,' said Molly, interrupting him as they passed a group of people 'I do so hate it when you talk to me like that.'

He glared at her.

'As my daughter, you should learn that you have a proper place in society.'

'And where is that?'

He waited until they were out of earshot of the group.

'I wish you'd stop doing that.'

'What?' she replied innocently. 'Look. Major…'

'Harry.'

Now it was her turn to glare at him.

'Look. I've got a headache. Can you just tell me what you found?'

A flash of concern passed across Harrys face before he guided her to a bench and sat her down.

'Whatever it is, killed again yesterday.'

'While we were at the warehouse?'

Harry nodded.

'Who?'

'Nobody. It was just some poor man. What was left of him was found near the river.'

'Nobody? Well he must have been somebody.'

Harry shrugged and Molly frowned.

'Did you go back? With soldiers?'

'No. I spoke to Harrington. He was of the opinion that if Sir Wilfred is involved, we should keep an eye on him and give him enough rope to hang himself. However, what with the recent killings and more yesterday, local people around the area are nervous.'

'But if he's keeping the beast in the warehouse, then that's enough. Isn't it?'

'Beast?'

'It's something a friend called it.'

'And is it?' he asked.

'What?'

'A beast?'

'Oh. I don't know.' replied Molly. 'She hadn't seen it. But she'd heard it. Said it howled like something out of a nightmare. I've asked her and another…' she thought for a moment before smiling slightly. '…and another *associate* to see what they can find out. I'm meeting them later.'

Harry nodded.

'Keep me informed please. This isn't a game.'

'I know.' she replied defensively.

The Major sighed.

'I don't like this one bit.'

'No.'

They sat in silence for a moment before Molly turned to him. He took one look at the smile on her face and shook his head.

'Whatever it is, the answer is no.'

'But father,' she said sweetly 'I'm sure that if I were to be properly introduced to Mr Hancock, the younger one that is, he and I would get along like a house on fire. I'm sure he knows all sorts of things. Things that a simple girl wouldn't understand…'

'No. Entirely out of the question.'

'Why not?' she demanded.

'That's taking too big a risk. I don't know why Harrington…'

'But he did involve me. I know what I'm doing. If Geoffrey Hancock knows something, I can get him to tell me.'

'No.'

'Fine. I'll go and see him myself.'

'You can't.'

'I bloody well can.'

Harry had to smile.

'You're as stubborn as a mule.'

'You're not the first person to tell me that.' she replied with a grin.

'Fine. Although I think this is a bad idea.'

'It's worth a shot.'

'Meet me here tomorrow and you can tell me what your contacts have found. In the meantime, I'll arrange dinner at my house for us and Geoffrey. I'll find an excuse to leave you two alone.'

'Alright.'

'But you have to promise me that you behave yourself.'

Molly placed a hand on her chest in pretend shock.

'But father, whatever do you mean?'

Collier walked through the dim street lost in his own thoughts. Lewis was being an arse. Sure, he'd fallen on hard times before, they all had, but Collier had seen him pick himself up before and carry on.

It was the drinking that worried him the most. It was getting bad.

Taking a left down a narrow road, he stopped in front of a small church. The fresh whitewash on the walls doing little to hide its dilapidated appearance.

Collier always came here if he needed some spiritual guidance. The Lord worked in mysterious ways and if there was a solution to his current problems, then this would show him the way. Removing his hat, he opened the small door and entered.

Inside was just as run down as the exterior. Two rows of worn looking pews faced an altar topped with a cheap brass crucifix.

Despite this, the cross had been highly polished and small candles were lit around the room giving it a homely feel.

Collier made the sign of the cross and approached the altar, stopping to light the stub of a candle which he placed next to several others on a low table at the side of the church. He crossed himself once more and knelt in prayer.

A few minutes later, he heard the door open behind him and steady footsteps come up the aisle.

Finishing his prayer, he stood and turned to the newcomer. It was an old priest. A slightly shabby cassock wrapped his thin frame but there was a kindness in his eyes that dispelled the obviously hard life he had.

Collier nodded to the old man and sat on the front pew. After a moment, the priest joined him.

'Do you want to talk about it?' he asked as he sat down.

'I'm worried for a friend Father. He's drinking himself to an early grave. He's lost a lot but won't listen to reason.'

'He should look to the Lord for guidance.'

'That's just it,' replied Collier with a sad sigh. 'I don't think he knows how.'

'Then as a friend, you should guide him. Bring him to the fold and he will thank you.'

'I don't expect he will.'

'The work of the Lord is never easy. Especially taking the word to those who don't believe. You must trust that your faith is strong enough for both of you. In time your friend will accept the Lord into his life.'

Collier nodded his thanks to the priest and stood up, feeling more positive than he had done for weeks. He had faith and knew it was enough for Lewis as well. Crossing himself once more, he turned and left the little church.

Outside, a heavy fog had closed in and he pulled his coat a little tighter around him to ward off the chill. He didn't need to be getting ill. Not at his age. Turning left, he headed back the way he'd come.

Hardly a soul seemed to be about and he only caught snatches of conversation from ethereal shapes as they moved past him.

Taking a left, he found himself at the riverside. The water lapped lazily against the bank and he paused.

Had that been a splash?

Straining to hear, he stepped closer to the water. There was nothing there. Must have been rats.

Shaking his head, he turned to go but stopped suddenly as a horrible screeching roar turned his blood cold. He'd heard that before. Back aboard the Amarantha. He swallowed dryly, a sudden fear gripping him. The roar sounded again, closer this time, and he ran as if the very Devil himself was chasing him.

Collier ran until he couldn't take another step. In his chest his heart was pounding and he was gasping for breath.

It couldn't be.

They'd pushed it over the side. It was dead.

Wasn't it?

He lent against a wall to try and get himself together. It couldn't be. He'd have to talk to Lewis.

The roar sounded again, but this time it came from somewhere above him. The last thing he saw as he looked up was a fanged maw and reaching claws plummeting out of the fog towards him.

Chapter Eleven

Dinner Date

Molly was sat stiffly in a leather armchair in Major Gould's drawing room, beginning to regret suggesting that they had dinner.

It had seemed like a good idea at the time but now the nerves were kicking in. Once more she cursed the fact that she'd had a poor upbringing. Formal dinners weren't something that she'd had a huge amount of experience with but she'd do her best.

It had all been arranged very quickly. Major Gould had gone to the warehouses to personally talk to Geoffrey and by all accounts the poor lad had nearly bitten his arm off at the invitation. His father on the other hand had initially resisted but gave his consent on the understanding that he was coming as well.

That was a complication that she'd have to deal with. Start by getting the drink flowing. That was the key. Get some wine down him and he'd be easy.

Failing that, there was always plan B.

The previous evening she'd met with Ruth and John. The inn had been busy but they'd managed to find a quiet corner to talk in.

'There's been another death.' Ruth had told her.

'I know. Do you know who?'

'Some bloke.' John had ventured until Molly glared at him.

'He, uh, was first mate on a ship.'

'Helpful. Which ship?'

He'd shrugged.

'Dunno.'

'The Amarantha.' said Ruth. 'It hasn't moved for months. It's tied up near the Osser warehouses.'

'How'd you know that?' John asked.

'Because I pay attention.' she answered with a scowl.

Molly sighed.

'Look. We haven't got time for this. Ruth, see what you can find out about this ship please.'

'What about me?'

'You're going to go see who this first mate was. He must have had a Captain. Find him.'

John nodded.

'I can do that. But…'

'But what?'

'I need some money.'

Molly had pushed some coins across the table.

'This is all you're getting.'

'Thank you miss.'

Molly couldn't mistake the look that Ruth gave him.

'Right, get going.'

John had stood up and after a hesitation, he left.

'I don't trust him.' Ruth told her. 'He's a thief and a cheat. He'll be off with your money. You won't see him again.'

'He knows better than that.'

'You sound sure.'

'I am.'

'I'm not.'

'Ruth. Please. He's all we've got.'

'I still don't trust him.'

'You don't have to. I have to.'

'Then you're a fool Moll.' said Ruth bitterly.

'Ruth…'

'I better get going.'

'Go back to Mrs Hopkins when you're finished. I'll see you there later.'

Ruth had nodded and left Molly alone.

There were voices in the hallway. This was it. Taking a deep breath, she stood up, smoothing out the creases in her dress to make herself as presentable as possible.

The door opened and in came Harry, followed by Sir Wilfred and then Geoffrey.

'Well this had better be worth it Major.' said Sir Wilfred as they came in. 'I dislike dining out, even more so when it's an establishment that I am unfamiliar with.'

'I'm sure everything will be to your satisfaction Sir Wilfred.' replied the Major smoothly.

The old man gave him a look which said "I don't expect it will" before pointing at Molly with his stick.

'You girl. Bring me a drink.'

'That's my daughter, Hannah, Sir Wilfred. You met her the other day.'

The old man peered at her through his spectacles.

'What's wrong with her eyes?'

'She contracted a rare fever, Sir Wilfred.' cut in the Harry. 'She's lucky to be alive.'

'Luck? No such thing. A man makes his own way in this world without relying on superstitious nonsense. Isn't that right Geoffrey?'

'Yes father.'

'In my opinion women should stay out of the way. They're only useful for keeping the house and producing babies.'

Sir Wilfred pointed at Molly with his stick again but addressed the Major.

'Is she dining with us?'

'Yes Sir Wilfred.'

'Why?'

'After their meeting the other day, she hasn't stopped talking about your son and I thought it might be nice for them to get to know each other. Isn't that right Hannah?'

'Yes father.'

Molly smiled sweetly and Geoffrey blushed.

'Pah!' spat Sir Wilfred before turning to his son. 'With those eyes, she'll have cripple babies. You could do much better.'

Molly looked at the floor, burning with embarrassment and also trying to supress the urge to punch the old man in the face.

'I say father…' began Geoffrey.

'You say what?' demanded the old man, prodding his son with his stick.

Geoffrey looked at his feet.

'Nothing father.'

The old man turned to the Major.

'I say as I find Major. I speak my mind and damn you if you don't like it.'

Harry smiled tightly.

'Quite, Sir Wilfred.'

'So where's this dinner?'

'Please follow me.'

Sir Wilfred followed Harry out of the drawing room, Geoffrey held back a moment and Molly could see the hesitation and abject terror in his body language. He was scared of her! A second later, some internal war won, he stepped forward.

'Miss Gould, um, may I …' he began hesitantly.

'Geoffrey!' Sir Wilfred yelled from the other room.

The young man looked at his feet and Molly felt sorry for him. Oh to have a father like that. She'd rather stay an orphan. Molly decided to help him out.

'Mr Hancock, I would be delighted if you would escort me to dinner.'

She offered her hand and after looking at it as if it might explode, Geoffrey took it gently.

'I'm sorry about my father. He has very strong views.'

'He's a very forthright man.'

Geoffrey smiled weakly.

'Geoffrey!'

Harry sat as the head of the table while Sir Wilfred and Geoffrey were to his left. Molly placed herself on the right, opposite Geoffrey.

'So, what's for dinner?' demanded the old man.

'I believe we're having duck, Sir Wilfred.'

'Duck? Can't abide duck.'

Molly and Harry exchanged glances.

From that point on, the meal was awful. Not the food, Major Gould's housekeeper had outdone herself, but the atmosphere.

Molly had drafted Ruth in to help serve the food as Harry didn't have many staff. At one point, Sir Wilfred had caught her smiling at Molly and rapped her sharply across the backside with his stick.

'Bloody servants ought to know their place. I hope you'll teach that one a lesson when we've gone Major.'

Harry had just smiled tightly.

Despite not liking duck, Sir Wilfred polished off quite a large portion, even demanding seconds.

The evening progressed slowly and as Ruth was clearing the plates, Molly couldn't help herself.

'Mr Hancock,' she enquired as politely as she could manage, 'If you don't mind me asking, is there a special, um, person in your life.'

Geoffrey, who had a glass of wine to his lips, almost choked, spilling the entire glass down his front.

'Hannah! That is not an appropriate question for you to ask.' Harry said quickly. 'I do apologise Mr Hancock sometimes I don't know where she gets her manners.'

'I told you Major. She'll become wilful and disobedient. You mark my words.' said Sir Wilfred. 'You should nip it in the bud now. Bring some discipline to this house.'

Geoffrey stood up and tried to wipe himself down while his father glared at him.

Harry turned to Molly.

'Are you going to apologise?'

'I'm sorry father.'

'It's not me you should be apologising to.'

'Oh, I'm sorry Mr Hancock. I didn't mean to cause you any offence.'

'I should send you to your room.'

'Please don't father.'

The Major winked and Molly caught a half smile.

'Be more respectful to who you're with. Do you understand?'

'Yes father.' she replied, glancing down and attempting to look suitably chastised but unable to do anything to hide the smile.

'Sit down Geoffrey, you're making a scene.' snapped Sir Wilfred.

'But...'

Harry stood up.

'Here.'

He helped Geoffrey out of his sodden jacket and handed him a handkerchief with which to mop the wine from his face.

'Should have a bloody servant to do that for you. Although from what I've seen, they're just as disrespectful and useless as your daughter.'

After that, any attempt at conversation from Molly, whether to the Major or especially Geoffrey, were quashed abruptly and quite rudely by Sir Wilfred. So Molly spent the rest of the meal in silence, her anger and dislike of the man growing with every minute.

They'd just finished the dessert when the butler came in followed by a smartly dressed man with his bowler hat in his hands.

He cautiously approached Sir Wilfred and whispered in his ear.

'What?' the old man exclaimed. 'Speak up man, I can't hear a bloody word.'

The man lent in again and repeated the message.

'Damn their incompetence.' shouted Sir Wilfred, standing up so fast he knocked his chair over.

'Is there a problem?' asked the Major.

'I should say so! Geoffrey, we're leaving.'

His son stood up with a longing look at Molly as Sir Wilfred swiftly headed out of the room.

'I…'

'Geoffrey!'

The young man sighed and followed his father. Molly watched them go in a stunned silence.

'So much for that plan.' said Harry, sitting back down and taking a swig from his wineglass.

'There's always plan B.'

'Which is?'

Molly smiled at him and dashed out of the room, catching up with Geoffrey outside as he was climbing into the waiting carriage.

'Mr Hancock.'

He turned back, the look of resigned sadness on his face brightening as he saw Molly. He climbed down from the step.

'I just wanted to say thank you for coming to dinner.'

She offered her hand and he shook it gently.

'It was a pleasure.'

As she let his hand go, she slipped a piece of paper from her palm into his. He looked surprised for a moment but Molly gave him an almost imperceptible shake of her head and smiled.

'Thank you again.'

From inside the coach, Sir Wilfred chastised his son.

'Geoffrey, let that silly strumpet go and get in.'

The young man glanced over his shoulder at his father.

'Now!'

With another sigh, he did as he was told and before the door had closed, the carriage was heading rapidly down the street.

'What was all that about?' asked Harry, standing on the steps of his house.

'Plan B.'

'And may I ask what that is?'

She smiled at him.

'I'm not going to like it am I?'

'Probably not.'

He sighed, shook his head and went back inside. Molly waited for a moment, until the carriage turned the corner, before she followed.

Chapter Twelve

A Walk in the Park

'I've got one hell of a bruise.' said Ruth as she and Molly headed into the park the next day. 'It hurts just to sit down.'

'Will you stop moaning?' asked Molly.

'It wasn't your bottom he hit.'

'No. But I expect you've had worse.'

'I suppose.' she said resignedly. 'But last time, I got *paid* for having my bottom smacked.'

Molly looked at her friend in astonishment.

'What?'

Ruth shrugged.

'I have to live as well, you know.'

Deciding she didn't want to know any more, Molly quickly changed the subject.

'Go and keep watch over by those trees. I won't be long.'

Ruth did as she was told and Molly headed across to the benches near the bandstand. Evening was creeping in and the first tendrils of a thick fog were squirming their way up from the river.

Sitting down, Molly waited. This was plan B. The note she had slipped to Geoffrey had asked him to meet her here tonight.

Harry hadn't been best pleased, even less so than the dinner he'd arranged. She told him she was going to go with or without him and eventually he'd agreed, but he would be keeping an eye on her as well.

He was somewhere nearby, although Molly couldn't see him. She'd brought Ruth for some additional support, just in case, and John was floating about somewhere too.

Not that she thought she'd have any problems with Geoffrey. The poor lad was smitten. She could see it in his eyes. She was sure that he really thought she wanted to be with him and that made her feel retched.

How was he going to feel when he found out the truth? Well she'd cross that bridge when she got to it. For now, she needed to know what was going on.

Sitting down, she waited.

Twenty minutes later, the fog had crept further in and she couldn't see the trees where Ruth was waiting. He wasn't going to come. She stood and was about to leave when a voice called out to her.'

'Miss Gould?'

Turning, she saw an out of breath Geoffrey hurriedly coming down the path.

'Mr Hancock?'

He was red faced and he looked sweaty and flustered.

'I was about to leave.'

'I'm terribly sorry. I couldn't get away.'

Molly smiled at him.

'Walk with me.' she said, 'I don't have long. Father doesn't know I'm out. He'll be quite mad if he finds out I've gone.'

Molly started to walk away from him and deeper into the park and he rushed to catch up.

'Well this is quite exciting, don't you think? Two people madly in love, overbearing fathers, clandestine meetings in the park. It's almost like a Shakespearian play.'

Madly in love? Molly opened her mouth in surprise.

'I'm sorry about yesterday, father can be a bit...'

She looked at him blankly for a moment before she recovered her composure.

'You both left quite suddenly.'

'There was something happening at one of the yards.' he hesitated. 'An accident.'

'Oh my,' replied Molly. 'I do hope no one was hurt.'

'Two of our workers were, unfortunately, killed.'

'Killed?' she said, feigning shock. 'What ever happened?'

Once more, Geoffrey hesitated, Molly took his hand, feeling awful for doing this to him and trying to block out thoughts of Marcus.

'Can you promise to keep a secret?' he said eventually.

'I promise.'

'It's quite awful really. I don't want to give you nightmares.'

She squeezed his hand and lent in close to whisper in his ear.

'I'm a big girl. I'm sure a few stories won't scare me too much.'

As she pulled back, he flushed crimson and she could feel the heat of his embarrassment pouring off him. Geoffrey looked around nervously.

'Do you really promise?'

Right then and there, Molly just wanted to grab him by his jacket and shake the information out of him, but she resisted, instead just managing to nod. He licked his lips, lent close and spoke in a conspiratorial manner.

'It killed them.'

'What did?'

He looked around once more, eyes darting from side to side.

'The monster.'

'Monster? I don't understand.'

Molly stared at him for a moment before guiding him to a bench and sitting him down.

'Mr Hancock. Tell me what is going on.'

He looked at her and she could see the turmoil in his head. Who was he more afraid of? In the end, he broke down in tears.

Gently, Molly put an arm around his shoulders and held him until he calmed down. He wiped his face with the back of his hand and sniffed loudly.

'What must you think of me?' he asked.

Molly decided that she better not tell him what she thought and placed a hand on his knee instead.

'It's very brave to show that you're upset.'

He smiled weakly.

'Father doesn't think so.'

'I don't expect he would.' replied Molly, anxious to find out what this "monster" was.

'Father doesn't think I'm enough of a man to run the businesses when he is gone. But I'll show him. I'm already showing him.'

Geoffrey was staring blankly, lost in his own little world. Molly grew impatient.

'If there's something out there that's killing people, don't you think you'd better tell someone?'

He looked at her.

'Oh, it's not killing people now.' he said absently.

'Why? Is it dead?'

'No. It's back home.'

'Geoffrey,' said Molly. 'Will you please tell me what is going on?'

'If I tell you, you must promise not to tell your father.'

'I promise.' she replied.

Geoffrey looked away and into the thickening fog.

'Father collects things.'

'I know. You showed me. Remember?'

He ignored her, continuing to talk as if she wasn't even there.

'He arranged for a shipment to come from China. He thought it was going to be a statue. But it wasn't. It was real. The thing escaped and killed some of the ships crew. They managed to force it over the side and into the sea, but it came back. It came looking.'

'Looking for what? Geoffrey, I don't understand.'

A frightened look appeared in his eyes along with something like relief at being able to unburden himself.

143

'It came to the warehouse. I was there alone. It tried to kill me, but I taught it a lesson. I tamed it.'

'What did you do with it?'

'I kept it. I can see the see the opportunities that it can provide. Father wouldn't understand.'

'It killed people.'

'Only at first.' he looked at her before adding proudly, 'I tamed it. Now it does as I tell it.'

'What happened last night?'

'It got out. Again.'

He lent in and whispered as if it were a confession of a naughty child.

'I let it out.'

Molly stood up quickly, she'd heard enough. Geoffrey followed.

'I have to go.' she said.

'Please don't.'

'I have to.'

Turning away from him, Molly took two steps before he grabbed her wrist.

'Don't go. I want to show you…'

Geoffrey yanked her back and almost pulled Molly off her feet. She cried out and twisted in his grip before stamping on his foot and pushing as hard as she could.

He let go and fell on his back where he lay for a second, a look of abject terror on his face. Molly took a step towards him, but he scrambled up and without a backward glance, ran off as fast as he could.

'Geoffrey!' Molly called at his retreating frame. 'Come back. I'm sorry.'

The thickening mist swallowed him and Molly swore loudly and colourfully. Both Ruth and Harry arrived at the same time.

'What happened?' asked the Major.

'Come on. Let's go somewhere warm and I'll tell you.'

She swore again and turned to go, but something caught her attention. On the floor where Geoffrey had fallen was a pipe.

She picked it up. It was about six inches long and looked like a fat penny whistle. Four holes were in the side and another in the bottom. The top was sculpted so you could blow in it. Harry took it off her.

'What've you got there? Looks like it's made of bone.'

He gave it an experimental blow and the noise it produced was discordant and ugly. Ruth covered her ears and Molly felt the same grating sensation as she'd felt in the warehouse, but this was a thousand times worse. Her head began to spin and she dropped to her knees.

'Moll!'

Immediately, both the Major and Ruth were by her side.

'I'm fine. Don't fuss.'

They helped her stand, Harry holding on to her in case she fell again. After a moment, she pushed away from him.

'I'm fine. Honestly.'

She took the pipe from Harry and wondered what the hell was going on.

Geoffrey arrived back at the docks breathless and flustered. She'd pushed him and that look on her face! His mind was whirling and he lent on a wall to compose himself.

Taking a deep breath, he straightened his tie and jacket.

He'd grabbed her. That had been wrong.

The poor girl must have been terrified.

That was it.

He'd scared her. Poor girl.

The more he thought about it, the more he was sure it was his fault.

Poor, terrified girl.

Geoffrey smiled to himself as he went into the warehouse. A faint light from the office signified that his father was still working. He went to see if the old man was alright.

'Where have you been?' he demanded as his son entered the chilly room.

'Out father.'

'With that crippled harlot?' Sir Wilfred replied, pulling himself stiffly out of his chair.

'No father. I was…'

'Don't lie to me boy.'

'I'm not.'

'Liar!' shouted the old man, smacking Geoffrey across the shoulders with his walking cane. 'I found the note she gave you. I'm not stupid you know.'

He whacked Geoffrey again, the young man cowering before the blows.

'Please father. I think she's the one. She's going to be mine…'

'What?' roared the old man, hitting his son so hard the stick snapped and Geoffrey was knocked to the floor.

Sir Wilfred regarded his son for a second before striking him three or four more times with the broken cane. Geoffrey curled up into a ball on the floor and sobbed quietly.

'Get up and stop your snivelling, I can't abide it when you act like that. You're pathetic.'

Geoffrey pulled himself up and stood in front of his father, eyes on the floor, not daring to look at the old man.

'I forbid you from seeing that girl again. Do I make myself clear?'

'Yes father.' Geoffrey whispered.

'What?' Sir Wilfred demanded, raising the stick up once more.

'Yes father.' he repeated, flinching back.

'Good. Now get out of my sight.'

The old man turned back to desk while Geoffrey scuttled away, closing the door behind him.

His back and shoulders hurt like blazes and he wiped his face with the back of his hand.

Limping away, he thought of Molly once more. Father wasn't right. Not this time. She was the one. The poor girl. The poor, frightened girl. She was the one.

Chapter Thirteen

Unravelling

Molly and Ruth were sat in the drawing room of the Majors house. Ruth was taking everything in. This was by far the grandest room she'd ever been in and had a silly grin on her face.

'Will you stop that?' asked Molly.

'What?'

'Smiling like that. It's unnerving.'

'What does that mean?'

'For God's sake Ruth.' snapped Molly. 'This is important. People are dying.'

Her friend looked down.

'Sorry.'

Molly sighed and pinched the bridge of her nose.

'No. I'm sorry. I've not slept very well.'

'Why?'

'I have nightmares.'

Since the park, the Major had insisted that Molly stay with him, so Ruth had been more than glad of the free bed at Mrs Hopkins shop. The old woman had tutted about it for a few minutes.

'She can stay here but only if she helps around the place. Cleaning and that.' Mrs Hopkins had said.

Ruth had quickly agreed, the opportunity for a warm bed and meals too good to pass up.

Now, two days later, they were sat, waiting for the Major to return from a meeting with Harrington.

There still hadn't been any word from John. Molly wasn't worried, but Ruth kept telling her that she shouldn't have trusted him.

'He's done a runner.'

'Shut up Ruth.'

'I'm only saying…'

'Don't please.'

She stood up and wandered around the room before sitting down again. She didn't like waiting. Harry had told her, in no uncertain terms, to stay where she was and she'd grudgingly agreed.

There was a knock at the front door and after a few moments, the butler came in. Molly jumped up.

'I'm afraid there's a Mr Hancock here again. I've told him you're not in, as per the master's instructions, but he insists on waiting until you are.'

'Tell him he can't. Tell him… I don't know, I've gone away for a few days.'

Ruth stood up.

'Let me handle this.'

She went out into the hall and Molly listened at the door.

'I'm afraid the mistress isn't in.' said Ruth.

'Well I would like to wait for her to return.'

'She will be out of town for a few days and we're not expecting her back before the weekend. She's visiting with her aunt in the country.'

There was a silence before Geoffrey spoke again.

'Well, make sure you give her this and these.'

'Very good sir.'

There was another pause.

'Are you sure she's not going to be back?'

'No sir. At least not before Sunday.'

'Very well. Make sure she knows that I called.'

'I will sir. Have a pleasant day.'

Before Geoffrey could say anything else, there was a heavy thud as Ruth shut the door. She came into the drawing room with a huge bouquet of flowers.

'These are for you.' she told Molly with a sly grin. 'He's fallen for you and that's a fact.'

Molly took the flowers and looked at them critically. They were actually quite beautiful. She put them on a table near the fireplace.

'Don't be so soft.'

Ruth grinned again.

'He also said to give this to you.'

She handed Molly a letter.

'To tell you the truth,' she told Molly, 'He looked a bit like he'd been in a fight. He had one hell of a bruise just under his shirt collar and seemed a bit stiff.'

'Very well spotted.'

They both turned as Harry came in. Ruth flushed with delight at the praise but also in embarrassment. She bobbed a curtsey.

'Thank you sir.'

He sat down heavily in one of the chairs.

'Harrington still won't do anything and there have been another four killings in the last two days.'

Molly looked up from the letter.

'What?'

'I said, that Harrington is being an arse. What've you got there?'

'It's a letter from lover boy.' said Ruth with a grin.

'Ruth!'

'Give it to me.'

The Major held out his hand and Molly gave him the letter. He scanned through it.

'What does it say?' asked Ruth.

Harry glanced at her and then at Molly.

'My dearest Hannah....'

Ruth giggled and Molly flushed with embarrassment.

'He says he was mortified by his actions the other day and is dreadfully sorry for scaring you. He would dearly like to show you that which you discussed....'

'Sauce.' interrupted Ruth with a nudge and a wink at Molly. Harry shot her a look but couldn't hide his own smile. He folded the letter in half and passed it back to Molly.

'I think you'd better read the rest on your own.'

She took it back and put it on the floor next to her. Harry sat forward.

'The boy is infatuated with you.'

'But…'

'Write back to him and have your maid…' he glanced at Ruth, 'Have your maid deliver it. I want you to say that you'll meet him again. Get him to show you this "Monster".'

'No!'

'You started this. I think you need to see this through.'

Molly glanced at Ruth.

'Don't look at me. It was your idea to invite him to dinner.'

'How would you know?'

'You told me.'

Molly folded her arms across her chest.

'Don't look like that.' said Harry, 'And besides, I think you should give him his pipe back.'

He placed the bone flute on a small table next to him and Molly felt the colour drain from her face.

'I can't.'

Harry levelled a finger at her.

'You can, and as your father, I'm telling you, you will.'

There was another knock at the door. This time the butler came in with the look of someone who'd just trodden in something smelly.

'There's a Mr Warner at the door sir. He says he's an acquaintance of Her Ladyship.'

Harry looked at Molly who shrugged before flashing an "I told you so" look at Ruth.

'Show him in.'

'As you wish sir.'

The man returned a few moments later with John. He was still as scruffy as he had been and the butler followed closely, obviously not keen on having such a reprobate in the house.

Molly stood up as they entered. John removed his cap and wrung it between his hands, he seemed just as uncomfortable at being here as the butler was at having him.

'John, we were wondering where you were.'

He shrugged.

'I found your Captain.'

'Where?'

'Drunk. He's at the Wagoner's Inn. Just off Yarldey Street.'

'I know the place.' said Ruth. 'It's a shit hole.'

Realising what she'd just said, she looked at the Major, blushed furiously and put her hand over her mouth.

'Oh, I'm sorry sir…'

Harry smiled and looked at Molly.

'So that's where you get it from?'

She shook her head with a grin.

'Not now father,' she turned to John 'What did he say?'

'He wouldn't talk to me. Too far gone. Kept going on about some "monster".'

Molly bit her lip thoughtfully.

'Ruth. You and John go and see what this Captain has to say.'

Her friend opened her mouth to protest.

'Just do it please.'

'Alright.' Ruth replied, although her tone suggested it wasn't.

'Meet me here in a couple of days and stay out of trouble.'

'I'll look after her miss.'

'Fine. Go.'

The look Ruth gave John as the filed out of room told him exactly what she thought about that.

'Now we're getting somewhere.' said Harry. 'Now all you need to do is get him to show you this "monster" of his.'

Molly nodded. Once more she glanced at the pipe. Somehow, she didn't think this was going to end well.

Three days later, she was waiting for Geoffrey.

Harry had been quite specific. She was to get him to take her to wherever this "Monster" of his was and then report straight back. She was *not* to do anything that would endanger her or anyone else.

Ruth and John had come back from the Wagoner's Inn empty handed, the Captain had disappeared. Molly was sure he'd turn up again and planned to go looking herself.

As she was back, Ruth had delivered her message and returned with another bruise across her backside. Sir Wilfred had been furious that she'd come and told her exactly what her mistress could do with the letter and it was not pleasant.

In the end, she'd hung around outside the yard until she'd seen Sir Wilfred leave before sneaking back in to find Geoffrey. He'd been overjoyed and wrote back straight away.

Now she was waiting. Again.

She seemed to spend quite a lot of time waiting recently. Patience had never been one of her strong points.

He'd asked her to meet him at a theatre, as it was somewhere his father didn't go, the old man despised the theatre. "It was a lot of pretentious nonsense and full of wastrels that should all get proper jobs."

The evening crowds were out and hawkers and street sellers were busy, loudly trading their wares to anyone and everyone.

Mollys stomach rumbled and she could smell all sorts of nice things cooking. She wished she'd eaten properly today.

'Hurry up Geoffrey.' she muttered under her breath.

Looking around, she spotted him straight away. He was trying to walk through the crowds without looking conspicuous, but in doing so, he stood out like a sore thumb. Molly shook her head. What was he doing?

He saw her and came straight over.

'Mr Hancock, it's…. hey!'

Grabbing her arm, he steered her quickly down a narrow road that ran down the side of the theatre.

'Please forgive me, Miss Gould. I'm so sorry about the other day, I shouldn't have grabbed you. I am so, so sorry if I scared you.'

Molly didn't say that he'd just done it again, instead she detached herself from his grip and smiled sweetly.

'There is no need to apologise Mr Hancock. I was just taken aback that was all. My father taught me to defend myself should anything happen and I'm afraid I panicked a little. It is me who should be saying sorry to you, and besides, you dropped this.'

She handed him the pipe and he looked at it with a mixture of horror and excitement. He glanced around before stuffing it in his jacket pocket and continuing as if it hadn't existed.

'Please call me Geoffrey and no I was at fault. I won't allow you to besmirch your beautiful character.'

Molly smiled again, making a mental note to ask Harry what "besmirch" meant.

'Shall we just say that it is water under the bridge and never happened?'

Geoffrey took her hand.

'Oh my dearest Hannah…' he hesitated, 'May I call you Hannah?'

'Of course.'

He smiled nervously and glanced around, and, still holding her hand, dropped to one knee.

'My dearest Hannah, would you marry me?'

'What?' stammered Molly, unable to keep the surprise from her voice.

'I know that it's quite sudden, but I love you. I can't stop thinking about you…'

Molly took a slow breath. What the hell was she going to do? In the end she looked him in the eye.

'Geoffrey. I mean, we hardly know each other, and I know your father doesn't approve of me.'

The young man looked crestfallen.

'I understand.' he said sadly.

He slowly stood and went to turn away, but Molly held on to his hand tightly.

'We have to take things slowly. I'm not sure my father would approve either. Not yet.'

Geoffrey turned back, a glimmer of hope flickering in his eyes along with something else.

'Then slow we shall be.' he said, 'My beautiful and dearest Hannah, you need never be frightened again. I will be there to protect you.'

Molly frowned. What was he on about?

'Geoffrey…'

He beamed at her.

'You've made me the happiest man in the world. I'm afraid I haven't got a ring yet. I would like us to choose one together. Money is no object. It will be the finest diamond for my bride to be.'

'But…'

'Come with me. I must show you something.'

Unceremoniously dragging Molly along, he took off down the alley.

'Where are we going?' she asked.

'To see *my* collection.'

Twenty minutes later, Molly and Geoffrey arrived at the yard by the river. He led her past the main gates to a set of narrow steps that went down to an old pontoon at the water's edge.

'Geoffrey?'

'Be careful my love, the steps are slippery.'

She frowned at him but he didn't see it. A mask of grinning stupidity had slipped across his face and he was only seeing what he wanted to see.

He went down the steps and along the pontoon, Molly following behind, lifting her skirts so that they didn't drag in the slimy moss that was growing on the aged wood.

'Here.'

He stopped at a rusty looking iron door and produced a key. The door swung open on surprisingly well-oiled hinges. Taking her hand once more, he led her into a long, narrow tunnel that smelled horrible.

Damp and moisture permeated the red brick walls and Molly shivered.

'Are you cold my love?' Geoffrey asked.

'A bit.'

'I will find you something warmer to wear in a moment.'

The tunnel ran on for a hundred feet or so before ending in a set of stone steps the top of which ended in another door. Geoffrey headed up and unlocked this one too.

'Come.'

He beckoned her up and she followed, hand slipping into a pocket in her dress which contained a brass knuckle duster, a present from Harry "Just in case".

The door led into the main warehouse and he placed his finger to his lips, indicating that she be quiet.

'My father is out at his club this evening.' he whispered, 'But it doesn't hurt to be careful.'

'Who...'

'Ssshhhhh.' he hissed angrily at her. 'Really my dear, you are going to have to learn to do as you are told.'

Molly bit her tongue so she didn't say anything that she'd regret later. She needed to see the "Monster".

'This way.'

Geoffrey took her hand once more, holding it so tightly it hurt. He was scared. She could feel him trembling.

Leading her through the deserted warehouse, he took her back up to the cavernous room that housed his father's collection.

Carefully, he unlocked the door and ushered Molly through.

'We'll have to be quick. This way.'

He led her across to the empty pedestal in the corner and with a theatrical flourish, pressed the hidden button. Molly pretended to be impressed as it sank into the ground.

'What's this?'

'A secret. The start of my collection.'

There was an odd edge to his voice and the nervous look in his eyes was being replaced by something else. He lit the lantern and headed down.

'Keep up my beloved. Really, must I tell you to do everything?'

Molly followed as closely as she dared. They reached the bottom and moved along to the heavy door.

Geoffrey unlocked it and she was assaulted by the awful smell, however it was much stronger this time. She covered her nose but Geoffrey didn't seem to notice. He turned to her and smiled.

'This way.'

The room beyond was as Molly remembered it, the far-right corner fenced off by the solid iron bars with the stagnant water inside.

The gate that sat on the wall was lowered down into the water this time and, huddled in the nest in the corner, was a "thing".

Geoffrey lit another lamp and cast its beam across the form. It moved like the wind, going from what appeared to be sleeping to madly thrashing at the bars in a vain attempt to reach him.

It was a good six feet tall with a long, almost rat like, snout. Thin arms and legs ended in large hands and feet with brutish looking claws that were covered in filth and dried blood.

Sharp yellowing teeth snapped viciously while black beady eyes looked on with mad hatred. Its body was bent and hairless with a long, wormlike, tail that arched up over its head while around its waist was a leather cord and hanging from that, a mouldy looking pouch.

Molly was reminded of a giant rat and couldn't stop the shudder that passed through her at its grotesque visage.

'My God. What is it?' breathed Molly.

'Honestly? I don't know. It came from a small island in the south China sea. Apparently the locals worshiped it as a God.' he laughed. 'Can you imagine such a thing? Backward natives looking to this... this creature. Idolising and worshiping it. Now it worships me. I am its God. The God of a God. How do you like that? Having a husband who is a God?'

Molly didn't have an answer for him.

'Father thought he'd bought a statue. But I knew. My friend Mr Dickenson told me. I gave one of mine to him. He gave me this.'

'One of your what?'

'All in good time my dear. I will show you everything. You will respect that. Respect me.'

Grinning madly, Geoffrey let her go and approached the thing, laughing as he taunted it by stepping closer to the cage but keeping just out of reach of those awful looking claws.

'Come here. It can't hurt you.' he told her, without looking around.

Molly had no desire to go anywhere near it and the stench it was giving off was intolerable.

'I'm fine here I think.'

Geoffrey turned slowly, the lamplight reflecting in his eyes and giving the look of a madman.

'Come here now. Don't make me tell you again.'

Slowly, she approached and when she was within a couple of feet, Geoffrey grabbed her and dragged her to him.

'I will need to give you lessons in how to obey your husband I think.'

He thrust the lamp into Mollys hands and pulled the pipe from his pocket.

Upon seeing the instrument, the thing in the cage redoubled its efforts to get to him and for a second, Molly was sure that the bars weren't going to hold.

Still grinning madly, Geoffrey put the pipe to his lips and blew a series of shrill notes which made Molly's head spin and knees buckle.

In the cage, the monster screamed and covered where its ears should have been. The noise it made was terrible, an awful discordant howling that made Molly just want to run away.

Geoffrey blew some more notes and the thing fell to the ground, thrashing and trying to scrabble away from them. Molly couldn't stop herself from falling either. She thudded to her hands and knees.

'Oh my dear, are you alright?' asked Geoffrey, helping her to stand on weak legs.

'Stop it. You're hurting it.'

'I'm taming it. Just as I will tame my wife.'

More notes followed and the thing screamed again, slowly dragging itself into the corner.

'Stop it!' shouted Molly, using all of her energy to try and grab the pipe from Geoffrey.

He rounded on her.

'You're just like the others.' he spat, 'Just like father. I can do whatever I want.'

'Your father? What has he got to do with this?'

'Nothing. He knows nothing. He's a pathetic old man.'

He blew the pipe again and in its cage, it screamed. Molly slumped against him, head whirling with bright lights.

She vainly tried to get the pipe once more but he shoved her away and she landed hard on her bottom. In a second he was next to her, helping her up again.

'My dearest Hannah, I'm so sorry. I...'

His remorse seemed genuine but the way he was switching between anger and docility was scary.

'You're mad.' she said breathlessly.

'No. No. I love you. You're going to be my wife.'

'I'm bloody well not.'

The anger returned and he struck out, catching her across the face with a weighty slap, knocking her to the ground.

'How dare you talk to me like that.' he shouted. 'You need to have time to reflect on your position. You need to think about what you've done.'

Grabbing her dress, he began to drag her along towards the door in the far wall. Still reeling from the blow, she couldn't stop him.

'You have to have respect, you stupid whore. Did your father teach you nothing?'

'My father?'

'Your father. What did that poor man do to have been lumbered with such an ungrateful daughter. When he is gone, you will do as you are told.'

'What?' stuttered Molly.

A serenity passed across Geoffrey's features and his spittle flecked mouth turning into a grimaced grin. He dropped her and walked to the bars of the cage, the thing still cowering in the far corner. From his jacket he produced a silk handkerchief.

'Your fathers.' he said to Molly before he pushed it through the bars.

It fell to the floor and the monster snatched it up sniffing deeply. It looked up at Geoffrey and he raised the pipe once more. It looked down and he smiled.

'You see. Tamed. It will do as I tell it.' he turned to Molly. 'As will you.'

'I don't think so.'

Molly stood up as straight as she could manage. The left side of her face was bright red from where he'd struck her and her legs were still a little wobbly from the effects of the pipe. Reaching into the pocket of her dress, she slipped the brass knuckles on.

'Oh, you will my dearest. I will see that you do.'

Geoffrey moved to the wheel and hauled it up, raising the gate on the other side of the bars.

'The creature has an excellent sense of smell. Now it has your fathers scent.'

Molly didn't understand what he was talking about until he turned to the cowering thing and uttered a single word with a demented smile.

'Kill.'

Chapter Fourteen

The Death of a Father

With barely a splash, the creature dived into the stagnant water, disappearing quickly. Geoffrey turned to Molly.

'Now come here like the good, obedient wife you will be.'

She backed away and he followed.

'You must do as you are told. They never do as they are told.' he muttered.

With a darting lunge he grabbed at Molly, but she sidestepped and caught his arm, twisting it viciously around until he doubled up, before she drove her knee as hard as she could into his stomach. He gasped for breath and she punched him in the side of the head. The brass knuckles knocking him to the ground and drawing blood.

'I think our engagement is over, don't you?' she said.

Molly turned to go, but Geoffrey grabbed the hem of her dress.

'You can't go.' he gasped. 'You can't...'

He yanked the dress and Molly turned as the material ripped.

'Get off me.' she shouted, stamping down on his hand, feeling a dark satisfaction as his fingers broke under her boots.

Geoffrey screamed in pain and pulled back.

'I'm sorry.' he shouted.

She didn't give him a chance to say anything else before she ran out of the smelly room into the narrow corridor, slamming the iron door behind her.

As she pounded through the warehouse, she couldn't help but think that this was her fault. Now the creature was after Harry. She had to stop it or at least warn him.

Taking the steps into the river tunnel two at a time, she began to mutter under her breath. The words were not in a recognised language, but they had a dark intent.

One that sent the chills of fear deep into the very soul.

Behind her a thick black mist began to form, trailing out in wisps of almost pure darkness.

The words grew in volume and as she shouted the last syllable she jumped through the door at the far end, the black mist rushing to catch her up and enveloping her in its chilly embrace.

Anyone watching the door would have seen the mist explode out, and from its depths, a huge eagle spear forwards, arcing sharply and soaring through the London night.

Of Molly, there was no sign.

She was in the Darkness.

It was the terrible space between worlds where the souls of the dead went, which was both a gift and a curse.

In India she had been marked by the Daughters of Kali and a huge eagle had been tattooed on her back by forgotten, painful, magic.

Each intricately inked feather was a link to the Darkness and it allowed her to summon the eagle.

Her mind transferred to the bird and giving her its clarity and killer intent while her body wallowed in the dark, surrounded by the souls of those she had killed. Their cold, dead hands grasping at her until she returned from that desolate place.

The transition to and from the eagle was painful and gave Molly a headache, not to mention the nightmares from which she suffered were always intensified if she had been in the Darkness.

All of that was a sacrifice worth making if she could save Harry. And, even though she tried to deny it, the sheer joy of flight was something else.

The eagle shot forwards, picking up speed as it flew through the night towards the Majors' house.

Riding in its mind, Molly guided it. She was sure she would get there before the creature but how much of a head start she'd have, she didn't know.

The journey across the city took mere minutes and, as she spied the house, she began to utter the words that would bring her back from the Dark.

Behind the eagle, the black mist returned, spreading out behind in lightless contrails as it dived towards the ground.

The bird swooped low as the mist engulfed it and after a pop of displaced air, it disappeared leaving a breathless Molly standing in the road.

She blinked a few times and screwed her eyes shut while her mind adjusted but she was running hard up the steps to the house within seconds. Crashing through the front door, she darted from room to room until she found the butler and housekeeper in the kitchen.

'Where's the Major?'

'Your Highness…' he began but Molly interrupted him.

'Just tell me where he is. Please. He's in danger.'

'I believe that he and miss Thomas were going to see Mr Harrington. They should be on their way back now.'

'Miss Thomas?' asked Molly.

The housekeeper smiled kindly at her.

'Ruth, Your Highness.'

Molly looked at her in surprise. She'd known Ruth for a good couple of years and didn't know that her surname was Thomas.

Why were they going to see Harrington? It didn't matter either way at that point, she had to find the Harry. She had to warn him.

'Is there anything I can do for you, Your Highness?' the butler enquired.

She looked up at him and pinched the bridge of her nose. She had a headache coming on.

'No. Thank you. But if he gets here before I find him, tell him he's in danger and to wait here.'

Before either the butler or housekeeper could reply, she'd grabbed a long kitchen knife, turned on her heel and was running out of the house.

The night had drawn in and the air was damp, with the first tendrils of fog beginning to form.

That was all she needed.

Running across the road and into the park, she began to speak the words once more, the thick black mist streaming out behind her.

With a cry, she jumped into the air as the transition to the Darkness took her and the eagle was summoned, the bird soaring high and cutting through the night.

Harry was sat in the carriage opposite Ruth. Neither spoke.

Ruth was enjoying the ride. Who'd of thought, a week ago, that she'd be riding in a fine carriage, wearing the nicest dress she'd ever seen and just been to the Palace? Not her, that's for sure.

Harry, on the other hand, was contemplating the recent discussion with Harrington.

God that man was an arse. He sighed and sat forward.

'So, what did you make of him?'

'Who sir?'

'Mr Harrington.'

'I only saw him for a second, sir.'

'And?'

'He's shifty sir.' she replied after a moments consideration, not really having the words to express herself more eloquently.

The Major smirked.

'That he is.'

'His man is a bit iffy too.'

Harry looked at her with a frown.

'Man?'

'Yes sir. He was waiting down the corridor from me. He was hiding around the corner and went into the room through another door as you came out.'

'What did he look like?'

'Scruffy. Messy hair and he had a scar across his face. From here to here.' She drew the location on her own face with a finger. 'And I'm sure I saw him at the inn we was in the other day too.'

The Major sat back with a sly smile.

'Mr Potts. I thought he was dead.'

'Sir?'

'I shot him. I thought he was dead. The bugger is more resilient than I thought.'

He saw the look that Ruth gave him and shook his head.

'Nothing for you to worry about. Well spotted though…'

Harry's words were cut off as the coach lurched to a halt and Ruth was thrown from her seat into his lap. She quickly disentangled herself, blushing furiously.

'I'm so sorry sir…'

There was a moments silence before the night was cut by a scream and the frightened whinny of horses.

Harry frowned as the coach lurched once more. He got off the seat, lifted it up, and pulled out brace of pistols.

'Wait here.' he told Ruth sternly as he readied the weapons.

She nodded in agreement.

Carefully, the Major opened the door and climbed out.

The scene outside was chaotic.

One of the carriage horses was dead in the harness, its throat torn out and the other was wild eyed next to it but unable to get away.

The driver, or what was left of him, was lying in the road while above the body stood a "thing".

It was taller than a man and sickly pale pink colour. A prehensile tale waved in the air above its rat like head and long claws were embedded deep within the unfortunate driver's chest.

As he watched, the creature tore out the mans' heart and took a bite, before dropping the rest into the pouch held at its waist.

Fighting his revulsion, Harry levelled one of the pistols at it and, sighting carefully, fired.

The ball hit the creature square in the back and it screeched in pain, the noise cutting through the thickening fog like a knife.

It rounded on the him and he levelled his second pistol, stepping backwards towards the carriage.

The thing sniffed the air a few times before fixing him with a glare from its beady eyes.

Licking his lips, the Major opened the carriage door, keeping the pistol pointed at the creature.

'Miss Thomas, do you know how to reload a pistol?'

'No sir.'

'Pity.'

The thing let out another horrible screech that set his teeth on edge and leapt towards him, clearing the ten or so feet between them in a single bound.

Harry fired as it landed, the shot driving deep into its shoulder.

Unfazed but shrieking in pain once more, it lashed out, catching Harry heavily and smashing him into the side of the carriage.

His vision blurred as he hit the ground and he felt blood in run down the side of his face.

Groggily he tried to stand but his head was swimming and his legs didn't seem to want to work.

Using as much strength and co-ordination as he could muster, he tried to crawl underneath the carriage but a cold hand grabbed him tightly and hauled him back out before it picked him up by the ankle and bodily swung him into the door of the carriage, smashing it from its hinges.

Dimly he was aware of someone screaming but had no idea where from.

There was also another sound. A long screech from somewhere above him.

He was dragged up once more and thrown across the street where he landed in a dazed pile.

Rolling onto his back, he couldn't do anything as the creature stepped over him, its tail waving hypnotically above its head.

Slowly it crouched and raised a clawed hand to strike him down. On the floor, Harry tried to block out the terrible stench from the creature and get his senses together.

Above him, the thing paused and sniffed the air, its head darting left and right.

It screeched in panic as, to Harry, something that looked like a blurred cross between a huge bird and Molly hit it feet first and knocked it sideways.

She came from a height and trailing a chilling black mist that looked like she had dived from the sky.

The creature skittered away, hissing madly. There were hands on his shoulders, dragging him up.

'Ruth. Get your backside out here now and help me.'

Another pair of hands joined the first and they heaved him to a sitting position. His head was swimming and something was grinding painfully in his side.

There was a none too gentle slap to his face and it resolved that it was Molly. She was crouched in front of him with Ruth to the side and looking scared.

'Harry. It's trying to kill you. Geoffrey ordered it. Can you stand?'

'What? Yes…' he began, groggily trying to get to his feet but his legs buckled beneath him.

There was some loud cursing.

'Ruth, you'll have to help. Get him out of here.'

They both dragged him up and, leaning heavily on the young woman to his right, he staggered back to the coach.

Molly watched her friend drag the stunned Major away before turning her attention to the creature. It was rising to its feet, hissing and spitting at her but not daring to approach.

Hefting the long-bladed kitchen knife in her left hand, she slipped on the brass knuckles on her right.

'Come on then.'

As if in answer to her challenge, it jumped forward.

Molly ducked and slashed the blade along its flank as it passed, eliciting another chilling squeal before it swung its tail wildly.

It caught Molly across the wrist and it was like being hit by an iron bar. She shouted in pain and the knife fell from her numbed hand.

It chittered at her and leapt once more, knocking her flat, its yellowing teeth and foul breath inches from her face. It opened its mouth, foul drool dripping from its maw, before it snapped downwards, only to find a brass encased fist coming the other way.

The punch landed solidly on the side of its snout and it staggered enough for Molly to squirm out from underneath it.

She stood, dropping into a fighting stance as the thing turned towards her once more. It screeched at her before turning tail and running away.

'Oh no you don't.' she muttered to herself as she made to give chase it but a shout from behind stopped her.

'Molly!'

Harry had slumped to his knees and Ruth was struggling to hold him upright. With a final look in the direction the beast had gone and with another loud curse, Molly went to help her friend.

The fog had descended and covered the city in a thick blanket by the time they managed to get back to Major Gould's house.

His butler took over straight away and guided him to a chair in the drawing room while the girls sank gratefully into chairs of their own.

Molly rubbed her eyes. God, she was tired. With a splitting headache too.

Harry had recovered some of his senses by the time they got him home, but he still looked at state. Dried blood plastered the right-hand side of his face and his clothes were dirty and torn.

Molly took a deep breath and went over to him.

'Let's have a look at you then.'

He smiled weakly and waved her away.

'It's nothing my dear, nothing that a strong drink won't cure anyways.'

She watched as Harry slowly stood, wincing as a pain flared in his side. Broken, or at least badly bruised ribs she thought, not to mention the gash on his forehead and numerous other cuts and bruises.

He stiffly walked across to the sideboard and poured himself a large scotch from a fine crystal decanter. Taking a large gulp, he topped it up and turned to the women.

'Would you ladies like a…'

'Yes.' said Molly. 'We would. Now sit down, before you fall down. I'll sort it out.'

He smiled weakly again before slumping back into his chair with a groan. Molly poured both her and the shaken looking Ruth a drink.

'What was that thing?' asked Ruth as she took the glass from Molly.

'I don't know.' she turned back to Harry. 'Geoffrey sent it to kill you.'

'And it damn near succeeded. Why does he want me dead?'

'He asked me to marry him. Kept going on about keeping me safe from harm, right up until the point where he slapped me and called me a stupid whore.'

'He did what?' spluttered the Major.

'That's not the half of it. He keeps the thing locked in that room we found. The pipe controls it, makes it do his bidding. He told it to kill you. Gave it your handkerchief to get your smell then sent it out after you. He said that with you out of the way, your ungrateful daughter will be his wife and learn to do as she's told.'

'He's mad.'

'Yes. He is. I don't think his father knows about it.'

'What makes you say that?'

'Just the way he talked about him. This is all Geoffrey. I think there have been other women as well. Ones that haven't managed to get away from him.'

Harry took a long sip of his drink.

'Harrington is going to have to do something now.'

'And you're in no fit state to do anything about it.' said Molly.

'Nonsense…'

He tied to stand but groaned in pain and sat down heavily.

'See.' she turned to Ruth. 'Are you alright?'

The girl nodded but there was fear written into every line of her face.

'Ruth. I need you to stay here and make sure he doesn't go anywhere. Can you do that?'

'What if that thing comes back?'

'Then go to the cellar and lock the door.'

'Alright.'

'What're you going to do?' asked Harry.

'First of all, I'm going to see Harrington. Then I'm going to stop this once and for all.'

Sir Wilfred returned to the yard after dining at his club. The food had been terrible and the service even worse. If that halfwit of a waiter was still working there tomorrow then there would be hell to pay.

His carriage dropped him outside and he walked in, silver topped cane clacking on the cobbles. Damn the waiter, if he had his way, the wastrel would have been thrashed to within an inch of his life already and be out on the street to boot.

He let himself into his office, laying his stick across his desk before lighting a solitary candle and slipping his coat from his shoulders.

'Hello father.'

The voice made him jump and he span around to find Geoffrey lurking in the shadows.

'What on earth are you doing back there?'

Geoffrey stepped into the half light of the candle. Dried blood painted the right hand side of his face and stained his shirt collar while his left hand was bandaged tightly. He wore a vague and distracted smile and was clutching what appeared to be a torn piece of cloth.

Sir Wilfred peered at him.

'What're you doing, you simpleton?'

'She's mine father. She's going to marry me.' his son replied.

'What?'

'I've been waiting to tell you. She's mine.'

'You've seen that little trollop again, haven't you?' snapped Sir Wilfred.

Geoffrey nodded dumbly, the smile never leaving his face.

'She's going to marry me.'

The old man picked up his stick and advanced on his son.

'I forbade you from seeing her again. Yet you disregarded my instructions. Do you need me to repeat myself? Do you need to be taught a lesson?'

'She's mine.'

Sir Wilfred raised his cane and slashed it down towards Geoffrey. Without seeming to move, the boy caught it in his right hand. The wood slapped hard against his palm and must have hurt but Geoffrey didn't flinch.

'What're you doing?' Sir Wilfred demanded, trying to wrench the cane from his son's grasp.

Geoffrey looked at him, his smile slipping for the first time.

'She's mine father. Neither you or the Major can do anything about it.'

'What?'

With a violent tug, Geoffrey pulled the cane from Sir Wilfred's hand. The old man backed away, his earlier bluster being replaced by fear.

'I'm going to marry her, and you won't stop me. Neither of you.'

'Geoffrey…'

The old man raised his hands as his son stepped forward.

'Geoffrey…' he said again, a pleading note in his voice.

'She's MINE!' shouted Geoffrey, lashing out with the cane and catching his father across the side of the head.

The older man stumbled backwards and sprawled across his desk. His son followed, dragging him up before slamming him back down.

His feet went from under him and his head cracked off the edge of the desk. He slipped to the floor and managed to roll over as Geoffrey stood above him with the cane raised above his head.

'Stop this now Geoffrey. Please.' he begged.

The young man smiled madly as he swung the stick down hard.

Sir Wilfred groaned and rolled over. He was lying in the dark on a cold stone floor. Somewhere nearby he could hear water and there was a terrible smell.

Stiffly, he sat up, touching his forehead and feeling wetness that could only be blood. His left arm was a blur of pain and he was quite sure it was broken.

'Damn that boy.' he muttered to himself, dragging himself along until his head bumped into a metal bar. From somewhere off to his left, he heard a soft splash.

'Who's there?' he demanded.

There was no answer.

Using the bar to haul himself up he began shouting.

'You hear me Geoffrey? You let me out of here this instant and stop all of this nonsense.'

Dripping water and a louder splash caused him to turn around in panic.

'Who's there?'

Behind him, a lamp was lit, and he spun round blinking in the sudden light. Geoffrey was stood nearby with a demented grin on his face.

'Geoffrey?'

The boy looked at him and spoke a single word.

'Kill.'

The lamp went out and plunged the room into darkness once more. Sir Wilfred gripped the bars tightly as from somewhere a heavy door was slammed shut.

'Geoffrey. Stop this now. I...'

He stopped talking as he felt a foetid breath on the back of his neck. The stink was so abominable that he closed his eyes as it washed over him. He swallowed, terrified.

'Geoffrey?' he whispered.

Chapter Fifteen

Designs of a Madman

'You're not going to see Harrington dressed like that!"

Molly stopped at the bottom of the stairs. She was wearing her leather jumpsuit with her sword strapped to her back. Another long knife was sheathed on her thigh.

She glanced up at Harry who was stood in the doorway. He had his shirt off and his ribs were heavily strapped up. She looked down at herself.

'What's wrong with it?'

'What's wrong with it? My dear, such a thing shouldn't be worn in polite society.'

'You didn't say that when we were breaking into Sir Wilfred's yard.'

'No.' Harry conceded 'But it was practical then.'

'It's practical now.'

'For hunting monsters, yes. For visiting Harrington, no. Go and find something more appropriate to wear.'

'But…'

'Now. We don't have much time.'

Molly sighed and headed back up to her room, muttering as she went. When she came back down five minutes later she was wearing a deep green, high-necked dress with long sleeves and her sword was in her hand.

Harry and Ruth were waiting for her in the hallway. He'd put a clean shirt on and Ruth was helping him into his jacket.

'Better?' she asked sullenly.

'Much.' Harry replied with a grunt of pain as he slipped his arm into the sleeve.

'Where do you think you're going?'

'With you.'

'Oh no…'

'This isn't up for discussion. You and your attitude won't get within a hundred feet of Harrington without me there.'

She scowled at him, but he ignored her, instead turning to Ruth.

'Miss Thomas, will you please go and make sure the cab is waiting.'

Ruth glanced between Molly and the Major before nodding and hurrying out of the front door. Harry straightened stiffly.

'Don't give me that look. I know how these things work. You need to do as you are told and listen for a change.'

'I listen.' she protested.

'Do you?'

She scowled again.

'See? Now we don't have much time. If we want to get this monster, then we'll have to convince Harrington to put soldiers on the streets. Tonight. And storming in there with your temper and sword are not going to do that. He'll need to see that there's something in it for him.'

Molly opened her mouth to reply but Harry cut her off.

'And I don't mean threatening to him. He's got more than enough strong arm both in the Palace guards and other, not so obvious, associates to hurt you and your family in ways you can't possibly imagine. So I want you to sit there, be quiet and let me handle this. Understand?'

She didn't reply.

'I asked you if you understand.'

Molly sighed heavily.

'I understand.'

'Good.'

They both turned as the door opened.

'The carriage is here sir.'

'Thank you Miss Thomas. I suggest you come too, I'd rather not leave you here on your own.'

Ruth looked between Harry and Molly once more, there was a tension in the air you could cut with a knife.

'I'll be fine sir.'

'That's as maybe,' he said, glancing at Molly, 'but maybe you can help Her Highness keep her temper in check.'

'It's, ah, late Major.' said Harrington without looking up. He was sat at his wide desk and was writing a letter.

'We need to get soldiers on the streets.'

The man didn't look up for nearly a full minute as he continued to write his letter. Eventually he put his pen down and steepled his hands with an unfriendly smile. He looked at the Major, stood in front of his desk, and then at the two women at the back of the room by the door.

'Your, ah, Highness. So delightful to see you, ah, again.'

Molly smiled tightly.

'Geoffrey Hancock has gone mad. He's in control of a creature. The one that's been terrorising the docks. He's using it to kill people.'

Harrington looked at him as if he were an idiot.

'And this is, ah, my problem because…?'

'He sent it to kill me! It damn near ripped my head off.'

'Do you actually have any evidence that Mr Hancock ordered this?'

'Yes.' said Molly. 'I was there when he sent the thing out.'

'I see. So, ah, correct me if I'm wrong, but if Geoffrey Hancock is responsible…'

'Which he is.' cut in Molly.

Harrington smiled crookedly.

'Quite…' he paused to see if there were to be any more interruptions before continuing. 'If Geoffrey Hancock is responsible then, ah, why are you both not out doing what I employed you to do? Primarily bringing the culprit to, ah, justice. Why do I need to order soldiers onto the streets and, ah, cause a panic?'

Molly tensed, and before she could say anything she felt Ruth grab her arm and hold her back. At the desk, Major Gould was fuming.

'Now listen here you little toad, I've been attacked and almost killed tonight. I'm in no mood for your petty games. If Geoffrey Hancock has lost his mind, who knows what he's going to do. He could unleash that thing of his across London…'

'Which is precisely why you should, ah, stop him now. Good night Major.'

Harrington looked back down at his paperwork as if dismissing them. Harry looked at Molly and Ruth before grabbing Harrington by the jacket and hauling him up over the desk.

'How much do you think I would mind if I killed you now?' he growled. 'The world would be a better place without one less pen pushing little rat at the helm. And don't think I don't know that you've got that bastard Potts still working for you.'

Harrington's eyes flicked to Ruth and back before a look of detached calm passed across his face.

'I suggest you let me go Major.'

Harry felt a gentle hand on his shoulder. He looked around to see Molly.

'He's not worth it.'

He turned back to Harrington.

'This isn't over.'

He thrust the man back into his chair and turned away.

'Good night Major.' called Harrington as he stalked towards the door. 'I will expect a full, ah, report of the matter tomorrow if you would be so kind. Good, ah, night Your Highness. Oh and of course. Miss Thomas.'

The Major left, slamming the door open and leaving with Molly and Ruth in tow.

Harrington watched them go and after a moment, stood and pulled a bell rope by the fireplace. A few minutes later a servant appeared.

'Yes sir?'

'Would you request that Captain McKay comes here at once.'

'Yes sir.'

The man hurried away.

'Come in Mr Potts.'

The door behind him opened and in came the scruffy man with the hat. He sauntered around the front of the desk. Harrington regarded him for a second before sighing.

'I assume you heard that?'

A sly smile graced Mr Potts lips for a moment.

'Aye.'

Harrington sighed again and turned away.

'Let them sort out this "monster" of theirs, then kill them.'

'It'll be my pleasure.'

'I'm sure it will. Make sure the women don't suffer unduly.'

'What about the Major?' asked Mr Potts, almost hungrily.

'As long as it can't be traced back to me, you can do what you like.'

Mr Potts smiled more widely.

'I'll see to it.'

'Good.'

The Major was down the end of the corridor by the time Molly and Ruth caught him up.

'I liked the way you handled that. Kept you temper and everything.' said Molly innocently.

'The man is a complete arse.'

'He is.'

They walked out of the building and to their waiting carriage. The Major helped Ruth in and offered his hand to Molly.

'I'm not going with you.'

'What? You can't…'

'Harry. You're in no fit state to fight anything. I know that you're hurting more than you want to admit. Otherwise you wouldn't have lost your temper like that. I'm going to see Geoffrey one last time.'

'You could be killed.'

'Yes. I could. But I don't think he'll do anything.'

'But you don't know that.'

'No.'

'Then you're not going.'

Molly reached past him and picked up her sword from the seat of the carriage. Harry grabbed her arm.

'Don't.'

She gave him a hard look which quickly softened into a sad smile.

'I'll be fine.'

'I can't let you do this.'

'Now you sound like my husband.'

He let her arm go and she took the sword.

'Ruth, take him to Mrs Hopkins, you'll be safe there.'

Her friend nodded.

'Be careful.'

'I will.'

Before either of them could say anything else, Molly turned and was running down the road.

'Damn girl.'

Ruth smiled weakly.

'She always did have a stubborn streak.'

'It's going to get her killed.'

Molly ran towards the river before ducking into a narrow alley to strip off her dress.

Underneath she had her jumpsuit and after strapping her sword to her back, she took off again.

The fog was thicker near the river, but she was glad of its cover as she neared the yard. Heading to the right, she went down the steps to the old pontoon, the door was still wide open from where she had left earlier but the tide had begun to come in and there were a couple of inches of water on the floor.

Leaving the door open she moved along the tunnel until she emerged into the warehouse proper.

She drew her sword as she walked through the empty space, and that's what it was, empty. There were a few crates and piles of sacks, but the place felt deserted.

She wished Marcus were here.

Taking a deep breath, she moved further in, surprised when she found the door to Sir Wilfred's collection wide open. Cautiously she crept in.

The place was a mess. Every single plinth had been turned over and every cabinet smashed. Broken artefacts littered the floor alongside shattered glass.

What the hell had happened?

Boots crunching on the broken glass and pottery she found the secret steps to where the creature was kept were also open. Ignoring the lantern, she moved down the winding stairs and along the corridor.

The door at the bottom was wide open and the foul smell was wafting out. As quietly as she could, Molly went into the room.

A small lamp was on the floor, its light illuminating the cage. The gate on the wall was down and it was empty but there was something slumped on the floor. Molly covered her mouth with her hand as she realised what it was.

'Oh dear God.'

Fighting her rising nausea and rolling stomach she moved up to the bars. On the floor of the cage, arms and legs broken and with massive tears to his chest and face, was Sir Wilfred.

'Help me.'

Molly gasped as the old man spoke, blood spilling from between his lips. She looked around for a second before grabbing the lantern and moving round the cage.

In the far corner, near the nest on the inside was a small gate with a large padlock on it. The lock wasn't closed but had been slipped through the bars to keep it shut. Moving the lock out of the way, she pushed the gate open.

The inside of the cage was filthy. The pool of water covered in a smelly green algae and floor slick with muck and blood.

Sheathing her sword, she knelt by the old man. His eyes widened when he saw who it was, more blood running from his mouth.

He tried to grasp at her but couldn't move his arms.

'Geoffrey…'

Molly nodded. How could he have done this?

'It's going to be alright.' she told him.

Sir Wilfred coughed a wet laugh.

'Liar.'

'Step away from him.'

Molly turned at the new voice to see Geoffrey standing in the doorway. He was in a pristine suit with hair slicked down.

The only give away that there was something amiss was the dirty bandage wrapped around his fingers and the look in his eyes. They were wild and darting from side to side, betraying the madman within.

Cautiously Molly stood and took a step back towards the gate.

'That's far enough.'

She stopped.

'Geoffrey...'

'SHUT UP!' he yelled, the sudden explosion of noise making her jump.

He took a deep breath and composed himself.

'The door. Lock it.'

'What?'

He snarled angrily and produced a pistol from behind his back.

'The door. Lock yourself in, you stupid whore.'

Molly backed away further until she was level with the gate, her eyes never leaving the gun. Reaching out, she pulled the gate shut and snapped the padlock in place.

Geoffrey advanced on her, the gun never wavering from her forehead. He checked the lock to make sure it was secure. Satisfied, he sighed angrily and lowered the pistol.

'I knew you'd come back.'

Molly didn't say anything, taking a step back towards the stagnant pool. As she moved, her boot caught the edge of the nest of blankets and filth and flicked it away to reveal the edge of a heavy iron trap door.

Geoffrey, oblivious to her, began pacing around, gesticulating wildly.

'As my wife you will do as you are told. You will be respectful and honour me in any way I see fit. You will be forbidden to travel unaccompanied and will not speak unless spoken to.'

He turned and while his back was to her, she kicked some more of the nest out of the way, her heart sinking as the huge lock on the heavy door became visible. The iron was rusty but bore deep scratches and gouges in its surface. Set in the top of the trapdoor was a small hatch which was bent and dented.

'Furthermore…' she looked up as Geoffrey turned around. 'Furthermore, you will wear what I say.' he waved the hand holding the gun at her. 'I can't have my wife wandering around looking like some dockyard slut, now can I?'

Molly didn't reply. Geoffrey lunged towards the bars, his teeth bared and spittle falling from the corners of his mouth.

'I ASKED YOU A QUESTION!' he screamed at her.

She took another step back, her boot heel reaching the edge of the pool.

'No. You can't.' she whispered back. She'd seen some scary things in the past year, but this madness was truly terrifying.

'You're just like the rest of them.' he raged 'Just like the others. They wouldn't listen. I taught them. They learned. Just as you will.'

'Geoffrey, please.'

He gripped the bars with his broken hand, the pain momentarily flashing across his face before once more being replaced by the madness.

'I am your Master. Husband and master of all. You will address me respectfully. Do you understand or do you need a lesson in humility and honour?'

He looked down at the broken body of his father.

'Like him. He learned.'

On the floor the old man groaned and tried to speak. A look of disgust passed across Geoffrey's face before he levelled the gun at the old man.

'Just die will you.'

'Geoffrey. No!' shouted Molly as the gun went off.

The shot found its mark, burying itself deeply in the head of the old man. Molly took a step back as blood and broken skull spread itself on the stone floor and splattered her boots.

'Never tell me what to do!' he shouted at her before tossing the gun to the floor. 'You're going to get a lesson.'

'Please. Geoffrey...'

He ignored her and strode to the wheel for the gate, heaving it around. Molly watched in horror as the gate rose up and from the murky depths of the pool, bubbles began to rise.

Geoffrey locked off the wheel and stormed back to the bars. He smiled and spoke softly.

'I won't let it kill you. I promise. But you will learn to do as you are told. You will be a good, obedient wife. Won't you?'

'I wouldn't bloody bet on it.'

Molly darted forward, reached through the bars and grabbed Geoffrey by the back of the head. In one swift movement she dragged him forwards as hard as she could.

The look of shock that crossed his face the second before his nose hit the unforgiving iron was something Molly would remember.

He fell back screaming obscenities, blood spurting from his broken nose. Without another word, Molly turned and dived into the stinking water, just as a rat like head broke the surface.

Geoffrey stumbled backwards, vainly trying to stem the blood that was running from his face as the creature pulled itself out of the water.

It turned a black, beady eye on the man and snarled menacingly.

It too shot forward, a long arm reaching through the bars and grabbing Geoffrey by the jacket and hauling him in.

He screamed and fumbled in his pocket for the bone pipe. The creature's teeth got within an inch of his face before he managed to get the pipe to his lips, his fear lending speed to his shaking hands.

Geoffrey blew the pipe as hard as he could and the monster let him go instantly. It screeched and wailed with its clawed hands over its head.

He smiled maniacally and blew again and again. In front of him the thing fell to the ground, thrashing around at the sound, pulping what was left of his father in its wild throes.

Eventually it cowered in the corner and Geoffrey stepped back, breathing hard.

'You'll learn.' he whispered to himself as he wiped the blood from his face with the back of his hand.

185

'You'll learn. I'm going to teach you a lesson.'

With his hands still shaking, he reached into his jacket pocket and took out a scrap of material. Material he'd torn from Mollys dress earlier as she'd run from him.

He dropped the fabric through the bars and it fluttered gently to the mucky and blood-soaked floor. The monster was on it in an instant, scooping it up in its long fingers and sniffing deeply.

'You're going to learn to be respectful. Honour your husband.'

Not really seeing the creature in front of him, glazed eyes staring off into the middle distance, he smiled.

'Kill.'

The water in the pool was dark and cold and Molly didn't want to know what floating horrors kept bumping into her as she swam down.

The wall loomed up in front of her and as she'd hoped, there was a narrow opening which led into a long brick tunnel.

She splashed upwards, relieved to find about a foot between the surface and the ceiling.

Gulping in stale and foetid air, she quickly made her way along, hoping that the thing wasn't too close behind. The tunnel ran for about forty feet before she hit another wall. Treading water, she closed her eyes.

'Saali?'

On her wrist, her bracelet blazed, the sapphire glowing brightly.

'I am here.'

The voice that materialised in her head was distant, as if the speaker were in another room and cut with echoes of other voices.

These were the essences of the Stones of Gunjai. Their power had been in her mind and she had been their vessel to take them to the Crown in India.

When the Crown and Stones had been destroyed, she thought that had been the end of them, but she had been wrong.

As a parting gift, they had given her a bracelet of finely worked silver with a perfectly cut sapphire set in it. Through the bracelet she could pull a portion of the power of Saali, the Air Stone.

The sapphire allowed her limited control over the air and the wind and also linked her to the mind and soul of the original Stone and through it, she could hear the others. They also seemed to give her the ability to heal. Cuts and scrapes disappeared quickly to leave just a vivid bruise. Right now, she needed their help.

'Concentrate and breathe deeply.' said the disembodied voice. 'I am with you.'

Molly did as she was told, feeling the power of the sapphire filling her. This wasn't the raw, unfettered power that the original Stone had possessed, but it was enough.

Taking a deep breath, she dived down.

The brickwork disappeared about five feet down to be replaced by a more natural feeling tunnel.

Visibility was nonexistent and Molly had to grope her way along. At one point she bumped into something solid that came apart in the water around her and she couldn't help but scream as a decapitated and rotten hand brushed her face.

Precious bubbles of air escaped her lips and she trashed wildly in panic.

'Breathe.'

Molly shook her head, she'd drown!

'Trust me as you have done before. Breathe.'

Molly screwed her eyes shut and took the deepest breath, fully expecting the foul water to flood her body and she would die in this lightless place.

Pure, clean air filled her lungs and she breathed once more, trying not to gulp in the oxygen.

'Be calm. Breathe slowly.'

Molly nodded and tried to do as Saali instructed, floating aimlessly for a few seconds and trying to get herself together.

She didn't like the water. She got sick when she was in a boat and now, well it would be another thing that gave her nightmares.

As if she didn't have enough memories to do that already. Saali's voice dropped into her head once more.

'Go. It comes.'

She took another deep breath and swam for it.

The tunnel was a hundred or so feet long, and if it weren't for Saali and the power she gave Molly, then she would surely have drowned. Feeling more than seeing, the tunnel gave way to the river proper.

She splashed to the surface and swam to a nearby pontoon, hauling herself out of the water where she lay for a second, only to be spurred into action once more as a splash and terrible screeching sounded from nearby.

'Give me a break.' she sighed.

Dragging her weary body up, she ran off into the fog, knowing that the thing was close behind.

Chapter Sixteen

Out of the Frying Pan

Molly dived down a narrow alley that led away from the docks and she could hear it behind her. It's grotesque and keening howl cutting through the foggy London night like a knife.

Marcus was going to have a fit! What was she doing?

Ducking into a doorway, she tried to catch her breath, pushing her soaking hair out of her eyes. Taking a deep breath, she tried to get herself together as from somewhere in the fog it howled again, this time accompanied by a horrible scream that cut off suddenly.

This was not good. Why hadn't she listened to Harry?

Reaching over her shoulder, she drew her sword and held it tightly and, although it gave her a little comfort, the blade still felt awkward.

She stood in silence for a few minutes. The fog muffling any sounds and making it difficult to hear if the thing was still after her. She hoped not.

'How do I get myself into these things?' she asked herself.

Taking another deep breath, she stepped out into the fog once more. The doorway was quickly swallowed up by the thick mist and she headed back towards the river. She moved quietly, her booted feet making hardly any noise on the slick cobbles.

'Where are you?'

As if to answer her question, a horrible howling came from somewhere nearby, but it was difficult to tell from what direction. The sound reverberated around the tightly packed buildings that made up this area of the docks.

She ran again, rounding a corner to come across the body of a young woman. This must have been who screamed.

Molly slipped her sword back into its scabbard and knelt by the body.

Her arms had been torn off and they lay casually discarded on the road and her chest was nothing more than a ragged hold from which her heart had been torn. Molly felt her stomach flip.

She moved away from the body and into the mist once more.

It was close.

She knew it and could feel it. Tonight, this would end. One way or another.

From somewhere to her left it howled again. It was an unearthly noise filled with pain and anger.

She turned slowly on the spot, trying to work out where it was. Suddenly it erupted from the fog, catching her in the chest with its full weight and sending her tumbling backwards.

Hitting the ground hard and cracking her head against the floor she managed to roll to the right as a hand that ended in claws as big as her fingers raised sparks where they gouged the cobblestones.

Panic guiding her, she scrambled up and ran again, trying to shake off the stars that were flashing in her vision.

She pounded down the road, taking random lefts and rights in and out of the maze of alleyways that made up the dockyard.

All the time, she was acutely aware of the thing behind her. Its heavy footfalls loud as they stomped across the cobbled streets.

Molly vaulted a low wooden fence and found herself on a slippery jetty. She turned to see if it was still following but the fog was thicker here on the river.

She began backing away as it howled once more before turning and breaking into a run as the fence exploded as the creature smashed through it.

Underneath her feet the wood was old and it gave a warning creak. The thing behind her was heedless of this and rampaged towards her. Its weight was too much and with a horrible splintering sound, the planking on the jetty gave way.

'Oh shi…' was all she managed before the jetty collapsed out from under her, and she pitched into the Thames, smashing into the edge of the pier on the way down. Behind her, the thing went too.

Molly hit the water hard. It was cold and dark and somewhere beneath her, she could feel the creature thrashing in the water.

She scrambled towards the surface, lungs bursting, eventually breaking through and splashing back towards the bank.

Gasping for breath, she hauled herself up and lay panting in the mud for a moment. There was the crunch of feet on the gravely bank and she looked up into the face of a man. His clothes were dirty and his face contorted into an ugly smile.

'Well if it isn't Molly Carter.' he said, before he punched her hard in the face and she blacked out.

Major Harry Gould was pacing up and down the little dressmakers shop, as he had been for the past hour.

Ruth was dozing in a battered armchair by the fire while Mrs Hopkins had taken herself off up to bed a few hours ago.

The old woman wasn't too put out by the appearance of Ruth and the Major but she made sure that everyone knew that it was her shop and as such, they'd do as they were told.

She'd made them some tea and found some bread and chicken for them to eat while she re-dressed the Majors wounds.

'You ain't the first man to be in my shop after a fight.' she'd told him as she strapped up his ribs again. 'But you mark my words, me and that girl are going to have a serious talk. I mean, I'm an old woman. I don't need to be woken up at this time of night 'specially by fugitives.'

Harry had offered to pay but she'd shaken her head, given him a lopsided grin and headed off upstairs.

Now dawn was beginning to break outside, the first rays of the weak autumnal sun were hazy through the fog outside.

Harry sat down in a chair opposite Ruth, grunting as his battered body protested. Taking out his watch for the fifth time in as many minutes he glanced at it before putting it away again.

'She should have been back by now.'

'What?'

Ruth rubbed her eyes and sat up stiffly.

'I said she should have been back by now. I shouldn't have let her go.'

'You couldn't have stopped her.'

'I should have tried harder.'

'She'll be alright.'

He stood up and began to pace again.

'I do hope so, Miss Thomas, I do hope so.'

Molly rolled over and let out a groan. Every bit of her ached. She sat up slowly, her head pounding. Where was she?

The ground underneath her was cobbled and there were a few barrels by the wall next to a solid looking door. A small window high up was letting in a little dull light but the place was cold and smelled of stale beer.

She ran a hand across her face and noticed her bracelet was gone. Quickly checking, she found her sword and the knife she had strapped to her leg were also missing.

She stood up and went over to the door. It was made of heavy wood and securely locked. She banged on it a few times.

'Hey. Let me out of here.'

No-one came.

Frowning, Molly inspected the barrels finding that all but one were full of ale.

Discovering an old tin mug behind the barrels, she helped herself to a drink and pondered what her next course of action should be.

Where ever she was, it wasn't too bad, but whoever had taken her things was going to be in real trouble when she got her hands on them.

While she was thinking, there was a solid thud as the door was unlocked.

She quickly jumped down from the barrel she had been sat on and almost automatically slipped into a fighting stance.

The heavy wood slammed back and she was glad she hadn't decided to hide behind it, it would have brained her. Four men stepped in, three of them fanning out while the final man hung back slightly.

Molly recognised him straight away. His name was Jack Gatling. Youngest of three brothers. Nareema, Mollys adopted sister, had killed the first, Jimmy, while Molly herself had killed the second.

All of the men were armed with swords and pistols.

'Jack.' she said, acknowledging she knew who he was.

'Molly.' he answered with a sly smile. 'It was lucky that I found you last night. Well lucky for me anyways. Mr Porkonicov in very upset with you. Very upset.'

'Where are my things?'

'What? The bracelet and that lovely sharp sword of yours? You'll have to ask Mr Porkonicov about that. You see, I sent him them as a bit of a down payment on some money that I owe him. They should just about clear my debt but being able to deliver you too? That'll see me free and clear and with a favour to boot.'

He grinned humourlessly.

'Take her.'

Two of the other men advanced on Molly, pistols pointed directly at her. Cautiously she backed away until she bumped into the wall behind her.

'Don't make them shoot you.' said Jack. 'Mr Porkonicov wants you alive, but he didn't say anything about you not being damaged.'

The man not pointing a gun at Molly moved to grab her but she dodged to the side before kicking him hard in the stomach.

He doubled up, gasping for breath as Molly rounded on the closest gunman. She grabbed his outstretched arm and span him around until the he was facing the final man before she squeezed his hand.

The pistol went off with a crack, the shot catching the other man in the leg and knocking him from his feet.

Before the sound of the pistol had finished reverberating around the small room, Molly had punched the man in the kidneys and shoved him towards Jack.

The pair went down in a tangle of confused limbs and Molly was running through the door, turning to slam it shut behind her.

The key was still in the lock and she turned it before taking the key. Turning around once more, she found herself in a bar.

Across the room was a narrow counter and she could just make out a couple of cowering figures who she assumed were the barkeep and one of the serving girls. No one else was in the place. She hurried over to the counter.

'Give me an hour and then let them go. One of them is going to need seeing to.'

The barman nodded dumbly.

'An hour.' she repeated, more sternly this time.

'Yes miss,' replied the girl, meekly.

Molly held her gaze for a few more seconds before she nodded once and headed out of the door into the morning, pausing only to drop the key down a nearby drain.

Pitor Ilaitch Porkonicov, or "Porky" as he was known to the people around the northern docks, although never within earshot, was a big man.

Obese to the point that he had to have a heavily re-enforced chair, he was a local heavyweight, both figuratively and realistically speaking in the local underworld.

Things didn't get done by the criminal fraternity without his say so. Partly due to the thugs he hired to do his dirty work and partly due to reputation.

It wasn't unheard of for those that went against him to turn him in four different parts of the city at once and it had been said that he once tore a man's head off for disrespect.

Molly didn't believe that for one minute, but she was wary as she crouched on a low roof overlooking the Turks' Head pub, the base of operations for the fat criminal.

It sat at a T-junction between two wide roads and was flanked on all sides by slums and abandoned workshops, all owned by Mr Porkonicov.

The place looked busy, even at this time in the morning, with mostly men hurrying in and out.

As she watched, Jack and two of the men from the bar came hurrying down the road. Molly cursed under her breath. She'd have to go and talk to that barkeep about his timekeeping. That most definitely wasn't an hour.

She watched for a few more minutes until Jack and a group of half a dozen other men quickly left the pub and headed down the street.

Taking a deep breath and letting it out as a long sigh she slipped from the roof, dropping lightly into a muddy alley that ran parallel to the main road. Moving almost silently, she edged along the alley, ducking back into the shadows as a cart rumbled past.

Once the coast was clear, she darted across the road and into the cover of another alley which led round to the back of the pub. Instinctively, she tried to draw her sword, cursing when she remembered it wasn't there.

The alley was dirty and strewn with detritus. Rats scampered out of her way and Molly didn't want to look too closely at what they'd been eating. She was sure that one of them had a finger in its mouth, nail and all.

She shuddered and pushed that thought away. Creeping along, she peered around the corner. Standing outside the back door was a guard. A heavy-set man with a stout cudgel in one hand and a face that was covered in scars.

Molly glanced around her for a weapon and picked up a wide piece of wood that had once been part of a packing crate. It would have to do.

She looked around the corner again and whistled softly. The man heard her and came along the alley to investigate.

To his credit, he didn't blindly charge around the corner, instead swinging the heavy cudgel at head height first to clobber whoever was hiding there.

It would have worked too, if Molly hadn't been crouched down by the corner then it would have taken her head off.

As it was, the cudgel bounced off the brickwork and the man's eyes widened in surprise as Molly jumped up, the piece of wood held in two hands, swinging hard at his head. It smashed across his face and he staggered backwards.

Molly followed, grabbing him by the scruff of the neck and ramming him as hard has she could into the brick wall. He hit the stone head first with a heavy thud and slumped face down in the muck. Checking that he was alive, she rolled him onto his side so he didn't drown in the mud, before picking up the cudgel and proceeding into the pub.

The back door opened into a narrow corridor. Doors to the left and right were closed but the one at the far end was wide open.

Hefting the cudgel in her right hand, she crept along the corridor. There were raised voices from the room beyond.

'I want her found!'

Quietly she crept up to the threshold and almost screamed as a heavy hand grabbed her wrist and dragged her into the room proper.

She lashed out with her left hand and it contacted sharply with the face of the man who'd grabbed her. He fell back but didn't let go of her arm, so she had no choice but to follow him.

As she moved, she twisted in his grip before aiming a kick at his groin. He moved at the last minute and her foot slammed into his thigh. He shouted in pain and anger before hauling her in and smashing her in the stomach as hard as he could.

Her breath left her instantly and she doubled up, gasping and unable to move out of the way of the backhand slap that sent her crashing across the room.

She hit a table with her side and fell into an awkward pile on the floor and he was on her in a second, grabbing a handful of hair and dragging her upright.

She squirmed and lashed out with her feet but he slammed her back down into the table. What little breath she had in her was driven from her again and she felt her nose break as it hit the unforgiving wood.

Stars flashed in her vision and she thought she could hear someone laughing as the man hauled her upright once more and then almost carried her stunned form across the room, throwing her down to the dirty floor.

She struggled to sit up, only to be knocked down again by a kick to the side.

'You must learn to stay down.'

She blinked away the daze and a fat face swam into clarity. Mr Porkonicov was sat at a wide table on an almost throne like chair. He waved a hand and the man next to Molly who wrapped his hand in her hair and dragged her to her knees.

'I'm fed up of people telling me what I should learn.' she muttered, wiping the blood from her nose away with the back of her hand.

Mr Porkonicov laughed out loud.

'Very good. Very good.'

He paused to take a huge bite from a chicken leg which was sat on a plate next to him. The juice dribbled down his chins, following a greasy path before dropping onto his expansive chest.

'You owe me money.' he said, waving the chicken leg at her. 'I don't take kindly to being stolen from.'

'I never…' began Molly, but the man next to her gave her a stinging backhand across the face which knocked her flat again. Mr Porkonicov smiled as she slowly sat back up again.

'You think I'm stupid? I remember. Even if you go away for a year. I still remember.'

He finished the chicken and threw the bone over his shoulder.

Wiping his hands on his shirt, he clicked his fingers, and the two men Molly had fought in the bar came forward. One was limping heavily, his left knee strapped up with a makeshift brace, the other was carrying Mollys sword and bracelet.

He put them on the table and stepped back. His nose was an ugly purple bruise where she'd hit him with the tankard. Both of them glared at Molly but there was an evil expectation in their eyes.

The fat man drew the sword and waved it around.

'Very nice. Where did you get it? Not that it matters. It's mine now.' he put in on the table and picked up the bracelet, smiling darkly. 'And so is this. Exquisite workmanship. Where does a penniless whore get such fine things?'

He nodded to the man stood next to Molly and he hauled her to her feet, one hand in her hair and the other tightly holding her wrists behind her back. Mr Porkonicov struggled up and plodded around the table. The bracelet looked like a ring in his fat fingers.

Stopping in front of Molly, he carelessly threw the bracelet back onto the table before gripping her chin in his chubby hand and forcing her to look at him.

'You owe me money. You hurt my men. I'm going to make an example of you for that. No one crosses me. Do you understand? This is going to be slow and painful.'

Molly snatched her head away from his grip and he grinned, showing teeth full of rotting food.

'Such spirit.'

He turned away and nodded to the two men that Molly had saved Ruth from. They grinned and stepped forward.

'You broke my knee, bitch.' said the first one as he punched her hard in the face, snapping her head to the side and splitting her lip.

Major Gould looked at his watch once more. It was a little after nine o'clock.

'I'm going to look for her.'

'She said...'

Ruth was interrupted by the shop bell ringing. Mrs Hopkins had gone out so they both looked at each other.

'Well I can hardly go, can I?' replied Harry.

The girl sighed and went through the curtain between the kitchen and shop. Stood in the middle of the room was a well-dressed gentleman.

He had tousled brown hair and a strong chin, but he looked lost. His blue velvet jacket had the right arm pinned up, to hide his missing hand and at his waist was a heavy

curved sword. Ruth took him in for a second, instantly
wary.

'Can I help you sir?'

He looked up, as if seeing her for the first time.

'Where is my wife?'

'Sir?'

He sighed and pinched the bridge of his nose.

'I know she's here. Go and fetch her.'

'I don't know…'

'Do as you are told and go and fetch my wife.' he snapped
angrily.

Ruth took a step back and almost bumped into Major
Gould as he came through the curtain. The man saw the
Major and a look of complete puzzlement passed across his
face.

'She's not here General.' said Harry. 'I don't know where
she is, and I'm worried.'

Chapter Seventeen

The Darkness Within

The strike from the man knocked Molly onto her side where she lay still for a moment. Blood ran freely from her nose and a cut across her forehead.

Something in her right side flared and grated and she suspected she'd broken at least one rib. Her left eye was swollen and almost shut, and she hurt all over. Seated on his reinforced throne once more, Mr Porkonicov waved his goons away.

'Does it hurt little girl?' he asked, taking a bite from the chicken he had in his hand and spraying bits all over the table.

Molly didn't reply so one of the men drove a kick into her kidneys and she cried out in pain. At the table, Mr the fat man smiled.

'I hope it does. But know this. We're just getting warmed up. This? This is nothing.'

He sat back with a chuckle as Molly heaved herself to her hands and knees, spitting out a mouthful of bloodied phlegm onto the floor. He laughed louder.

'The little bitch has spirit. I think you'd better make sure you knock that out of her.'

Deep within Molly, she felt something stir. Something dark. She'd felt it before, when she was at Marcus parents' house in the country after they'd hurt Gwen. Then again in the ruins of the abbey when the Herald of Carnothal was trying to kill her.

Her anger boiled up and flooded every nerve with its overwhelming rage. Slowly she looked up at the fat criminal, her white eyes now nothing more than glowing pits of blackness. He looked at her, his bluster momentarily gone.

'You talk too much, you fat bastard.' she snarled through bloodied teeth but her voice was strange. As if four or five people were speaking at once but all slightly out of synch.

Mr Porkonicov waved his goons back in and one aimed a kick at Mollys stomach.

At the last second, she sat up straight and the blow sailed past. Grabbing the booted foot, she pushed it up, allowing the momentum and arc of the kick to continue and throw the man off balance.

As it reached waist height, she shoved back and the man went down on his backside.

Before he'd hit the ground, Molly was up and diving for the table.

Her hand closed around the hilt of her sword just as Mr Porkonicov grabbed at the blade.

She yanked the weapon back and the fat man lost three fingers as it sliced them clean off. He fell back with a cry, blood spraying from his severed digits as the other men looked on in surprise.

Slowly, Molly stood upright with her sword held at her side.

'Kill her!' roared the fat man which snapped the men from their daze.

The few seconds seemed to happen in slow motion.

As one, the three men launched themselves at her. With a skill she didn't know she possessed, Molly gracefully pirouetted out of the path of the first and cut his right arm from his body with a deft sweep of the blade. The second lost a leg as she dropped below his clawing arms and cut it off at the knee.

The third man, the one with the leg brace received the point of the sword through his chest. Molly ran the blade though him, right up to the hilt, before she twisted it and yanked it out sideways. He fell to the bloodied ground with a gurgle as he died.

Hearing a pained and angry roar, she moved to the side and swung the blade once more as Mr Porkonicov charged at her.

His weight driven momentum was so great that he couldn't compensate for her quickness and the blade entered on the left side of his stomach, tearing him open from side to side and easily splitting his clothing and the mounds of flesh beneath.

He carried on running for a few more steps before his brain caught up with the damage done to his body and he slumped to his knees.

The floor shook as he went down, vainly trying to hold his intestines and distended stomach in. Slowly Molly walked around him.

'Please.' he begged.'

Molly looked at him with her black eyes and face full of disgust and anger for a second before she smiled widely.

Deep down, she was horrified at what she'd done but at that moment she couldn't have been happier, and a thin laugh escaped her lips.

Slowly she raised the blade, his piggy eyes watching the light play off its blood covered surface.

'Please.' he begged once more which made Molly smile further.

The sword sang through the air and with a thump, Mr Porkonicov's head rolled from his fat shoulders and his blubbery body pitched forward onto the floor. Slowly she reached down and picked up the decapitated head, holding it by the lank and greasy hair until it was at eye level.

'Bastard.' she said, before spitting in the face.

At that moment, two things happened.

Through the front door came Jack and a couple of other men. They took in the scene before them in total confusion. Molly was stood, covered in blood, in the middle of the room with Mr Porkonicov's head in one hand and a sword in the other.

Around her lay the bodies of four of the hardest men Jack had known, all spreading their life fluid in a pool around her feet.

The second thing that happened was the door to the alley exploded inwards and the creature came crashing through.

Its rat like head weaved from side to side as it was assaulted by the overpowering smell of blood. Molly took one look at it, grabbed her bracelet and scabbard then ran, heading as fast as she could out of the front door, pausing only to throw the severed head to Jack who caught it by instinct and then dropped it again just as quickly.

She barrelled out of the door and down the road taking random lefts and rights, dodging in an out of the dockside crowds. The screams and crashes behind told her that the thing was hot on her heels.

Rounding a corner she was relieved to find a group of soldiers lounging outside a small inn. She dashed up to them.

'Thank God. I need your help.'

A couple of them raised an eyebrow and grinned at each other, taking in Mollys leather suit.

'I'm sure we can help. Or maybe you could help us. I've got an itch that needs scratching...'

Molly made an angry noise and punched the soldier square in the face.

'I haven't got time for suggestive remarks! If you don't hurry up, it's going to kill us all.'

'What is?' said the youngest of the group, a lad no more that fifteen with spots and unruly hair sticking out from under his shako.

She turned and pointed back down the street as the creature rounded the corner.

'That.'

The soldiers began to back away.

'Well what're you waiting for? Shoot it!'

They hesitated and with a curse, Molly snatched the rifle from the one she'd hit and raised it to her shoulder before sighting along the barrel and pulling the trigger. The rifle went off with a bang and the kick nearly broke her shoulder.

'Bloody hell!' she shouted.

She threw the now empty weapon to its owner.

'Reload.'

Behind her, the others had begun to get themselves together, the youngest bringing his rifle up and firing at the oncoming monstrosity.

Mollys shot had gone wide, but his found the mark. The shot punching the thing in the side. His companions likewise raised their guns and fired. The roar of half a dozen muskets was loud, and Molly covered her ears.

In the street, the creature had stopped. As the soldiers frantically reloaded, Molly drew her sword.

She raised it high and with a glance at the men, she charged towards the monster. It was bleeding heavily from the wounds inflicted by the gunshots but it hadn't slowed at all.

She swung her blade towards its head but it ducked at the last minute, lashing out with its tail and sweeping Mollys feet out from under her.

She hit the ground hard and the sword skittered out of her grasp.

'Stay down.' shouted the youngest soldier and Molly glanced up at them before covering her head with her arms. This time, all of the half dozen men fired at once, the shots striking the monster with accuracy borne of countless practice hours.

It screeched wildly, thrashing around as the shots hit home. Black blood fountained from its pale body, splattering the muddy ground.

With a final defiant screech, the thing turned tail and ran, springing through the gathering crowds. Molly scrambled to her feet and grabbed her sword. She turned to the soldiers.

'Come on. We can't let it get away.'

Without waiting to see if they were following, she charged after the creature.

Marcus, Harry and Ruth were in the kitchen of Mrs Hopkins shop. The old woman had come in, tutted at yet another person in her shop, before putting the kettle on.

'I may as well open a bleedin' boardin' house. At least them customers would pay!' she waved a finger at Marcus. 'You want to have a word with that girl of yours. She's going to get herself into trouble one of these days.'

He'd smiled sadly.

'She can't seem to stay out of it.'

Now they were sat at the kitchen table with Harry filling in Marcus on the last two weeks.

'And you let her go? On her own?' said Marcus disbelievingly.

'I'm sorry General. She didn't give me a choice.'

Marcus frowned and looked at Ruth.

'What about you? Didn't you try to stop her?'

'She wasn't having any of it sir. She was away before we could do anything.'

He sighed.

'No. I don't expect you could.'

Harry and Ruth exchanged glances before Ruth spoke.

'How'd you know she was here sir? If you don't mind me asking?'

'Gwen came back after a few days and told me everything. Poor girl was beside herself with worry.'

'And Gwen is?' asked Harry.

'She's her maid.' added Ruth.

Marcus sighed again.

'I thought I'd give her a week to, I don't know, get it out of her system. I can't say I wasn't worried, but I know she can take care of herself.'

'That she can.' added Harry.

Marcus rubbed a hand over his face.

'The week turned into ten days, then two weeks. My butler heard about some creature attacking a coach last night and I decided I couldn't wait any longer. So here I am. And she's not here.'

'No.'

Marcus stood up.

'I'm going to find her. Major, will you tell me where this warehouse is please? That seems as good a place as any to start looking.'

'I'll do more than that.' said Harry, standing himself. 'I'm coming with you.'

'Thank you.'

Now it was Ruth's turn to stand up. She saw the look on Harry's face and raised an eyebrow.

'Don't say it. I'm not coming. I've got to go and meet at idiot John although why should I let Molly have all the fun, I don't know.'

They headed out of the back door and into the little yard behind the shop. Ruth stopped and cocked her head to one side.

'What's that noise?'

Both Marcus and Harry looked at each other as a concussive echo rolled across the docks.

'Gunfire.' said Harry.

'That's probably not a good thing, is it?' asked Ruth.

'No.' replied Marcus. 'It isn't.'

They all hurried out of the gate and down the road towards the river.

Molly pounded after the thing. It ran straight towards the river, twisting and turning down narrow alleyways and ploughing through the crowds where the route took it through more populated areas.

They entered a wide road and she could see the river at the far end. The creature charged a horse and cart, jumping over the animal at the last second.

The horse reared up and dumped the entire cartload of cabbages across the street. Molly vaulted through the mess and over the back of the cart, just in time to see the thing dive into the river.

She stopped at the waters-edge, breathing heavily. A few seconds behind her, came the soldiers, puffing madly.

'Where'd it go?' asked the youngest soldier.

She pointed to the river'

'In there.'

She sighed angrily and slammed her sword back into its scabbard.

'Come on. I know where it's going.'

Chapter Eighteen

Reunions

Molly and the soldiers arrived at a run, skidding to a halt outside the large gates to the yard and warehouses. They were flung wide open with the yard beyond deserted. Cautiously Molly drew her sword.

'What now?' this was a whispered question from the Corporal who, until Molly had shown up, had been in nominal command of the soldiers.

'It'll have gone into that building.' she pointed with her sword, 'There's an underwater tunnel and it can swim really well.'

'So what do you want us to do?'

Molly looked at him in confusion.

'How should I know. Do some soldiering.'

He looked at her blankly and she sighed.

'Take your men over there, two through the small door and then the rest through the large. Try not to shoot anything that isn't the monster. There might be workers around and we don't want to kill them.'

'What if it's that…, that thing?'

'Then shoot it as much as you like.'

'Right you are ma'am.'

He saluted and began issuing orders to his men. As he did, the youngest came running up to them. He saluted Molly crisply.

'There's two men outside ma'am. Said they're looking for someone called Molly.'

'That'd be me then.' she replied distantly as she watched the soldiers move carefully across the yard using the stacks of crates for cover.

'Shall I bring them in?'

'What?'

'My God. Molly. What on earth happened?'

She turned to see Harry walk through the gates, behind him came Marcus. He looked at her in shock.

'Oh. Marcus.' she said, a knot of guilt forming in her stomach.

He walked over to her, pushing past Harry and Ruth.

'What happened? You look terrible.'

Her suit was covered in mud, grime and blood. It plastered her face too along with the vivid bruises from Mr Porkonicov's men.

'Well it's nice to see you too.' she looked down. 'I might have gotten into a fight.'

'Might have? You look awful.'

Her reply was interrupted by one of the soldiers who saluted.

'We're ready to go in ma'am.'

'Alright.' she told him.

'Molly...'

She looked at her husband.

'Can this wait until later? I know you're angry with me, but this isn't the time or place. We've got to stop it now or more people are going to die.'

Without giving him time to answer, she turned on her heel and headed across the yard. Marcus looked at Harry who shrugged.

'Don't ask me. She's your wife.'

The youngest soldier came hurrying over.

'She, um, that is...' he pointed vaguely across the yard to Molly and the soldiers.

Harry and Marcus looked at him expectantly.

'She wants to know if you're coming too or if she's got to do this on her own.'

Marcus shook his head but couldn't hide a small smile.

'Honestly, that girl is going to be the death of me.'

'Me too if she keeps this up.' added Harry.

Marcus drew his sword. It was heavy, the curved blade covered in deeply etched whorls and lines.

'Come on then.'

The corporal was talking to Molly when they got there.

'Both sets of doors are locked ma'am and there are boards on all the windows.'

'Is there any other way in?'

'No ma'am. We can break the doors down but that'll make a mighty racket.'

She glanced towards the river.

'How high is the tide?'

The Corporal looked at her with confusion.

'There's a tunnel that runs in but it's below the waterline.' she explained. 'If the tide is high, then it'll be no use.'

The soldier quickly despatched someone to look. The news wasn't good.

'High tide ma'am.'

She bit her lip while she considered the options. There weren't many. She looked at Marcus who shrugged resignedly.

'Go on then, but you and I are going to have a serious talk about this later.'

She grinned and gave him a peck on the cheek before turning to the doors. Marcus gently pulled Ruth to the side and addressed the soldiers.

'Corporal, get all of your men over here now then take cover.'

'Why? What's she going to do?' he asked.

'Knock.'

He began shouting orders as Molly placed her hands on the doors, one on each. She looked at the group next to her.

'Duck.'

As the others watched in amazement, the bracelet on her wrist began to glow with a blinding blue light.

Molly closed her eyes and then from nowhere a hurricane erupted from her hands. It smashed the heavy doors apart like they were matchwood, flinging debris in all directions. The soldiers, Marcus and Harry all flung themselves to the floor.

'Bloody hell.' exclaimed the Corporal as he looked up into the clearing dust.

Harry glanced at him.

'Language Corporal. There are ladies present.'

The Corporal swallowed nervously.

'Sorry sir. But still, bloody hell!'

Molly drew her sword as the soldiers assembled around her.

'What now corp'?' asked one of the men, eyeing Molly with a mixture of awe and suspicion.

The Corporal shrugged and turned to Molly.

'Ma'am?'

'Follow me.'

She strode off into the warehouse, the soldiers moving quietly with muskets raised.

Harry and Marcus were a couple of steps behind.

'Where'd she learn to do that? Was it magic?' asked Harry.

Marcus didn't answer immediately, trying not to get drawn into a conversation he had few answers for.

In truth, he didn't understand it himself. Molly had been the conduit for the powers of the Stones of Gunjai and when they had left her, one of the Stones at least, had left a little portion of its power behind. Molly could channel the wind through the bracelet she wore. Eventually he settled on,

'It's a bit like magic. She can use the wind.'

Harry didn't seem satisfied but let it go.

'And how'd she get the soldiers to follow her? I know that corporal. He's a scheming little bastard who would sell his own grandmother for a penny and has an uncanny knack of getting out of doing anything that looks like work. I've never seen him salute *anyone*, let alone some random woman that he's just met in the street. I mean, look at them...'

They watched as the soldiers fanned out and Marcus could see what he meant. Molly was in the centre, striding purposefully through the warehouse while the men formed a defensive cordon around her. All were alert and ready for anything. Marcus shrugged.

'She's got a way with people.'

Harry gave him a sideways glance that conveyed exactly what he thought of that answer and shook his head.

'Well it's about time the little bugger did something worthwhile anyway.'

They went upstairs and through the wrecked collection until they came to the steps leading down. Molly went to descend but the Corporal stopped her.

'Let a couple of the lads go first ma'am. Just in case.'

She smiled at him and nodded.

Quickly, the Corporal organised his men. Three of them went down the stairs with Molly, Marcus and Harry next followed by the Corporal and the young lad. The sixth was left at the top to keep watch. Harry overheard the Corporal before they went down.

'No wandering off to see what you can nick.' he gestured to Molly. 'She...' he faltered for a second before continuing. 'This feels important, so we'd better not muck it up. If I find you kippin' when we come back then there'll be hell to pay.'

The other soldier nodded, an understanding in his eyes. The Corporal gave him a slap on the shoulder before heading down.

'Right. You know what you're doing.'

At the bottom, the iron door was wide open and flickering lights could be seen from the room beyond. The soldiers fanned out quickly when they reached the bottom of the steps. The room was empty.

Four lanterns were burning on the floor, the poor flickering light they gave off suggesting that they were nearly out of oil. The gate on the far wall was up but the cage was empty.

'Corporal, will you see what's behind that door please?'

She gestured to the other door in the right-hand wall. The man nodded and organised two of the soldiers to check.

Molly walked over to the door in the bars. It was unlocked and swung open as she touched it. The nest had been thrown across the cage and lay in a dirty pile next to the mangled body of Sir Wilfred.

The trap door with the little hatch was open too and the smell from the room below was terrible. Picking up one of the lanterns, Molly peered inside.

'Help me.'

She passed the lantern to Marcus while two of the soldiers lowered her down.

The room was barely six feet square with a low ceiling. Heavy iron chains with manacles were fixed to the far wall by a large iron ring. The whole room was coated in excrement with pale bones sticking through the muck.

Molly bent down and examined a meaty lump that was below the trap door, almost gagging when she saw it was a heart. Badly chewed but still recognisable. She took a deep breath and closed her eyes, fighting down the rising nausea.

'Right. Get me out.'

Two pairs of hands reached down and hauled her out. Harry came over while she got her breath back.

'Where is it?'

'Loose.'

'What?'

Molly looked at him.

'He's mad. He's taken the only bargaining tool he's got and now he's run for it. The creature will follow him. We've got to find him before it's too late.'

'Bargaining tool?'

She looked at his as if he were stupid.

'There's more than one of them. A female, a child, I don't know. Geoffrey has them and with the pipe, he's got the first one doing his bidding. The hearts. It's been collecting food. The hearts. It's been feeding the other one.'

'Oh shit.'

Molly laughed, despite herself.

'Father! Language! Come on.'

She saw a pale faced Corporal emerge from the far doorway and headed over to talk to him as Marcus came over.

'Father?' he asked innocently.

Harry smiled.

'Only for the purposes of this investigation. It was a good ploy. She's young and...'

'You're old enough to be her father.' finished Marcus.

'That's about the size of it. Look...'

'It doesn't matter.' said Marcus. 'But if you would please stop encouraging her...'

'She doesn't need any encouragement.'

'No. She doesn't.'

They both glanced down into the small room, lost in their own thoughts for a moment.

'So as her father, did she take as much notice of you as she does of me?' asked Marcus.

Harry couldn't help but grin.

'Less I would say.'

'Less than what?'

They both turned to find Molly standing behind them, lantern in one hand a sword in the other.

'It doesn't matter.' said Marcus.

Molly frowned at him.

'I'll tell you later. What's through the door?'

'Cells and bodies. Looks like I was right. I wasn't the only woman who Geoffrey has had designs on. He must have been keeping them from his father. I got away. They didn't.'

'That's terrible. Can we do anything for them?'

She shook her head, reply interrupted by one of the soldiers

'Over here corp.'

They all went over to the door.

'What?'

The soldier pointed at a spot on the floor. Molly knelt down and ran her fingers through the oily looking substance that covered the cobbles. It was a dark reddish brown and felt slimy on her skin. She sniffed it. The odour it gave off was rank.

'What is it?'

'Don't know.' she replied, wiping her hands on her leg. 'Could be blood. The Corporal and his men shot it. Maybe it's hurt.'

'So what now? Where's Geoffrey and where the hell is that thing?' asked Harry.

'I don't know,' she snapped. 'Do I look like I've got all the bloody answers?'

Taking a deep breath, she screwed her eyes shut and pinched the bridge of her nose.

'I'm sorry. I'm a bit tired.'

'Are you alright?' asked Marcus, concern evident in his voice.

Molly opened her eyes and smiled tiredly.

'I'm fine. Don't fuss.'

Marcus frowned.

'Honestly. I'm fine.'

She sighed.

'Let's get this finished. They can't be too far ahead of us. Corporal, will you and your men take the lead please, we're going to search the rest of the warehouse.'

The soldier glanced at Harry and Marcus and then nodded.

'Yes ma'am. Rutter, Williams, you two go first. Newmore, you bring up the rear.'

The soldiers split and headed back up the stairs.

Leaving the collection room and moving back down, they began to search. In the left hand side, below the collection room, the office, and the first floor were empty.

'Must be in the other half.' said the Corporal.

Cautiously they moved into the other side of the warehouse, finding the ground floor, first and second floors empty. Even the rats seemed to have better places to be.

They found more spots of the oily blood on the stairs as they ascended to the third floor.

'Careful now lads.' whispered the Corporal.

The floor was the entire width and length of the building and was densely packed with crates. To their left was a wide path led down the centre, while the right was a maze of little alleys between the boxes while almost lost at the end a set of three large windows overlooked the river.

'Which way?'

Molly looked around before shaking her head.

'Don't know.'

Without a word, the Corporal split his men up, sending three to the right, the rest staying with Molly as she cautiously headed left.

A dozen feet down the wide path, the Corporal held up his hand to stop everyone. He crouched down and looked around nervously, musket held ready in his hands. Molly joined him.

'What is it?'

'More blood.' he pointed to a large patch on the floor. 'It's hurt.'

Molly saw more drops running in a line away from them. They pooled at the bottom of one of the crates and more was smeared up the side. Immediately she looked up.

'It's above us.'

Privates Newmore and Rutter moved through narrow spaces between the boxes. There wasn't room for them to walk two abreast, so they went back to back, guns held ready.

'What do you think is going on?' asked Newmore.

He was a stocky man who'd seen plenty of fighting in France and Spain. His scarred face, a souvenir from a close range French musket shot, did more to enhance his hard attitude than his gruff voice.

He was a career soldier and would be until he died on some pitiful battlefield. His companion on the other hand was the opposite.

Rutter was slender, almost feminine in appearance, with a seemingly gentle nature that was at odds with the job he did.

People often underestimated him which is when they found the point of one of the many blades he kept hidden about his person slipping between their ribs.

He and Newmore were as thick as thieves.

'Dunno. Something though. Bet we won't get paid for this either.' Rutter whispered back.

'Corp'll see us right. He always does.'

Rutter laughed.

'Ain't that the truth. Remember that time…'

Newmore shushed him into silence.

'What?'

'Where's Blinky?'

Rutter's brow furrowed.

'He was right with us a few minutes ago. Stupid bugger.'

They looked around.

'He can't have gone far.' replied Rutter before calling out. 'Blinky, you stupid sod. Where are you?'

'Shut up.' snapped Newmore. 'Do you want to bring that thing to us?'

Rutter's answer was cut off by a musket shot, closely followed by a chilling scream.

'Newmore? Rutter? Where are you, you bastards?' hissed Charlie McCrannon. The other soldiers in their little band called him "Blinky" due to a nervous twitch he had which meant he blinked a lot.

He'd picked up the habit while in France. He remembered the padre before they took the frogs on at Salamanca. 'Battles change a man.' he'd said. 'But trust in the Lord and you will be saved.'

Change a man it did. He'd seen some horrors that day. And more than enough in his career to say that God wasn't picky as to who he called to his side.

He moved along a narrow path between stacks of wooden crates.

'Where are you? This isn't funny.'

He'd been with the other two but he must have got turned around. One minute they were there, the next, they'd gone. It'd be just like those two smart arses to piss about like this.

Blinky cursed them under his breath. When he got his hands on them…

The path ended and he found himself in a small square of space in between the stacks. It wasn't more than ten feet to a side, but it was a nice relief to be in an open space.

Blinky didn't like enclosed spaces. Leaning his musket up against a box, he took out his tobacco pouch and rolled himself a smoke.

There was nothing here. They were all on a wild goose chase. Why the Corp' was listening to that woman, he didn't know.

True, he'd seen and shot at the thing in the street and then without thinking, come tearing down here. But it wasn't here, was it?

Who was she anyway?

Looked like a whore in all that leather getup. An expensive whore mind you, but a whore all the same.

He smiled to himself as he took a long drag from his cigarette and thought of all of the things he could do with a woman like that.

Closing his eyes, he rested his head on the crate behind him and blew out a thin stream of smoke.

'Yeah,' he thought, 'I could have some fun with that one. Teach her a thing or two.'

His fantasy was interrupted by a drip of water hitting him full in the face. As second followed quickly and he wiped them from his skin.

'What the...'

He looked at his hands.

It wasn't water.

It was an oily red liquid that stank something terrible. Another drop splashed onto the back of his neck and he glanced up, right into the fanged maw of the creature.

He fell backwards, scrabbling for his musket as he went. His fingers managed to brush the edge of the weapon which fell to the ground and went off with a bang.

In an instant, the thing dropped from the top of the crates and began tearing into him.

Blinky's scream echoed around the warehouse for a second before cutting off as the thing tore his throat out in a spray of blood.

Rutter and Newman pelted through the maze of boxes towards the scream, muskets ready.

They hurtled around a corner and found themselves in the small clearing amongst the boxes. On the floor was the torn remains of their friend and crouched above him was the creature.

Its bloodied face whipped around as they skidded to a halt and its hands it held the still bleeding heart of their comrade.

With exaggerated slowness the thing took a bite, swallowing the chunk whole before hissing at the men.

Both soldiers looked at each other before turning tail and running the other way. They took lefts and rights at random as the thing thundered behind them, smashing into crates and sending boxes and cloth bales flying.

'It's gonna get us.' shouted Rutter as the creature swung a wicked clawed hand at him. He ducked at the last second and it scored a deep set of grooves in a crate.

'Shut up and run you pillock.' snapped Newmore, a few feet in front of him.

They rounded a corner and burst out into the wide avenue in the east side of the building, almost crashing into Molly and the other soldiers who were running towards them.

'Down.' yelled Molly, and the two soldiers threw themselves flat. A second later, the thing emerged. It jumped clean over the prone men to skid across the floor.

'Fire!'

As the Corporal shouted, three muskets barked, and the creature roared in pain. The shots hit it in the side with sprays of blood.

It roared once more then jumped at the soldiers, knocking them out of the way like skittles before bounding away down the wide avenue.

'We can't let it get away again.' shouted Molly, already running after it.

'Molly. Wait!' called Marcus before cursing under his breath. He looked at the others. 'Come on then.'

Molly ran after the thing as it bounded along the length of the warehouse towards the large windows at the end.

It didn't even pause as, with a powerful leap, it went through them.

Molly skidded to a halt at the edge and looked down to the river three stories below just in time to see the creature splash heavily into the water. She cursed loudly as a few seconds later, it hauled itself up the bank on the other side.

'It's gone. We can't follow that.' said Marcus as he reached her.

She turned to her husband.

'I can. Get them downstairs.'

'Why? What…' he saw the look on her face. 'Molly, are you sure that's a good idea?'

'No. It's not. But it'll just about cap off the day I'm having so far. Please Marcus. Get them downstairs and ready. When I call the eagle, follow me.'

'Molly…'

'We don't have time for this Marcus. Just do it.'

She turned away from him and closed her eyes.

'Get moving.'

He sighed before turning to Harry and the others.

'It's gone. Come on, we can follow it on foot but we need to move now.'

Harry looked past him to see Molly standing, staring out of the broken window.

'What's going on?'

'Major, just move yourself please.'

Marcus began to usher the confused soldiers back the way they'd come, his protestations becoming more urgent as Molly began to speak the dark words and the black mist began to form.

Around the window the temperature began to drop and each of the retreating men felt the ice-cold bite of fear begin to form like a knot in their stomachs as they retreated.

Marcus almost shoved the last man into the stairwell. He'd felt this before, he'd even been taken into the

Darkness while they were in India, but it didn't get any less terrifying.

He hoped to God that she knew what she was doing.

Chapter Nineteen

Under Construction

Ruth walked up to the Wagoner's Inn. John had sent her a message, he'd found the Captain again and wanted her to meet him. Even though it was just after eleven, the place was busy with people coming and going and there was an excited buzz to their hushed conversations.

Something had happened to Mr Porkonicov.

Something bad.

Ruth was about to ask what was going on when she was hissed at from a nearby doorway.

'Oi. Ruth.'

She frowned as she glanced over to see John standing in the shadows.

'What?'

He grabbed her arm and hauled her into the doorway.

'Hey!' she snapped, before pulling out of his grasp and slapping him on the arm. 'Where do you get off, grabbing me like that?'

'Sshhh.' he hissed, placing a finger to his lips, 'He's in the Inn. I don't want him to see me. He'll run again.'

Ruth narrowed her eyes at him.

'What did you do?'

'What?' he protested, looking shocked but far from innocent.

'You stupid bugger. Did you threaten him?'

'No! I just said that he might like to come and have a chat with the Princess. Next time I saw him, he took one look at me and did a runner. It's taken me two days to track him back here. Cost some too.'

Ruth sighed.

'What does he look like?'

John shrugged.

'Small man, greying hair. Was wearing a blue jacket.'
'Wait here.'
Leaving John in the doorway, Ruth went into the inn. She spotted the Captain straight away, sat at a small table in the corner with two empty bottles on the table next to him. She went to the bar, bought a bottle of gin for herself with some of the money Molly had given her, and went over to hm.
'Can I join you?'
He looked up.
'No. Piss off.'
'Charming. And here was me thinking you was a gentleman.'
She sat down, before pouring them both a drink. The Captain scoffed and knocked his back in one.
'I don't got time for whores.'
'Well it's a good job I'm not one then isn't it.' she replied, handing him the bottle.
He poured himself another, spilling some of it on the table.
'What do you want?'
'You. Information.'
'Pah.' he spat, knocking back another shot. 'Information. I wondered how long it'd be before someone else came looking.'
'Looking for what?'
He stood up and tried to put his coat on, succeeding only in getting his left arm through the right sleeve
'I told the other bloke. I don' t know nothin'.'
'You ran from him.'
'Aye.'
'Did he hit you?'
'Nah, he's a big streak o' piss. He couldn't worry a fly. I ran 'cus I knew the likes of you would be looking.'
Ruth couldn't help but smile as he described John.
'People are in danger.' she said after a moment.
The Captain dragged his coat off and threw it on the floor.

'You think I don't know that?' he shouted, drawing eyes from all over the room. 'You think I don't know what we brought back? We should've killed them, like we killed the other one.'

'What? Them?'

'Ah, not so bloody clever as you think are you? There were three of 'em. A big one, a medium one and a small one.' he sat down again and picked up the bottle, taking a long swig. 'Jus' like the three bears. Father bear, mother bear and baby bear.' With a bang that made Ruth jump, he slammed the bottle down on the table before leaning in. 'But they wasn't bears, they was monsters. Killed half my bloody crew before we got the big one. Then the others went mad. We managed to shove the mummy bear over the side.'

'What about the other one? The little one?'

The Captain gazed at her before seeming to sober up as his memories flooded back.

'Sold it.' he replied eventually.

'Who to?' Ruth asked, refilling his glass.

'Don't know. Some posh bloke paid for it and took the crate away. Don't know any names, all of the business was done through a starch arsed lawyer. All I know is that I'm glad I'm rid. Worst job I ever took.' he grabbed his glass and downed it in one.

'Did you know that your first mate is dead?'

This appeared to be news to the Captain. A whole swath of emotions passed across his face before settling on anger.

'It'll bloody be me next. Well I ain't waiting around for that.'

He stood quickly, grabbed the bottle and his coat and hurried out.

Ruth cursed under her breath before following. She met John in the doorway.

'He's just left.'

'I know that you idiot.'

'Hey, I was only trying to help.' he replied, genuinely hurt.

'Get out of the way.'

Ruth pushed past him and out into the street. The Captain was heading through the crowds towards the river. She called out to him and he turned around.

'Wait.'

Once more, he turned away but stopped dead in his tracks. From down the road came screaming and the entire street erupted into blind panic. People fled left and right as a creature bounded up the middle of the road.

Ruth recognised it instantly. It was the monster.

The thing was bleeding heavily from multiple wounds and had its nose close to the ground as if it were tracking something.

Anyone too slow to get out of the way was trampled beneath it as it ploughed up the carriageway.

Suddenly it skidded to a halt and raised its head to look directly at the Captain who was stood in the middle of the road.

A look, akin to a look of recognition passed across its face and it snarled before letting out an unearthly howl.

'What the hell is that?' gasped John.

'Trouble.'

The Captain seemed to be rooted to the spot as the thing roared again and began to advance on him.

'We've got to do something.'

'Like what?'

Ruth looked around and grabbed a stone from the floor. Throwing it as hard as she could, she shouted at the creature.

'Hey. Over here.'

John joined in, throwing his own rock which bounced off the creatures' head. It turned to regard them.

Ruth threw another stone, this one catching it on the shoulder. With its attention diverted, she shouted at the Captain.

'What are you waiting for? Run, you bloody idiot.'

As soon as the Captain turned to run, the creature snapped its attention back to him.

Ruth cursed loudly, grabbed a nearby plank of wood and heaved it towards the thing. It roared again before rounding on the pair.

'I think we pissed it off.'

The look that Ruth gave John would have felled even the hardest of men.

'You think?'

'Well…'

'We've got to get out of here.'

John didn't get a chance to reply. He had barely turned to run when the creature hit him from behind, sending him flying into Ruth. They went down in a tumbling pile.

'Miss Thomas. Stay down.'

From underneath John, she saw Harry and a group of soldiers run into the road and level their weapons at the creature. The world exploded in a barrage of shot and smoke as they fired simultaneously.

Above her, the monster roared in pain before taking off again and loping up the road. Harry ran over as Ruth extracted herself from underneath John.

'Are you alright?'

'I am.'

She looked down. John wasn't. His right arm was bent at an unnatural angle and there was blood on his back. Immediately she crouched down.

'John?'

He groaned and tried to sit up, crying out in pain as he moved.

'Get him inside,' Harry instructed two of the soldiers.

They slung their muskets and began to drag him in.

He turned to Ruth.

'Help him as best you can. Get inside and lock the door.'

Harry held her gaze for a second.

'We can't stay. I've got no idea where Molly is and that thing is loose. She thinks there's more than one of them.'

'There is. A little one. The Captain told me.'

'Where is he?'

'Don't know. Did a runner.'

Harry shook his head.

'Here.' he handed her a pistol. 'It's loaded. If that thing comes back. Shoot it.'

She looked at the weapon for a second before taking it and nodding once.

'Take care Miss Thomas.'

'And you sir.'

She watched the soldiers come out of the pub, form up and then head off after the creature. Looking down at the pistol in her hands she shook her head.

What the hell was she doing?

She shoved the weapon into her belt before striding into the pub and slamming the door behind her.

The eagle circled high above the city and, from behind its eyes, Molly searched.

She had picked the creature up easily enough, for it was doing little to hide its path through the docks.

It was weaving backwards and forwards, up and down and Molly knew that it was searching for the other one. Geoffrey had said has much himself.

It had come looking.

She spotted Marcus, Harry and the soldiers and swooped low, narrowly avoiding being shot at by one of the men as he panicked at the sudden sight of a giant bird sweeping towards him.

Marcus had pushed the gun aside at the last second, sending the shot wide but it still ruffled the eagle's feathers.

She cawed out loudly and arced away, leading the soldiers onwards.

'What the hell do you think you're doing?' yelled Marcus.

'It was going to attack us!' replied Newmore.

Marcus clenched his fist before shouting at the others.

'The next man who fires on the eagle will not need to worry about the creature. That I promise. The bird is leading us. Just follow it.'

They set off at a pace in the direction the eagle had taken. Harry fell in beside Marcus.

'It's her isn't it?' he whispered.

'I don't know what you're talking about.' was Marcus' terse reply.

'Come on. I know it is. I thought I saw a huge bird right before she let me into the yard the first time. There's no way she could have gotten in there.'

'She's a good climber.'

'Rubbish. Then, when she saved me last night, it looked like she came in from the sky. There was a blurry bird then. I thought it was just the knocks I'd taken.'

Marcus set his face in a grim line.

'She won't thank me for telling you and it can go no further. I need you word.'

'You have it.'

'I mean it Major. Her sisters will kill you if they find out you know.'

'Sisters?'

'The Daughters of Kali. In India, she was marked. Her tattoo. It gives her the power to summon the eagle. I don't like it and neither does she. The bird comes and she goes... elsewhere...'

'Where?'

'The Darkness. The worst place I've ever been. It's where the souls of the dead go and is terrifying. Imagine a battlefield. The smell, the fear, the death. Now multiply that by a thousand and you won't be close.'

'Then why does she do it?'

Marcus laughed sadly.

'Because it's necessary.'

'I don't understand.'

'You don't have to. Just add it to the list of things that you will never understand about Molly. I've got quite a long list myself.'

The Major looked at him but didn't say anything. Turn into a bird, control the wind, what else could this girl do?

The creature threaded its way through the dockyard before moving arrow straight towards a construction site and Molly circled as it barrelled through the yard, sending workers running.

Knowing that she had found it and that Marcus, Harry and the soldiers were close, Molly began to return from the Darkness, speaking the words to bring her back into the light.

The black mist spread out behind her as she neared the ground and with a pop of displaced air, she was back, sprawling forward to lie on the ground.

Her head was spinning. That was the worst transition she'd experienced.

The dead that surrounded her were an unwelcome surprise. Nareema had said that the souls of those she had killed surrounded her when she was in the Darkness and Molly could still feel the cold dead touch of more than a dozen as she returned to her body.

Even though she hadn't seen them, she knew Porkonicov and his thugs had been there. The fat criminal would torment her for the rest of her life.

Pulling herself painfully to her hands and knees, she vomited a stream of black mist as somewhere ahead, there was the splintering of wood before there was a gentle hand placed on her back.

'Are you alright?'

She nodded before looking up at Marcus. He and the soldiers were breathing heavily. Behind him there were some stunned looking men and fearful mutterings.

'How'd she get here?'

'Impossible…'

Taking an offered hand, Molly hauled herself up. God she was tired.

'You look terrible.'

'Thanks.'

'No. I mean it. You really don't look that well.'

'I'll rest in a few minutes. I promise. But we need to stop this. Geoffrey must be here. The creature has come to find the other one.'

'It's a baby. Ruth found the Captain and he told her.'

'Then let's find them both.'

Without giving Marcus a chance to protest, she drew her sword and went after the monster.

Geoffrey huddled in the corner of the first floor. Across from him, tethered to a brick support was the little one.

It looked like a miniature version of the creature but had a steel muzzle around its face along with thick chains around it's wrists. A wide metal collar bounded its neck with a heavy chain like leash running up and around the support. It hissed madly at him and gouged deep furrows in the wooden floor.

His father had commissioned the building of the new warehouses alongside the river last year and construction was well under way. Most of the floors were in and they had made it up as far as the roof.

Father would be please.

He giggled to himself.

Would have been pleased.

It didn't matter now. No one knew he was here. Not the creature, not the soldiers, not *her*.

She didn't matter. But when this was over. He'd find her and she would honour him. Just as a wife should. The poor, terrified girl.

He giggled again while across the floor the little thing hissed once more.

'Shut up. Shut up, shut up, shut up!' he screamed at it, reaching into his jacket to produce the pipe.

He put it to his lips as from outside there came screaming and shouting. Jumping up, Geoffrey looked out of the glassless window. There were men fleeing and standing in the middle of the yard was the monster.

He whimpered pathetically. It had found him.

Grabbing the chain, he began to haul the little creature along. He had to get away.

Ahead of her the creature smashed through a door and bounded up the stairs, Molly skidded into the stairwell, just in time to see it crash through the door to the roof.

Taking the stairs two at a time, she emerged onto the roof. It was flat and across from her was the thing, slowly advancing on Geoffrey.

The man was stood near the edge, dragging something along. The smaller creature was resisting, gouging deep furrows in the roof as it was dragged forward.

Geoffrey shouted at it and produced the pipe which he blew hard.

Both of the creatures thrashed in pain as the discordant note sounded across the rooftop and Molly staggered before falling to her knees.

The smaller of the two began mewing pitifully and with a vicious yank, Geoffrey pulled it towards him. The large creature shook its head and advanced but was floored by another harsh blast of the pipe.

'You see?' shouted Geoffrey as he saw Molly. 'It does as it is told. It obeys. Just as you should have done. Just as you *will* do.'

'Stop it Geoffrey. That's enough.'

'Don't tell me what to do!' he yelled.

She stood unsteadily as behind her, she heard the rest of the group arrive.

'It's over. You've nowhere to go.'

'When you're dead, I can go anywhere I like.' he said, his tone like a petulant child.

Behind Molly, the soldiers began to fan out, guns trained on the beast. It dipped its head and snarled, trying to watch all of the men at once.

'Geoffrey.'

He smiled madly before he put the pipe to his lips he blew again.

'Kill her!'

The creature rounded on Molly instantly, the beady eyes focusing on her as she slumped back down, the sound of the pipe tearing through her mind. Marcus helped her up and she pushed away from him then, without taking her eyes off the thing, she shouted to the Corporal.

'When I move, I want you to keep this thing busy. Don't kill it.'

'What?' he called back. 'That bloody thing killed Blinky.'

'I know but don't kill it.'

'Molly...' that was Marcus.

'Do as I damn well say!' she snapped before launching herself at the thing. It reacted at almost the same time as her, charging forwards in a flash of claws and snapping of teeth.

At the last second, Molly jumped. Her booted foot caught the creature on the side of the head as she used it as a springboard to vault clean over it.

She landed hard but rolled and was up in a single movement. Geoffrey saw her coming and backed away until the back of his legs hit the low wall around the edge of the roof.

'Don't come any closer.' he shouted, 'I'll drop it.'

With a heaving pull, he dragged the little creature up and over the edge of the roof. It flailed around madly as it hung above the four-storey drop to the cobbles below.

'Let it go Geoffrey.'

'No. Its mine. You could have been too. You *should* have been mine.'

'Geoffrey, that was never going to happen.'

'Don't speak to me like that!'

He thrust out his arm, holding the thing further out over the edge.

'I'm going to ask you one more time.' said Molly calmly, stepping to within a few feet of him. 'Let it go and we can talk about this.'

'Don't talk to me. You should obey you husband! Be seen and not heard you stupid whore!'

'I've given you all of the chances you're going to get.' replied Molly with an edge to her voice.

Taking another step, she brought her sword down. The blade cut cleanly through Geoffrey's wrist, severing it completely.

He cried out in pain and shock and fell to the floor as Molly darted forward to grab the chain.

Hauling for all she was worth, she dragged the little creature up and back onto the roof. Immediately it bounded away from her, straight to the larger monster.

Geoffrey sat up, cradling his arm against his body. Molly walked up to him and hauled him upright. He was deathly pale from the shock and blood loss.

Holding him by his jacket, she stared at him. He looked back, unable to tear his gaze away from the spinning blackness in Mollys eyes.

He whimpered pathetically and wet himself, the tell-tale smell and patch staining his trousers.

'It's gone.'

Molly looked over her shoulder at Marcus who had come up behind her.

'The thing. It's gone. Both of them.'

She nodded once and turned back to Geoffrey.

'Keys. I want the keys to the chains.'

He obeyed without question, she took them and clipped them to her belt.

'Now give me the pipe.'

He did as he was told, quickly handing over the bone pipe with bloodied fingers.

'Please help me.' he begged.

Molly looked at the pipe and then up at him. He whimpered again and tried to pull away.

Her eyes were just pits of blackness.

All trace of the white had gone and he was scared beyond belief.

'You're a bad man Geoffrey.' she said softly.

She looked at the pipe again and then with a shove, sent him tumbling backwards over the edge of the roof.

'Molly!'

Marcus dashed to the edge in time to see Geoffrey hit the cobbles below with a wet smacking sound. From the way his body lay, Marcus was sure the man didn't have an unbroken bone in his body.

Molly didn't look. She just walked away.

'What did you just do? That was murder!'

'No. Necessary.' she replied coldly.

Marcus ran to catch her up, grabbing her and spinning her to face him. She slowly looked at the hand on her arm and then up at Marcus.

He took a step back. There was something in her face. Something dark. Something terrifying.

Her eyes were black with an unfathomable depth that spoke of hatred and power. Her face was pinched and pale, giving her a deathly, unearthly look.

'Molly?'

She regarded him for a second more before the black began to disappear.

'Where has it gone?'

'What?'

'The thing. The *things*. Where'd they go?'

With a nervous glance between Molly and Marcus, the Corporal stepped up.

'When the little one came running, it picked it up and then jumped off the roof. It hit the water pretty hard and we didn't see it come up again.'

'It's still alive.' she said.

'Are you sure?'

Molly looked at the pipe in her hand once more.

'I know.'

She strode from the roof, leaving the men looking confused and bewildered.

Chapter Twenty

Home again

The carriage pulled up outside their home and Marcus got out, turning to help his wife. She was battered and bruised and ached all over from the beating that she'd received from Mr Porkonicov's men and the fight with the creature.

After they'd left the warehouse, Harry had sent one of the soldiers to fetch Harrington. The detestable man arrived four hours later and declared the matter closed.

Molly had said nothing, even though Harry had protested that the creature was still out there and could kill again.

Harrington had given his word that he would honour his pledge and provide Molly with the deeds to the Scottish castle, along with which came the title of "Laird and Lady of Tioramney".

She'd only nodded and then climbed in to the carriage Marcus had arranged then they'd sat in a tense silence all the way home. Molly was greeted by her maid, Gwen. The poor girl looked sick with nerves.

'Are you alright Your Ladyship?' she had asked anxiously.

'Run me a bath please.' replied Molly, more sternly that she had meant to.

The girl nodded and hurried away.

That had been three hours ago. Now Molly was sat in her parlour staring blankly at the fire.

The powers of the Stones of Gunjai had done their work and not a scratch remained on her body, but there would be some stupendous bruises and she ached awfully.

Marcus came in and sat opposite her. There was another stony silence.

'Go on then.' said Molly eventually, unable to take the tension any longer.

'What?'

'Go on then. Tell me off. Shout at me. Tell me all of the things that I shouldn't have done. All of the things that aren't suitable for a lady. Unbecoming of a wife.'

Marcus looked at the fire, searching for the right words. She was right. There were things that he wanted to say. How she'd put herself in harm's way again, endangering not just her but others too.

But he couldn't. He knew why she'd done it and deep down, he'd have been disappointed if she hadn't, but that wasn't the point.

'You lied to me.' he said eventually.

'Yes.' she said. 'I know.'

'Why?'

Now it was her turn to search for the words.

'You'd have tried to stop me.'

'Of course I would, but...' he said but tailed off. 'Please don't do it again.'

She looked at him. Her white eyes boring into his and making her face unreadable.

'I'm sorry.' she said after a moment.

'So am I.' he replied.

She looked down.

'I can't be the wife you deserve. You should have married Lady Samantha's daughter. Jane would be reliable and dependable. She knows how to behave correctly. I'm different and it sets me apart from everyone else. I can't change who I am.'

'Even if it gets you killed?'

'Even then.' she replied softly, unable to look at him.

Marcus moved and knelt in front of her, gently lifting her chin. Her fair skin was coloured yellow and purple from emerging bruises.

'And if I ask you not to?'

She smiled sadly.

'You won't.'

He shook his head.

'No. I won't. But next time, tell me. I'm coming too.'

Eventually she nodded, pulling away from his hand to stare once more into the fire.

'What's the matter.'

Molly didn't answer straight away. Giving voice to the thoughts in her head was difficult. She didn't understand them herself but she had to talk to someone.

'There's something wrong with me.'

Marcus was instantly full of concern.

'What is it? Are you hurt?'

She laughed sadly.

'I ache but that's not it. There's something wrong Marcus.' she hesitated. 'Today I killed some men. I was angry. So angry I couldn't stop myself. I butchered them Marcus. Killed them. Even when one of them was on his knees begging, I killed him and even though I should have felt as disgusted with myself as I do now, I enjoyed it. I killed them and I laughed while I did it.'

He didn't know what to say, instead he took her chin once more before giving her a gentle kiss.

'I love you Molly Kane. Whatever it is, we'll sort it out.'

'But what if I hurt you? Or Gwen? Or…'

'Don't. It will be alright.'

'I'm sorry Marcus.'

'Don't be.' he whispered.

She hugged him tightly, trying not to wince as her battered body protested. Eventually she let him go and he stood walking to the sideboard and pouring them both a large brandy.

'Owain has written to us.' he said, handing his wife her glass. 'He's having a wake for Mr Davis. Wanted to know if we were going.'

Owain Brody had been the Captain of the ship the Endurance and had taken Molly to Portugal, Iceland and then to India and back.

His first mate, Mr Davis had been like a father to Molly. Looking after her and being there when she needed someone.

The old sailor had been killed by the demonic Heralds of Carnothal during the incident near Brillington Abbey. Molly owed him.

'Of course. When is it?'

'Next week. I said that we'd be attending.'

Molly smiled at him.

'Thank you.'

Marcus finished his drink and stood up.

'I'm going to bed. Are you coming?'

'In a minute. I need to talk to Gwen first.'

He took her hand and kissed it gently.

'Don't be too long.'

'I won't.'

She watched him go.

How had she managed to find a man like that?

'Just get yourself kidnapped!' she laughed softly to herself and took a sip of her drink.

Reaching a decision, she picked up an empty glass and the decanter and went upstairs. She stopped outside Gwen's room, took a breath to compose herself and knocked.

There was no answer, so she opened it and went in. Gwen was stood near the dresser, a guilty look on her face and half a packed bag on the bed.

'Going somewhere?'

The girl looked down.

'I didn't think you wanted me here. You were angry and…'

Molly sighed.

'Stop it Gwen. Please. My head is all over the place at the moment. Please stop assuming you're going to be fired. I don't care what other houses do, you've got a job for as long as you want one.'

Molly put the glasses and decanter on the floor, shoved the bag aside and sat down heavily.

'I'm sorry. I put you in a difficult position and I shouldn't have done that. I don't want you to leave. I need you.'

Molly picked at a trailing thread from her sleeve.

'As much as I don't want to admit it. I do need help. From Marcus. From you.'

'I thought…'

Molly shook her head.

'No. You did the right thing. It was me that didn't. I need to learn that I can rely on other people. I've not been able to for such a long time that…' she sighed again. 'Look. You can leave if you want. I'm not going to stop you, but I'd rather you didn't.'

Gwen looked at her for a long moment.

'I'd like to stay if you want me to. If…'

'That's settled then.' cut in Molly. 'Drink?'

She poured them both a generous measure and handed a glass to the girl.

'For God's sake, sit down. Please.'

Gwen perched on the edge of the bed. She was still a little uncomfortable at the familiarity with which Molly treated her.

None of the other maids that she knew would dare sit down in the presence of their employer, let alone drink their brandy.

Well, not with their employer knowing anyway.

True, they'd already been through a lot together, what with the things that happened at the Abbey, but it was still strange.

Molly took a long swig, relishing the warming feel of the liquor as it went down.

'Marcus and I are going to Gosport next week,' she said 'then I think we'll go down to Somerset. For real this time. A lot has happened that I want to tell Uncle Tobias about.'

Gwen nodded and took a delicate sip. Brandy like this was expensive and she wanted to savour it. Still, she coughed as it went down.

'Your sister is getting married soon isn't she?'

'Yes.' replied Gwen, between coughs. 'In a couple of weeks.'

'I don't think we'll be back by then.'

Gwen's face fell and Molly smiled.

'I never said you had to come with us. Take some time to yourself. I'll manage without you. Go to your sister's wedding. I promised you could take the carriage, and I order you to have a good time. I'll arrange for food for the party afterwards. Spend some time with your family.'

'But you said you needed me.'

'I do. But not as a maid. As a friend.'

Molly patter her on the knee.

'I don't expect you enjoyed your last visit did you?'

'I never made it that far. Stopped at an inn for two days then came back.' she replied, wretchedly.

'Then go. It'll do you good to go home…'

Molly tailed off then stood up suddenly, the glass slipping from her fingers to smash on the floor.

'Your Ladyship! Are you alright?' Gwen asked, jumping up too.

'I know where it's gone.'

The girl looked at her, bemused.

'Where what has gone?'

Molly's reply was a smile and a wink before she headed out of the room.

Harry had watched Molly's carriage roll away before turning to the Corporal and his men.

'Get yourselves back to barracks. You've done well today. All of you.'

'But what about Blinky, Sir?' asked the Corporal.

'I'll sort it out. I'll also sort out a few bottles of something so you can toast him until you can't see straight.'

The assembled men smiled and exchanged some knowing glances amongst themselves.

'Now go on. Get out of here.'

Forming up and shouldering their weapons in a display of martial prowess that Harry didn't know they had in them, the men swiftly marched away.

He watched until they were out of the gate before going across to the body of Geoffrey. The man had hit the cobbles face first and was completely unrecognisable.

His neck was snapped and the rest of him lay at unnatural angles. Harry sighed and went back inside. When he left five minutes later, a fire was raging through the lower floor with a similar fate destined for the other warehouse.

Once out of the yard, he hurried up the road to the pub by the river.

'Miss Thomas. It's all clear.' he shouted as he banged on the door.

There was silence for a second before the heavy door was pulled back and he found himself looking straight down the barrel of a gun and behind that, Ruth. She smiled and shrugged an apology as she lowered the weapon.

'Sorry...'

'Don't worry about it. It's safe. It's gone. You can all come out now.'

Behind Ruth, the gaggle of men, women and children that had taken shelter with her in the building, began to stir and head out.

Some looked scared while some of the older boys were talking animatedly about the monster. He was sure that by the time they got home it would be fifty feet tall and almost have eaten them alive.

Ruth waited until they were all out before coming out herself, handing the pistol back to Harry.

'How's your friend?'

'He's not my friend. We just both happen to know Moll.'

'Ah. Still, how is he?'

'Drunk as a skunk. It's only a couple of bad scratches and a broken arm. He's got himself some sympathetic help. He'll be alright.'

Harry glanced past her and into the pub. Propped in a chair with a bottle in his hand and right arm strapped up was John. Sat to his left and right were some pretty girls, gently cooing over his injuries and bravery at saving everyone from the monster.

The Major laughed and turned to Ruth once more.

'He'll do fine. I must say, you handled yourself admirably miss Thomas.'

She shrugged and began walking down the road. Harry smiled and followed her.

'If it were agreeable, I would like to give you a job.'

She stopped suddenly and turned, giving him a suspicious look.

'Why?'

'Why not?'

'I'm not a snitch. I don't want to be trailing all over London for you, just so you can bang up some criminals.'

Harry almost laughed.

'My dear, that is far from what I do.'

She began to walk away again.

'I'm still listening.' she called over her shoulder.

He jogged to catch her up.

'I, and a very few others, are used when more direct methods aren't suitable. We operate clandestinely, doing the jobs that need to be done with the minimum of fuss and publicity.'

'What does "clandestinely" mean?'

He couldn't hide his smile.

'In secret. We work in secret.'

'Why me?'

'You're a smart girl. I had the idea while working with Molly. Sometimes it is necessary for me to attend functions and such. It would be most advantageous for there to be another pair of eyes and ears around.'

'And I'd look good on your arm?'

'Obviously.' replied Harry smoothly, 'and of course, you have certain, um, charms that may come in handy.'

She stopped dead and glared at him.

'Just because I don't have a home doesn't mean I'm a whore. That's not for sale at any price.'

'I never said you were and that never crossed my mind.'

She considered this.

'So what's in it for me?'

'Very mercenary and direct. I like that.'

Ruth just continued to stare at him.

'I would arrange a suitable recompense. Along with lodgings, food, clothes, an education, all of the things you're going to need.'

'Why me?'

Harry caught the movement out of the corner of his eye and it saved Ruth's life. Without thinking he shoved her hard and she fell backwards into the mud.

She rolled over just in time to see the iron pipe swung by the shady man she'd seen at the palace tear through the air where she had been standing.

If Harry hadn't pushed her, it would have smashed her head in. As it was, it struck Harry across the shoulders and knocked him to the ground. The man cursed and rounded on the Major.

'I was going to make it nice and easy. She wasn't going to suffer.'

He swung again but Harry scrambled to the side just in time.

'But now? Well. I'll have some fun with her when I'm finished with you.'

From a crouch, Harry launched himself up and grappled with the man. They toppled back into the muddy street. The Major managed to get on top and drove a ferocious punch into the mans' face.

'Potts, you bastard. I should have killed you last time you...'

The snarled words were cut off as the man swung the pipe again. It clattered off the side of Harry's head knocking him senseless. He rolled over, trying to blink away the stars from his eyes as Mr Potts drove a solid kick to his stomach, knocking what little breath he had from his lungs.

He kicked Harry again before throwing the pipe down and pulling a long knife from his belt.

'I'm going to enjoy this. Harrington said I could do what I like to you, and what Mr Harrington says, goes.'

He smiled cruelly and knelt next to Harry, wrapping a hand in his hair and yanking his head up. Slowly he brought the point of the blade towards Harrys left eye.

'Get off him.'

Ruth cracked the pipe down across Mr Potts wrist and he cried out in pain, dropping the knife in the mud.

He whirled as she swung again, the pipe catching him on the shoulder, knocking him over. Quickly, Ruth scrabbled at Harrys waist and came up with the pistol, just as Mr Potts stood with murder in his eyes. He looked down the barrel.

'You won't shoot me girl. You ain't got it in ya. I can see it in your eyes.'

Ruth raised an eyebrow.

'Really?'

Mr Potts moved as she pulled the trigger. The gun went off with a crack and the shot hit the man in the shoulder rather than his head. He cried out in pain and took off down the road, barrelling through Ruth and sending her flying once more.

She rolled over in the mud to look up at Harry who had pulled himself to a sitting position.

'Is it always going to be this much fun?'

He laughed.

'Probably.'

Molly and Marcus arrived at the dock at a run. They ducked into a narrow alley opposite the area the ship was being held in.

'Tell me again what we're doing?' asked Marcus breathlessly.

'It came here on a ship. I guess they both did. Now it's free of Geoffrey, I think it's come home.'

He didn't look convinced.

'So what now?'

She smiled at him.

'We go and have a look.'

Molly ran across the road and scrambled over the fence. Marcus shook his head. Honestly, she was going to get him killed.

He followed, landing on a cobbled street. To the right was a row of single story warehouses while to the left was the river. Three or four ships were tied up on the quay and Molly was nowhere to be seen.

'Molly?' hissed Marcus.

'What?'

She was stood right behind him and he almost jumped out of his skin.

'Don't do that! You scared me half to death.'

She grinned warmly.

'There are things more scary than me around.'

'Yes. I know. But none of them sneak up behind me.'

'I don't sneak!' she replied in a mocking hurt tone.

'You just did.'

'Didn't!'

'Now you sound like Nareema.'

She winked at him. Marcus thought she was enjoying this a little too much.

'Come on.'

Keeping to the shadows of the buildings, Molly and Marcus made their way down the quay.

'It came in on a ship called Amarantha. She came in from the far East in May. The crew jumped ship as soon as they docked. Not even the Captain stayed aboard.'

'How'd you know?'

'I did a little digging and Geoffrey filled in the rest.'

Marcus frowned.

'So why is it here?'

'The insurance people don't want to pay and no-one else wants it. They think it's cursed.'

'Is it?'

'What do you think?'

He shook his head.

'From some of the things we've seen, it's difficult to tell.'

They drew up opposite the ship. It was third in the line. A rickety looking gangplank ran up to the deck and there were no lights visible.

'Wait here.' she told him.

'Not likely. Let you go on board alone with that thing there?'

'It might not be there.'

'Yes.' agreed Marcus. 'But there's a chance that it will. How many people has it killed?'

'I don't know. But if it is there, then it won't hurt me.'

'How do you know?'

She reached into a pocket and pulled out the bone pipe.

'This. If I blow this, it'll do as I tell it.'

'Molly...'

'Please. I don't want it to hurt you. It knows me.'

She didn't add "It tried to kill me".

He frowned.

'You've got ten minutes.' he said eventually, 'If you're not out by then, I'm coming aboard.'

She smiled and gave him a kiss.

'I won't be long.'

'Take care.'

Quietly she drew her sword and moved up the gangplank, leaving Marcus in the shadows.

The deck was empty, and she moved lightly to the steps below. There was a whiff of something horrible and Molly knew she had been right. Most of the deck was pitch dark and only a little light filtered in from above.

'What're you doing?' she asked herself. 'Why didn't you let Marcus come too?'

The answer was easy. She was fairly sure that the creature wouldn't kill her.

Probably.

But it would attack Marcus in a second.

On the deck at the bottom of the stairs was a small lantern. Sheathing her sword across her back, she lit it and looked around.

The smell was stronger down here.

She moved as quietly as she could, wincing at every creak and groan of the wood beneath her feet. As she neared the steps to the cargo hold, she heard a pathetic mewing and an answering growl from below.

'They're both down there.'

The voice was quiet but Molly still jumped in shock, hand immediately going to her sword. She span around and there, in the dark shadows in the corner, was a man. He was dirty, his face smeared with grime although there were clear paths down his cheeks where he had been crying. With a sluggish motion, he raised a bottle to his lips.

'Who are you?'

The man wiped his mouth with his sleeve.

'Phillip Lewis. Captain of this death-ridden pile.'

'Captain?'

'Aye. This is all my fault. The monsters. The deaths. Collier.'

'Who's Collier?'

'A man. My friend. No one. He's dead now. That thing killed him.'

Captain Lewis emptied the bottle and dragged himself to his feet.

'Time to finish this.'

Unsteadily he moved to the door to the cargo deck. Molly grabbed his arm.

'What are you going to do?'

'What I should have done ages ago.'

From inside his jacket he pulled out another bottle, this one had a rag stuffed in the top.

'You're going to burn them?'

'Them and me. I'd get out of here girl if you know what's good for you.'

'No.'

He shrugged her off and aimed a drunken punch at her which she easily sidestepped.

'I'm sorry, I can't let you do that.'

In one swift movement, she pirouetted and kicked him in the face. The Captain went down hard and lay still.

Taking a deep breath, she went down. The cargo hold was split in half, with a wide door at the far end leading to the forward compartment.

Cautiously she went up to the door and peered through.

There it was.

There *they* were.

Both of them. The little one still had the iron collar, muzzle and shackles on. It was lying on the floor while the large one prowled around it. She closed her eyes for a second.

'You're mad.' she told herself.

Steeling herself, she opened the door wide and stepped in. Instantly the larger creature hissed and bounded towards her, smashing her back into the bulkhead before she'd even registered it had moved.

Her vision was filled with a fanged maw and behind that a tail, frantically whipping to and froe.

It opened its mouth wide and Molly lashed out with the power of her bracelet, giving her space to scramble to the side, pulling the pipe out as she moved.

The thing looked surprised but was ready again in an instant.

As soon as it saw the pipe it stopped, backing away and putting itself between Molly and the little one, hissing madly. Molly raised her hands.

'I know this hurts you. It hurts me too. I know you don't belong here and what you've been through was wrong.'

It hissed again.

'What Geoffrey did was wrong, but he's dead now. Gone.'

As slowly as she could, she placed the pipe on the floor. The creature followed every movement, tail swishing behind it.

Molly straightened and then with a sudden movement, stamped on the pipe, smashing it into a hundred pieces.

'It's gone now. It can't hurt us now.'

The creature backed further away, as if it was unsure what to do. Reaching to her belt, Molly took out the keys that she'd taken from Geoffrey, holding them up for the thing to see.

'I can help the little one. But you have to trust me.'

She held her breath, not knowing if the creature even understood her. It hissed once more before glancing at the little one on the floor.

Slowly it moved to the side, allowing Molly access. Carefully, her eyes never leaving the larger thing, she moved to the small one on the floor.

The collar, chains and muzzle were too small for it and there was fresh blood from where it had struggled against its bonds.

The thing hissed at her as she reached towards it but there was no threat in it. It sounded weak and tired.

The collar came first, followed by the shackles and then finally the muzzle.

As the metal hit the deck, the creature lashed out, scoring a deep line across her thigh with its claws. She fell back as above her the larger thing hissed too.

Molly fully expected them to kill her now but when no attack came, she shuffled backwards out of the way until she was clear of them.

The big creature wrapped its tail around the little one and pulled it close. Molly stood up.

'Go.' She said. 'Leave the city. If they know you're still alive then they'll hunt you down and kill you.' she glanced at the little one. 'Both of you.'

Both creatures moved to the door and Molly stepped out of the way. As they drew level with her, the larger one reached into the pouch around its waist and pulled out a small object which it handed to Molly.

It was a small brass key, no longer than her little finger.

She looked up at the creature in puzzlement. It tilted its head before speaking in a thick, droning voice.

'Ooonddurrrr Loooonndooonnn.'

Then, without another word, they both headed out and up the stairs. Molly looked at the key, then out of the door before she let out a breath she didn't know she had been holding.

Beneath her, her legs turned to jelly and she had to hold on to the wall to steady herself. Taking a few deep breaths, she got herself under control.

It could talk!

It could have killed her but didn't. It really did understand.

She looked around. At the back of the room, was a heavy door. It had deep gouges in the thick wood and was badly splintered but it still held.

She went up to it to find a large padlock holding it closed. She closed her eyes and channelled the power of her bracelet once more, feeling the wind and air build in her hands.

With a concentrated blast, the door exploded into a thousand pieces.

The room beyond was small, not even six feet square with a low ceiling that Molly would have had to crouch under.

In the middle of the floor lay a body. It was like the other creatures but larger, barely able to fit into the space.

Heavy iron rings and chains pinned it to the floor and she knew it was dead. The jaw was broken and stuck out at an odd angle from the face.

Its claws were chipped and worn from where it had scratched at the deck beneath it and it was covered in multiple deep wounds and gashes.

Molly turned away in revulsion.

Why?

Forcing down her growing anger she looked around once more before picking up the lantern.

Throwing it as hard as she could into the small room it smashed and the oil inside quickly caught light. Closing her eyes, Molly channelled the wind and the body began to burn fiercely.

Turning, she headed out, stopping only to drag the still unconscious Captain off the ship.

Marcus was at the bottom of the gangplank with his sword drawn when he saw his wife.

He'd given her fifteen minutes and was getting worried. More so when he was sure he heard some splashing in the shadows.

He'd drawn his sword and was about to board the ship when she came on deck. He couldn't have been more happy.

'Marcus, help me.'

She was dragging a semi-conscious man along with her. Quickly he sheathed his sword and slipped an arm under the man.

'Who's he? I thought something had happened.'

She smiled weakly.

'Are you alright?'

'Yes. I'm fine. We better get going. This place is going to get really busy soon.'

'What happened? Is it dead?'

'It's over, Marcus. That's it. It's over.'

He frowned.

'What…'

'Come on.'

They dropped the man on the wharf before Molly grabbed his sleeve and led him back into the shadows on the other side of the wharf. He glanced over his shoulder to see the edges of flames dancing around the gunwales of the ship.

'Come on.'

He let himself be led along until they reached the fence and scrambled over. Behind them, the early morning sky was beginning to brighten as the fire took hold.

'Will you tell me what happened?'

She shook her head.

'No.'

He opened his mouth to protest but she put a finger to his lips to silence him.

'Can we go home? Please?' she asked softly.

Marcus nodded once and took her hand, leading her away.

They walked in silence for a few minutes before Molly turned to him.

'Marcus,' she asked, 'what does "Besmirch" mean?'

Mr Potts sat in his chair by the fire. A small table held a candle, bloody knife and a large bottle of whisky.

He winced as he dug his fingers into the hole in his shoulder, grinding his teeth together and stifling a groan of pain as he pulled out the shot.

He dropped the metal ball onto the table and picked up the bottle. Taking a large slug, he tipped the bottle up, emptying some of the liquor onto the wound, again holding back a shout.

God that bitch was going to pay. He'd make sure of it. Her, her friend and then that bastard Gould. They'd all pay. And he'd make it hurt.

Taking another pull from the bottle he began wrapping dirty bandages around his shoulder, flopping back into the chair when he was done.

They'd pay alright.

He'd make Gould watch while he had the women before he killed them. Slowly and painfully. Right in front of him.

They'd pay.

He raised the bottle to his lips once more but paused.

Something didn't feel right.

The fire to his right, which had been burning ferociously a moment before had dimmed to embers. The candle was guttering, flickering pitifully in the light.

A knot of tension formed in his stomach.

Something wasn't right. Carefully, he lowered the bottle and leant forward towards the knife.

He reached out, stopping suddenly when he felt a blade press against his throat. A female voice, thickly accented whispered in his ear.

'The eagle has her destiny written in prophecy. It is not for you to change that.'

The last thing he felt was a hand wrap in his greasy hair and yank his head back before the blade ran across his throat.

Molly will return in

"Parisian Blood"

Printed in Poland
by Amazon Fulfillment
Poland Sp. z o.o., Wrocław